Phantom Detectives on Vacation

The Third Sleuths and Serpents Mystery Anthology

by Greensburg
Writers Group Members:

Thomas Beck, Marge Burke,
Judith Gallagher, Barb Holliday,
Michele Jones, Ed Kelemen,
Barb Miller, M. A. Mogus,
and Ronald J. Shafer

Weavers Old Stand Publishers
722 Armbrust Hecla Road
Mount Pleasant, PA 15666-3135

ISBN-13: 978-1535555326
ISBN-10: 1535555327

ACKNOWLEDGMENTS

"My Summer Staycation" by Ronald J. Shafer. Copyright 2016 by Ronald J. Shafer. Original story used by arrangement with the author.

"Murder 101" by Barb Miller. Copyright 2016 by Barb Miller. Original story used by arrangement with the author.

"The Fourth Treasure of Ireland" by Judith Gallagher. Copyright 2016 by Judith Gallagher. Original story used by arrangement with the author.

"The Nittany Needles" by M. A. Mogus. Copyright 2016 by M. A. Mogus. Original story used by arrangement with the author.

"Ding Dong the Witch Is Dead" by Michele Jones. Copyright 2016 by Michele Jones. Original story used by arrangement with the author.

"What Happens in Vegas" by Marge Burke. Copyright 2016 by Marge Burke. Original story used by arrangement with the author.

"I'll Have a Brandi" by Thomas Beck. Copyright 2016 by Thomas Beck. Original story used by arrangement with the author.

Contents

PROLOGUE

Manelli dragged his feet as he approached the basement door in the Falls Bend Town Hall. The sign on the arterial-red door said Archives, but it was so much more. It was – or had been – the meeting place of the Sleuths and Serpents writers' group, a collection of unique characters who, with their psychic sidekicks, managed to solve cold cases that the Laurel Falls District Office had charged him with eradicating. In other words, they had made his professional life bearable instead of the living hell he'd expected.

Now he was going to have to tell them they had lost their room. Even though he arrived early and with a box of donuts, Jessie, Lazlo, and his son Bob were already sitting there chatting.

"Donuts!" Bob said and leaped up to claim his favorite. Manelli looked around at the comfy nest they had made for themselves among the filing cabinets. There were as many odd chairs as odd people in the group, some salvaged from home, the library upstairs, and possibly the streetcorners on trash pickup day. The chairs, not the writers.

He glanced up at the clerestory windows of the lowest level of Town Hall. It was summer and still light outside. He poured himself a mug of coffee from the ancient coffeemaker that must have been bought at a yard sale and sat down as the rest of the group filed in.

Cassie carried her tray of cream puffs carefully. Manelli figured she had something to spring on them because she had gone to so much trouble. When she finally slid the tray onto the table, he arched an eyebrow at her. The rest of the writers were busy filling their mugs.

"Why the high-caloric offering?" Jessie asked.

"I'm going to miss some meetings because of my delayed honeymoon. Actually it's a working honeymoon," Cassie said.

"What?" Mary Alice almost choked on her coffee.

"I have a writers' conference in Nashville. Sam is going to drop me off there, then go on to shoot egrets in Louisiana."

"With his camera, I hope," Colleen said.

"That's right. Then I'll go join him for our often postponed honeymoon."

"In the swamp." Night Train seemed amused.

"I'll be away as well," Colleen said. "I've won a literary prize and a free trip to Ireland for the acceptance ceremony." She bowed at the general applause and whooping.

"This makes my news easier to deliver," Manelli said. "They have discovered mold down here since the flood, so our meeting room and the archives will be off limits for the whole summer. Everything will have to be packed and moved out of here until they completely renovate the room."

A universal groan went up from the group. "What about our furniture?" Merris asked.

"The chief of police who is overseeing the project assures me they will pack and preserve all of it."

Gwyneth sighed and her puppy tried to comfort her. "Good timing. My boss included me in a business trip to Las Vegas, and Tazz is invited as well."

"I know how you all love to solve cold cases, then come back here to dissect them, but we are all going to have to take a short vacation from sleuthing," Manelli said. "My advice is to actually go on vacation, get some sun, have fun, and come back fresh for more work in September. I know that's what I'm going to do."

Lazlo looked at his son Bob. "Disney World, here we come."

"No way, Dad. I'm headed for the Outer Banks."

Nick Oakley nodded and said, "I really need a vacation."

"It's staycation time for me and Lindsay," Night Train said. "I'm planning on a fun staycation."

"Me too," said Mary Alice. "With no money in the bank for me right now, I'm planning an undercover vacation. I have a client who wants me to keep an eye on her husband and her money, says she can't wait any longer. It should be fun sharpening my disguise skills."

Manelli held up a hand to get their attention. It helped that there was a cream puff in it. "I know we'll all miss each other, murder, and pastries for the duration, but we still have one meeting left before our hiatus. Who has something to share?"

Character Bio from Ed Kelemen

Detective Brendan Manelli takes cold cases—and some hot ones—to a local writers' group, the Sleuths and Serpents, who meet at the library in the small town of Falls Bend. Manelli works out of the Laurel Falls Police District Office, which often helps local police with murder cases countywide. He presents the cases at the Sleuths and Serpents' regular meetings. Each amateur sleuth seeks the inspiration of a fictional detective from literature to solve cases.

Brendan stands an even six feet tall and weighs an athletic 180 pounds, though his shoulders sag a bit with the weight of twenty years on the job and forty-two years on the planet. His curly black hair has a sprinkle of grey here and there, and his startling blue eyes exude sympathy from a ruddy, crinkly face with a winsome smile. His ability to portray a sympathetic father confessor has allowed him to wring information from the most recalcitrant of criminals.

Brendan enjoys an occasional beer with his cronies and is fond of hand-rolled cigars made by Cuban refugees. The cigars are shipped to him by a friend in Puerto Rico. However often he is seen gnawing on one of these expensive beauties, the only time he actually lights one is as he descends the courthouse steps after a homicide case has been brought to what he considers a proper conclusion. (This usually means a guilty verdict.) He does not actually smoke.

Character Bios from Ronald J. Shafer

Curtis "Night Train" Dupre is a retired police officer who now owns his own agency, Dupre Investigations. He joined the Sleuths and Serpents seven years ago, when he began writing fiction to escape the tedious monotony of working on police reports. A lifelong resident of Greensburg, he now runs his agency out of the house he shares with his adopted daughter, Lindsay King. His inspirational detective is Anna Pigeon from Nevada Barr's series about a national park ranger.

Lindsay King, the youngest member of the Sleuths and Serpents, began writing stories at the age of eight. She joined the Sleuths and Serpents four years ago and now writes a biweekly column for her school newspaper.

She works part-time answering phones and doing filing for Dupre Investigations, but she has helped solve several cases. Her psychic detective is the 1930s-era Nancy Drew.

When not writing or working, she can be found practicing the piano and clarinet, attending Girl Scout meetings, drawing, reading, and hanging out with her best friend, Chelsea Beacon.

Chelsea Beacon is the second-youngest member of the Sleuths and Serpents. She is an aspiring poet, songwriter, and artist. Her short-term goals are to become a rock star and to have her own art exhibit, but her long-term goal is to become a partner with her best friend Lindsay King in Dupre Investigations. Chelsea and her family live in Greensburg.

My Summer Staycation

Ronald J. Shafer

"Uncle C," Chelsea asked, "where's your license plate?"

"I'm in no mood for jokes this morning, Chelsea," I said. Chelsea is Chelsea Beacon, a dark-haired fourteen-year-old white girl who has known me nearly all her life and calls me her uncle, though we're not related. She's the best friend of my fourteen-year-old adopted white daughter, Lindsay King-Dupre. Both girls spend their summers and weekends working in my office. I'm Curtis "Night Train" Dupre, Black, former cop, and the owner of Dupre Investigations.

It was a typical early August morning in Greensburg, our little slice of western Pennsylvania. Temperatures had already climbed through the mid-seventies on the way to a high somewhere in the nineties, and the humidity was so high that just thinking about moving made a person break out in sweat. I was wearing a T-shirt and shorts and feeling overdressed, and the girls were wearing halter tops and short shorts. And as if the heat and humidity weren't enough, the air-conditioning in the house had stopped working.

"No joke," Chelsea said. "Your plate's gone. See for yourself."

The girls followed me out to the driveway. Sure enough, the plate was missing.

"When was the last time you saw it?" Lindsay asked.

"Yesterday, when I washed the car." I said a few words to myself that I couldn't use in front of the girls, then said aloud, "Can this day get any worse? I was supposed to get the car inspected this morning. Now I have to call the shop and cancel." I reached for my cell phone as we walked back to the house.

Charlie Watkins, the shop's owner, answered. I explained the situation. "No problem," he said. "In fact, you're doing me a favor. My helper called off again, and I'm already running so far behind I think I'm in front."

"That worthless bum's always complaining he has no money, but he hasn't worked a full week in over two months," Charlie said. "I'd like to fire his lazy butt, but I haven't been able to find anyone else who wants to work for what I can afford to pay."

We rescheduled for the next week, and I hung up.

"I need to see about a new plate," I said to the girls. "You can come up to the state police barracks with me, or you can stay here and run the office. Your choice."

"We'll stay here and wait for the repairman," Lindsay said. "We'll call you if he comes."

I grabbed my keys and headed back out to the car. I knew I shouldn't drive because of the missing plate, but I didn't want to walk the mile or so to the police barracks in the heat. Beads of sweat formed on my forehead before I had even settled into the front seat, and I cranked my Chevy's AC to the max as soon as the engine turned over. Within minutes I was talking to a dark-haired, late-thirties trooper I knew from my days as a city cop.

"This has been going on for a month," she said. "I haven't even had my coffee yet, and you're already the third person to come in about a lost plate. How'd you lose it?"

I told her the story, and she handed me a booklet. "You should know what to do," she said. "Make sure you get this notarized, and don't forget, no unnecessary driving."

"No problem," I said. As I turned to leave, a sixtyish-looking woman dressed in capris and a tank top walked in. "Who do I see about getting a stolen license plate replaced?" she asked.

"Looks like I'm giving up coffee today," the trooper said to me. To the woman she said, "Me."

I hung around to listen. The woman's name was Autumn Ishikawa, and she was from Washington state. Her plate had been stolen from the parking lot of the motel where she was staying.

The trooper finished her report, then said, "I'm afraid there's not much I can do for you. You need to contact the Washington state DMV to get your license plate replaced."

"Can I still drive my car?" Autumn asked.

"Not unless you want to get pulled over by every officer who sees you. My advice is to get a rental till you get a new plate.

"And that goes for you, too," the trooper said, looking at me. "We have some new people around here who'd ticket their own mothers for not using a turn signal; they wouldn't think twice about writing you up, even if you are a former cop."

I followed Autumn out the door and introduced myself. "If you'd like," I said, handing her a business card, "I can follow you to your motel and then drive you to the car rental place. Bus and taxi service around here is nothing to write home about, and I'm going there anyway."

She stared at the card, looked at me, then held out her hand. "You're on, Mr. Dupre," she said.

"Most folks call me Train or Night Train," I said.

We drove to a motel on the south end of town, about ten minutes from the barracks. She pulled her car into a spot near the office and climbed into mine. "What brings you to western PA?" I asked.

"I'm on my way to D.C.," she said. "I was tired of staying at places along the interstates, so when I saw the billboard for a motel in Greensburg, I thought I'd give it a try. I wasn't expecting to make it a long-term layover, though."

"Maybe the plate won't take long. What's in D.C? Relatives?"

"The Vietnam Memorial. I go there every year."

"You were in the service?"

She nodded. "Army nurse. Some of the guys I knew have their names on that wall."

"Same with me. I'm ex-infantry."

"Have you ever been to the Wall?" she asked.

"No."

"Why not?"

"That's a part of my life I try not to think about." A slight nod of her head told me that she understood.

We didn't say much more till we got to the car rental, where Autumn got a Camry and I picked up a Sentra. She followed me to my place, where I pulled my Chevy into the garage, then drove me back to the car rental.

"Thanks for the lift," I said as I reached for the door handle. "If you need help with anything while you're in town, call me. You have my card."

I got back to my own house just before the air conditioning guy arrived. An hour later the unit was working again and I was feeling much cooler.

"I'm not going outside again till November," I said to the

girls.

"Did you forget about your new plate?" Lindsay said.

"Not really. I'm just in denial." I called my friend Gwyneth Gates. Gwyneth works at a car dealership and includes notary work among her many job duties.

"Come on over," she said after I told her my story. "That won't take long to fix."

The girls and I piled into the rental, made a quick stop at the grocery store, and drove over to see Gwyneth. Though her office door was open, I knocked anyway. Gwyneth, dressed in a Snoopy T-shirt and dark jeans, sat at her desk, which was almost invisible amid the stacks of papers, mail, and license plates that covered it. The girls said hi, then wandered off in search of snacks at the customers' waiting area.

"How's the rat race going?" I said, handing her the grocery bag.

"As you can see," she said, waving her hand over all the mess, "the rats are winning." She peeked inside the grocery bag. "M&Ms and dog biscuits. Tazz and I thank you very much."

Gwyneth and I belong to the same writers' group, the Sleuths and Serpents. She waives her notary fee for the group's members, so we always bring a gift of appreciation for her and her dog.

"Okay," she said while putting the bag on the desk with one hand and reaching toward me with the other. "Let's see that booklet."

We chatted while she worked. "We've had a number of people come in for the same reason," she said. "The rumor is that it's college kids looking for back-to-school decorations for their dorm rooms, but I don't think so."

"Why not?"

"Because I've worked here for nearly fifty years, and in all that time, I have never, ever seen this many plates disappear in one summer."

It didn't take long to do the paperwork. I herded the girls out of a showroom Mustang they had been sitting in, and we left. I told them about what Gwyneth had said as I drove.

"I agree with her," Chelsea said. "It doesn't sound right to me."

"Yeah," said Lindsay. "If it was just one or two plates, sure. But not when this has been going on for weeks."

We talked about the case off and on until late that afternoon, when I drove the girls to Chelsea's house for a sleepover. I had just gotten home from that when my cell phone rang.

"Is there any place to eat around here that isn't a chain or fast-food restaurant?" Autumn asked.

"Absolutely," I said. "Do you like fish?"

"Sure."

"Then I'll pick you up at seven. No need to dress up." I changed into jeans and a Pirates T-shirt and drove off.

Autumn was sitting in a chair by the pool, wearing jeans and a sleeveless top. We drove through town till we came to an old wooden building near the downtown section. A neon Budweiser sign in the lone front window gave the only clue that the place was a bar.

"Welcome to the Greensburg Grille," I said as we stepped inside. "Home of the best fish sandwich this side of the Mississippi."

The place had two rooms. The smaller room held a bar, a juke box, and a half dozen tables; twice as many tables filled the larger room. I said hello to some of the regulars as we made our way to a table near the back of the larger room. Menus already sat on the table. I picked one up out of habit, while Autumn looked around.

"It's gotten a lot quieter in here since we walked in," she said. "And people are staring at us."

"Ignore them," said the waitress, who had walked up behind Autumn. "They're staring because Train hasn't brought a woman in here since his wife left. And that's been years."

"Hello, Rosa," I said to the short, pear-shaped woman. I introduced her to Autumn.

"It's about time you found someone," Rosa said in her slight Italian accent. "You spend too much time by yourself."

There didn't seem much point in telling her that Autumn was just passing through town, so I let her comment slide. She left after taking our orders for fish sandwiches, fries, and a couple of drafts.

"So you don't date much?" Autumn asked.

"Not much. At least not since Lindsay and I became a family."

"I'm flattered that I'm the first. But why don't you go out

some?"

"Too many responsibilities, not enough time."

"Is that the only reason?"

"I'm over the divorce, if that's what you mean. I moved on a long time ago."

"But you haven't gotten over Vietnam yet. Why not, if you don't mind my asking?"

"I just don't like talking about it," I said. The edge in my voice caught her by surprise.

"Sorry," I said. "You didn't deserve that."

"No, I'm the one who should apologize to you. I didn't mean to pry."

Rosa brought two iced mugs to the table. I took a long drink from mine, then looked at Autumn. "I was still in grade school when Kennedy sent the first troops over," I said. "The country supported them. Then by the time I got out of high school, everything got turned upside down.

"I had wanted to be a soldier for as long as I can remember. That was going to be my career. I gave up a football scholarship to enlist, even though Americans were turning against the military and what was going on over there."

Rosa brought the food over. Autumn took a bite while I went on. "You remember what it was like. The protests, the violence. People spitting on us, calling us murderers. But they didn't know what it was really like. All they knew was what they saw on TV, what they read in the papers.

"I didn't expect to come home to a ticker-tape parade," I said. "But I didn't expect to come home to all the hatred, either."

Rosa brought another round of drafts, and we made small talk for the rest of the meal. It wasn't until we were driving back to the motel that Autumn said, "I felt the way you did when I got out. It was my late husband's idea for us to make the first trip to the Wall. He thought it might help me heal. I had my doubts, but it turned out he was right.

"At some point going there stopped being about me and became about the people whose names are on that wall. I don't go there to remember the war, I go there to remember them. Going there helped me get over what happened, and I'm betting it would help you, too."

We reached the motel, and I pulled into the lot.

"I'm not asking you for an answer right away," Autumn said. "Just give this some thought. I'll be here for a while yet, but when I leave, I wouldn't mind having some company."

I promised to sleep on it, and then I drove off.

The next day brought no break in the heat wave. Chelsea's mom dropped the girls off, and the three of us ate breakfast. When Chelsea left the room, Lindsay said, "I had the strangest dream last night. I dreamed that I found a license plate, and all of a sudden Nancy was there. She told me that she couldn't help with the case because she was on vacation."

I nearly dropped my slice of toast. "I had the same dream, only it was Anna who showed up. She said she was on vacation, too."

Nancy and Anna are Nancy Drew and Anna Pigeon, our muses. They come to us and provide inspiration whenever we're stuck on a case. Every member of the Sleuths and Serpents has one.

"So I guess we'll just have to do this on our own," Lindsay said.

"Do what on your own?" Chelsea asked as she sat back down. I glanced at Lindsay. She glanced at me. The only sound came from the air-conditioning vents.

"Break up this theft ring," I finally said. "No cops or writers' group help."

"What's wrong with your muses?"

Lindsay had the same deer-in-the-headlights look that I was sure I had. "What muses?" I asked.

"Oh, come on. Anna and Nancy. Don't even think I don't know. I've been to some of your meetings, remember?"

Chelsea has started writing and occasionally brings a piece in for feedback from the group. "Do you know how much time you guys spend talking about everything but writing while you're there? It's amazing that you get anything accomplished. And you don't care who's around when you're talking. If that group worked for the CIA, there'd be no such thing as the phrase 'Top Secret.'"

"Well," Lindsay said, "since you already know about our muses, you might as well know that they've turned this case over to us."

"Really? Cool. Now we can work the case like real detectives."

"Whoa," I said. "What's this about we? I'm the P.I. You two handle the phone and the filing, remember?"

"For now," Chelsea said. "But you're old. You can't do this forever. Eventually Lindsay and I will take over, so we might as well start training now."

"Besides," Lindsay said, "we've worked together before. The three of us make a good team."

Though I hated to admit it, the girls had a point. More than one point, actually. Every time I looked in the mirror I seemed to have less and less hair, and what was still there had more and more grey. Though I weighed the same as I did when I was a cop, much of the weight had shifted so that my stomach now hung over my belt. It had been a long time since I'd solved a case without a tip from Anna Pigeon, and with her gone, I might need some assistance.

"Okay," I said, "here's the deal. You two have Girl Scout camp next week. When you get back, you can help. And when I get done eating, I'll call Manelli to see what he knows about the thefts."

Brendan Manelli is a detective for the Laurel Falls Police. After he spoke at one of our writers' meetings a few years ago, the members helped him get rid of some of his cold cases, which earned him a bunch of bonus points with his bosses. He was grateful, and we've had a good relationship with him ever since.

"License plates are way down on the totem pole," Manelli said when I called. "There's so much crime around the county right now that all the departments are overwhelmed. The chief even reassigned me. I've been working on car thefts for the past month. Why do you want to know about plates?"

After hearing about what happened to Autumn and me, he said, "I'll see what I can find out and get back to you." I thanked him and hung up.

The girls worked on getting packed for camp while I took care of some paperwork. Around lunchtime, my cell phone rang. "What are you doing for dinner tonight?" Autumn asked.

"Probably throwing a few burgers on the grill for me and the girls," I said. "Why?"

"I'm in the mood for Chinese. The phone book lists a bunch of places. If you help me pick one, dinner's on me. Bring the girls. I'd love to meet them. And I won't say a word about Vietnam."

"Cooking in the hot sun suddenly lost its appeal," I said. "What time?"

Autumn pulled her rental into the driveway at five-thirty. After introductions, we all discussed the pros and cons of the local restaurants, finally deciding on a buffet at a strip mall on the east end of town. "Leave your car here," I said. "It'll be quicker if I drive."

The evening was sunny and the sky cloudless, though rain was in the forecast for later. Traffic was heavy on both sides of the highway. "Looks like no one feels like cooking tonight," I said when we pulled off into the plaza. "We may not find a place to park."

We didn't. After circling the restaurant's lot twice, I found a spot two businesses down. As we walked back to the restaurant, Chelsea said something to Lindsay and pointed to a silver SUV pulling into a newly emptied parking space.

We had better luck getting seated than we did finding a parking spot, and we started making trips to the buffet tables. We shared stories about life on the eastern and western ends of the country as we ate. By the time we left, the sun hung low in the sky.

As we drove through the lot on our way back to the highway, Chelsea leaned forward.

"What's wrong?" I said.

"That SUV in front of us," she said. "I saw it when we pulled in. The license plate's different now."

"Are you sure that's the same one?" I said. "There are probably at least twenty silver SUVs in this lot."

"I'm positive. The rear window's smudged, like some little kids wiped their hands all over it. And I know the plate's different because I showed it to Lindsay. The one that was on it had my mom's initials and my and Lindsay's birthdays. And I'll bet that when the driver hits the brakes, the light on the driver's side is out."

As if on cue, the brake lights came on. The one on the driver's side didn't work.

"Okay," I said, "I'm convinced. Lindsay, call Manelli and let him know what's going on. Ask him to run the plate. I'll follow the car till we hear from him. But if it pulls into someone's driveway and a couple of innocent kids get out with their parents, Chelsea owes us all breakfast for a week."

"Deal," said Chelsea. "And when you find out that the plate is stolen and probably the car, and we catch the thieves and solve the case, you owe us lunch for a week. And I don't mean at your house. I'm talking real food, like that all-you-can-eat buffet."

I stayed far enough behind the SUV to keep its driver from getting suspicious, an easy job in the evening traffic due to that burned-out light. After a couple of miles, the SUV turned onto a two-lane highway, past a couple of housing plans into the farmland, and then onto a two-lane blacktop. "It looks like our suspects are heading for the mountains," I said.

The road narrowed and the number of houses along the road decreased as we climbed, till we were soon winding our way through nothing but woods along the top of the mountain. The curves made it harder to keep the SUV in sight.

Lindsay's phone rang. "That was Detective Manelli," she said. "The plate's stolen."

"Way to go, Chelsea," Autumn said. "What made you check the license plate?"

"I've been looking at license plates since before I could read. My family and I play games every time we go anywhere. We try to see who can find the most out-of-state plates, the most vanity plates, the plate from the farthest away. You name it, we look for it. I can tell you the plate colors of nearly every state and most parts of Canada."

"It's true," Lindsay said. "Try going out with her family sometime. It is so annoying. Two minutes and you're ready to jump out of the car."

"You did a good job, Chelsea," I said, "but we're going to have to break off soon. We've been following them a long time, and if we go on much longer, we might spook them."

Mother Nature broke the chase off for us. A doe and two fawns stepped out of the woods and stopped on the road between us and the other car. We watched as the SUV rounded one more curve and disappeared. By the time the deer moved on, there was no hope of catching it.

I turned around, and we headed back to the city. "What do we do now?" Lindsay asked.

"We," I said, "do nothing. At least for now. You two, on the other hand, will be going to camp tomorrow. Meanwhile, we need to call Manelli and let him know what we found."

Manelli agreed that the stolen plates could be connected to the rash of car thefts and promised to look into it. We also agreed to keep one another posted on what was happening. Before she left for her motel, Autumn and I decided that tomorrow we'd drive back through the area where we had lost the SUV.

The rain that had been in the forecast fell for most of the night, driving out the heat and humidity, leaving partial sunshine and a more comfortable temperature. Chelsea's parents picked up the girls after lunch and drove them to camp. I had just begun getting used to the quiet in the house when Autumn pulled smoothly into the driveway.

"I thought we might take my car today," she said when I opened the front door. "It's silly to rent a car and then just have it sit. Is that okay?" Though we were both dressed in jeans and T-shirts, she looked a whole lot better than I did.

"I was thinking the same thing," I said. "No sense in having the thieves see my car again so soon. If they're even in the area, that is."

I had borrowed a couple of Chelsea's and Lindsay's old backpacks and stuffed them with food and water. "In case we need to go exploring," I said, handing her a pack. "We'll just look like a couple of senior citizens out on a hike."

Traffic was light, and once we passed the spot where we had stopped the previous night, we kept our eyes open for any sign of the missing SUV. A number of side roads branched off from the blacktop. "They could have taken any one of these roads," Autumn said.

"Or they could have stayed on this road and driven anywhere. We knew this wouldn't be easy. Let's give it another couple of miles, and if we don't find anything we'll go back and explore the other roads."

We drove on without seeing anything. Just as I was about to suggest turning around, we passed an overgrown road with a chain stretched across it. "Find a place where you can pull over," I said. "I want to take a closer look at that."

"Why?"

"It's out of place. No other road or driveway that we've seen was blocked off. Why this one? It may not be anything. It may lead just to a gas well, a sawmill, or someone's hunting camp. But it's the only promising thing we've seen so far."

She found a spot a quarter mile up the road. We grabbed our packs and started walking. When we reached the overgrown road, we noticed that the chain and lock were new and the tire tracks in the mud were recent.

"Let's follow the tracks," I said, "but from inside the woods. If we see anyone coming, it'll be easier to hide."

The road eventually led to a clearing, where we saw an old two-story wooden house, two wooden outbuildings, and a small barn that had recently had its sides and roof replaced. There was no sign of vehicles or people. "What should we do now?" Autumn asked.

"Stay back here in the woods and watch to see if anything happens," I said. "We still don't know what this is, so there's no sense bringing in the police."

We watched the property for the next two hours. Nothing happened. "I've been thinking," I said, "and my thought is that we're wasting our time sitting here in the middle of the afternoon. The car we saw was stolen late in the day. Maybe the others were, too. If that's the case, we need to be here around sundown."

"Why don't we just sit here and wait till then?"

"Because your car's in plain sight. We can pass ourselves off as hikers during the day, but not after dark. We need to rethink this."

We hiked back out of the woods to Autumn's car and drove home. "How about some coffee?" I asked when she pulled into my driveway.

"How about a beer instead?" she said.

We formed a new plan over a dinner of beer and backpack leftovers. I would contact Manelli in the morning to see if the vehicles were indeed being stolen late in the day. If so, we would shift our surveillance to the evening hours. Then I'd call in some favors and recruit people to drive us to the site and pick us up again. We would go into the woods a couple of hours before sundown and stay till a couple of hours after dark. If nothing happened, we'd call our driver to pick us up. If anything was going on there that shouldn't be, we'd call Manelli. And if whatever was going on out there was totally legit and we were barking up the wrong tree, we'd go back to square one. And Chelsea would keep the group well fed.

Though I tried to talk Autumn out of coming along, she

wouldn't hear of it. "You shouldn't be out there alone," she said. "What if something happens? You could trip in the dark and get hurt, or even get caught. You need someone there to help, just in case."

She added, "I promise to listen and do whatever you tell me. You're the professional; I'm not. But you're not going out alone."

Truth be told, I was glad she was being stubborn. Though I'd prefer having someone more experienced with me, I enjoyed her company.

"If you're going to be on the team, then you need to do some of the work," I said. "While I'm doing research, you're in charge of supplies. Pick up some water, food, flashlights. I have binoculars, but you may want a set for yourself. If we need anything else, I'll get it."

The next morning brought more rain. I drove over to Laurel Falls to talk to Manelli. As I suspected, the license plates were getting stolen overnight, while the cars were taken just before sundown.

The rain continued the next day, varying between light showers and downpours. Neither Autumn nor I was excited over the thought of sitting in the woods and getting soaked, so she visited tourist attractions and I called Charlie to cancel my inspection.

"That worthless, no-good helper of mine didn't show up again today," he said. "That loafer's so lazy he won't even answer his phone. I've had it with him. I found a guy willing to work part-time, so if Mister Useless ever does show up, he's fired." I told him I'd be in touch when I got my new plate and spent the rest of the day working in my office.

By the next day the rain had moved off to the east, and we were ready to go. Chelsea's dad agreed to drive us out to the site and pick us up for as long as we needed. We would rotate among his car, mine, and Autumn's so that the same vehicle wouldn't be seen in the area each day. We'd also stagger the times that we came and went so as not to show a pattern.

Autumn and I picked out a spot close enough to the buildings for us to see anything that was going on, yet far enough back in the woods that we wouldn't be seen.

The first two nights brought a nearly full moon, which made traveling in the woods easier, but there was no sign of the thieves or of anyone else. On the third night, Friday, Autumn and I went out with Chelsea's parents for dinner. Then they dropped us off at the site.

After checking out the area and again seeing no sign of activity, we settled in just before sunset. "We had better catch these guys soon," Autumn said. "I can't stay in town much longer."

I didn't know what to say. She had been here only a week, but we had spent so much of that time together that I was starting to feel like she was another member of the agency.

"So when do you need to leave?" I finally said.

"Monday at the latest. Much as I've enjoyed spending all this time here, I need to get to D.C. My sister's been housesitting for me, but she's a teacher and has to go back to work soon."

"That still gives us time. Maybe we'll catch a break and get these guys before then."

We spent the next several minutes in silence. I pretended to watch the area, but I couldn't stop thinking about Autumn. There was a part of me that wanted her new plate to never come. Though I loved Lindsay and Chelsea, it was nice to just spend some quality time with an adult for a change. Especially an adult as attractive and pleasant as Autumn.

"I wish you'd change your mind and come to D.C. with me," she said, interrupting my thoughts. "We can leave Monday morning and visit the Wall, and you can be back home before bedtime. And you could bring the girls; it would be a good history lesson for them. I really believe that going there would do you good."

Before I could answer, we heard a car engine behind us. We turned and watched as a pickup truck pulled into the clearing alongside the garage. I pulled the binos up to my eyes and saw a man get out, unlock a side door, and go inside.

"I know that guy," I whispered. A few seconds later the main door opened, allowing us to see in.

They've sure got a lot of tools and equipment in there," Autumn said. "What should we do?"

"I'll text Manelli and let him know what's happening. You text Chelsea's dad and tell him to come and get us. If something illegal's going on, I don't want us to be here when the cops come. If this is all nothing, then there's no use wasting our time."

We sent our messages and waited. Inside the garage, a compressor started. Then another vehicle came up the road. The car, a late-model sedan, was driven inside the garage. The door closed, but not before I got a good look at the license plate.

This time I called Manelli and asked him to run the plate. It didn't take long. "Stolen," he said. "Cars are on the way."

"Make it fast," I said, "it sounds like they're going to chop it. We're heading out, so this is all yours. If anyone asks, you got an anonymous tip. Call me tomorrow with the details."

The next morning I drove up to scout camp to pick up the girls. During the trip back, I filled them in. Chelsea wanted to stay with us till I heard from Manelli, so I headed for the house. Autumn was waiting on the front porch, looking as if she lived there.

"Bagels and fruit," she said, holding up a couple of bags. "You supply the coffee."

The weather was sunny but comfortable, so we ate outside. Manelli called to say that he was in the area and would stop by with the story of last night's arrests. He soon pulled into the driveway and joined us on the porch. "This is Autumn," I said. "She helped us with the case."

"I only sat and stared at empty buildings," she said. "Chelsea solved it. Had it not been for her, those thieves would still be out there."

"Here's to Chelsea," I said, raising my coffee cup. The others joined me as Chelsea's face turned the color of one of Autumn's strawberries.

"You broke up a pretty big operation," Manelli said to her. "This theft ring covered two counties. The guys doing the stealing were local." He took out his notepad and read off the names.

"I recognize that last guy. He works down at Charlie's, my mechanic," I said.

"Not anymore," Manelli said. "He's going to be taking some time off. A lot of time."

Thank goodness Charlie had found a new helper, I thought.

"These guys would steal a bunch of plates and then switch them out when they stole a car," Manelli said. "So if we were looking for a blue Camaro with a certain license plate, and we saw a blue Camaro with a plate that didn't match what we were looking for, we had no reason to stop the car. A pretty slick trick.

"One of the other guys had the property. It was a hunting camp, but he figured he could make some extra money by using the place year-round."

"So how did this become a two-county operation?" Autumn asked.

"The guy's cousin has a body shop in Fayette County. He'd call when he needed parts for a certain model car. The thieves would steal one, chop it, and truck the parts over to him. Anything that was left over went along, and the body-shop owner would sell it for scrap. Then he'd bill the insurance company for the parts, and all the guys would split the money."

Manelli finished his coffee. "I've got to run," he said. "The family's going on vacation tomorrow, and I have a to-do list a mile long."

The girls went inside to unpack Lindsay's gear, leaving Autumn and me alone on the porch. "It looks as if everyone's going places this summer but you," she said. "I've got to get back to the motel, but my offer still stands. If you change your mind, call me."

I watched her drive off, then walked inside and sat down in my office. Maybe she was right, I thought. Maybe it was time to let go. It wouldn't hurt to try. If nothing else, I'd have one more day with Autumn, and the girls would get a history lesson. I picked up the phone and called Chelsea's parents.

The girls joined me. "I've been thinking while I was at camp," Lindsay said. "What if this thing about Nancy and Anna being gone was a sign?"

"What do you mean?" I asked.

"What if this whole vacation story was a scam?" she said. "What if they're trying to tell us that we don't need them anymore? You didn't have a muse when you were a policeman. I didn't have one till I joined the writers' group. And Chelsea doesn't even have a muse. Maybe they're trying to tell us that we can run this business on our own. Or maybe," she added, "we already have a new muse. Chelsea."

"You may be onto something," I said, "but let's not rush into it. Remember, good detectives gather evidence, analyze the data, and then come to a conclusion. Let's give this some time and see what happens."

"No offense to Nancy and Anna," Chelsea said, "but I

don't want to be a muse. I have bigger plans. I'm thinking long term here. Junior partner at least. What about you, Lindsay? Do you want to take over when we ship the boss off to the old folks' home?"

"Don't look for that to happen anytime soon," I said. "But speaking of going away, how would you two like to take one last summer trip, to our nation's capital?" I told them about Autumn's offer.

"Your parents are okay with it," I said to Chelsea. "I told them we'd be over soon, and they'll bring you back here tonight.'

"Cool," Chelsea said.

"Works for me," Lindsay said.

"Then I'll call Autumn." The girls headed back to Lindsay's room, and I reached for my cell phone.

"How about dinner tonight?" I said when she picked up. "The four of us. A celebration."

"Do you always celebrate when you close a case?"

"Not the case. Something else."

"What?"

"Healing," I said. "Letting go."

"Then pick me up at six," she said. "I'm looking forward to it."

Character Bios from Tom Beck

Mary Alice Brandon is twenty-eight years old, five ten, blond, 138 pounds, with icy-blue eyes. Because she is blonde and large breasted, many people assume her mental capacity must be limited, but she's smart, has always been nosy, and naturally rebels against what people think. It just seemed normal for her to expand those abilities and become a private investigator. Many people, especially men, say things in front of her that may incriminate them. Mary Alice's muse who helps her solve crimes is the ghost of actress Mae West.

> Private eye Brandon
> used womanly attributes
> with Mae West, solved crimes.

I'll Have a Brandi

Thomas Beck

"May I help you?" I asked.

Mrs. Florine D'Amato walked into my second-floor walk-up office. She was a rather substantial woman in wealth and body shape, an influential woman in the community of La Crosse. I easily recognized her from her frequent pictures in the society section of the La Crosse Chronicle. She took a seat at the front of my old, wooden desk. It was a battered, secondhand monstrosity topped by a large, last-year's calendar and a small metal plaque announcing that I was Mary A. Brandon: private investigator.

"Well, you see—" She hesitated, not quite sure how to proceed. "I have a problem and I think I need your help," she said.

"Please, tell me what I can do for you."

"I'm worried." Again she paused. "I financially backed my second husband, Ray, in a business venture. Now I need a full accounting of my husband on several fronts. I need to know, is his business acumen as sound as he presented it to me at first and is he being faithful to me? I'm having second thoughts about my investment in him and the business." Once she started, it all began to tumble out.

"I am in love with Ray, but trust in that emotion only extends so far. My love for him may have blinded my vision. Needing a complete accounting of my money, I came to you. You were recommended to me by one of my dear friends.

"She hired you to follow her womanizing husband, before she sued for divorce. You apparently impressed her with the thoroughness of your investigation, and the fact that you're a woman and could understand what she was feeling helped too.

"I've already had words with my husband and his accountant, Cal, about a full financial disclosure, but I've been pushed aside. Ray assured me that the business was new. He was still getting everything in order. The books were a mess. He told me that he was trying to work with Cal to put the flow of the money that Ray spent and the profits that the company's earned into a more easily recognizable shape. Cal and he were butting heads over the best way to do that. Ray liked his way of record keeping and Cal had his way. As soon as they worked it out, he would share them with me. And that makes me nervous."

While she was talking, I was able to assess Mrs. D'Amato. She made my casual business attire seem downright ratty. I wore a pale yellow silk blouse and tan slacks. She was a beautiful full-figured woman, well dressed in a champagne-hued Armani suit and a diamond ring on her finger that would make a glass doorknob hide in shame.

"Oh my, honey," Mae West crooned. "Just look at that rock. It makes me drool, and her clothes are so beautiful. She's so shapely. She fills her suit quite well, don't you think?"

By now I was used to Mae's voice appearing out of nowhere and talking to me. She shared her intelligence and sensuality whenever she felt like it. Only I could hear her voice, and she seemed to read my thoughts.

"You can't trust a skinny woman. You're excluded of course, my dear." Mae gave a little snort of a laugh. "As you can tell."

A picture of Mae sliding her hands over her curves came to mind. "I've never believed in diets. The only carrots that have ever interested me were the number that I could get in a diamond."

Mae, I'm so glad that I am the only person that can hear you.

She frequently embarrassed me, like she just had. She was often very blunt with me, but I was thankful to have such a beautifully glamorous, worldly, and sexy woman as my muse. A blonde queen of the risqué in Hollywood, she'd filled the silver screen with her racy innuendos. I never would have been able to become a femme fatale for my next case without her guidance.

"Ray started a used car lot in LaCrosse. His plan was to sell high-priced, high-end cars in an indoor sales arena. At the time, I didn't think too much of it, but I researched it and there seemed to be a market for it. The place he chose was at the intersection of two busy highways. A lot of rich businessmen and wealthy people drive by that intersection. Most live or work in the area. A traffic light caused people to stop at the crossroads. As they waited, they would look at the inventory that appeared as advertising," Mrs. D'Amato said. "The population base and the volume of traffic that drove by his salesroom supported the idea.

"I felt it was a great strategy until he invited me for the grand opening. I was aghast when I saw the reality behind his plan." She raised the hand that had been resting on her lap to finger the gold locket at the base of her throat.

"Are you okay, Mrs. D'Amato?" I asked.

"I'm fine, but please call me Florine."

"When I drove out to see the property, I thought that it was very clean and businesslike. Even the signage was upscale. Ray had a huge flat display screen installed that filled the window next to the entrance, presenting photographs of the vehicles that were being offered inside. One picture slowly faded into the next car. The photos would alternate with the logo for the business. It read 'TOOTERS' and in smaller lettering beneath it 'quality vintage vehicles.'

"At first, that play on words didn't bother me at all. That is, until I walked inside and saw all of the salesgirls in tight short shorts and well-filled halter tops. I began to question my reasoning and Ray's integrity. I need you to get inside and investigate. One of the girls is pregnant and has decided to quit in a few weeks —" Florine left the unfinished sentence hang between us. It said much more than she could have said in words. Her hand left her throat and fluttered in midair.

Mae shared in her rich, husky, feminine voice, "You are all woman and you're going to have to flaunt two of your best attributes for your next assignment. You know, I'm not the woman who discovered curves. I only uncovered them; just like you will need to do."

"It's a good thing to know ahead of time that you'll have to put all of your ASSets on display," she cooed. "There are no good girls gone wrong, just bad girls found out, you know."

I saw Florine's concern. Who wouldn't be upset if her husband forced salespeople to wear revealing outfits? I was mulling over the requested assignment when Mae said, "Pregnant? With all of those beauties under him, no wonder she's questioning her investment in the business and in her husband. I'm sure she wants to be sure the business he's into isn't monkey business. I'm no model lady; a model is just an imitation of the real thing, but I can see why she's worried."

I was reluctant at first, trying to decide whether I actually wanted to take the job or not. I had never flaunted my 38 DDs, especially in public. I wasn't ashamed of them, but I had never put them on display either. Now I was being asked to do so for money.

It almost made me feel like a prostitute.

"Packing a pair of 38s could be dangerous, but she's not asking you to be a hooker, honey. She just wants you to show off your breast attributes." Mae's seductive chuckle at her own pun danced in my ear. "You only live once, but if you do it right, once is enough."

Mae helped me make up my mind. I had bills to pay and minimal funds in my checkbook. With no other prospective clients at present, I reached into the desk drawer to pull out the necessary forms, explaining to Florine my standard rates and prices. "My normal charges are $300 per day plus expenses. I will be charging an extra $50 per day because of the, uh ... unusual nature of the disguise I will have to wear. This is not one of my normal cases."

And I will never feel comfortable in that costume.

Mae's sultry voice interrupted my thoughts and my spiel. "I can see that you're soon going to be somewhat exposed to unexpected danger, but a dame who knows the ropes isn't likely to get tied."

Thanks, Mae. That's all I needed to hear. But the need for cash flow overrode the minor, temporary discomfort that I would have to bear.

"The money I pay you is less important than finding out the truth. You'll have to go to the dealership for Ray to interview you. He will have to hire you. It would never do for me to put you on the payroll or he'd be suspicious." Florine signed my contract, then broke down and began to sob.

I pulled a tissue for her and said, "I'll go down to Tooter's warehouse in the morning and see if I can get hired." I needed to do some shopping before I went on the interview.

I stopped my old, silver-blue Reliant K car off to the side of the parking lot to study the building. The exterior of the warehouse was immaculate. The landscaping was well manicured and the parking area was smooth. It had just been resurfaced. The whole of it looked like a highclass spa or health club, if not for the signage to explain that it actually housed luxury cars.

I had already decided to use the nickname of Brandi to complete my undercover persona when I applied for the job.

As I stepped through the wide double door, I was

welcomed inside by a soft bell tone. I was immediately impressed by the faux marble floor and the variety of bright and shining automobiles glistening under the overhead lights. Each vehicle was spotlighted and surrounded by soft dimness. Each machine was an island of color in a sea of darkness. Displayed as though it was singled out as a special offering, each auto was lit as if it was the only auto on the showroom floor. The smooth, sleek surfaces glistened under the blue-white mercury lights spilling down from the darkness high above. No windows kept the showroom dark, lit only by the lights overhead.

Parked just inside the entrance was a vibrant, vintage electric-blue Lotus Europa holding the place of honor. In staggered rows behind it were Lincolns, Mercedes-Benzes, a Rolls Royce, BMWs, a Hummer, a Bentley, and a Land Rover. The least expensive car that I could see was a GMC Denali. I was impressed with the inventory.

"Oh yes, everything is so luxurious. The autos are so beautiful," Mae reminisced. "This makes me wish I still had my 1934 Duesenberg. It was a great gift and a beautiful car. I loved driving it and listening to its magnificent engine purr."

You must have been awfully good to get a car like that. "Darling, goodness had nothing to do with it." Mae laughed her rich, sultry laugh.

Ray's "office" was a raised dais surrounded by glass panels and sales cubicles. From his perch, he had a view of the entire sales floor, the cars, and the buxom women workers as well. Their sales offices surrounded his. The women had been chosen by Ray because they were able to put more on display than the cars.

Florine had told me during the initial interview, "Ray never had an original idea in his entire life. This was as close to an original thought as he ever had. Before this, he just copied the lives of other people. I found that out after I'd married him. I married him for life, but that doesn't stop me from keeping track of my assets."

"Marriage is a great institution, but I'm not ready for an institution," Mae murmured.

My attention was drawn to Ray as he stood on his raised dais. He was wearing a dark suit and a red striped tie. His silver hair glistened beneath the lights and his teeth glittered as he smiled. He strode purposefully toward me, his Oxfords lightly tapping on the "marble" floor.

A handsome man, I thought. No wonder Florine was drawn to him.

I was wearing a contour-hugging pair of jeans and a tight-fitting coral-colored blouse that had several more buttons left undone than usual. My lipstick matched the blouse. I used the lipstick to emphasize the bow-shape of my smile. I was wearing the new bustier I'd purchased just for this interview to lift my 38 DDs, and they definitely caught Ray's attention.

"You're looking good, honey. Now throw your chest out and stand up straight. You're applying for a sales position, not a librarian," Mae advised.

"Put on the performance of your life. It's better to be looked over than overlooked. You need to keep those 38s locked and loaded."

Although there were other saleswomen in the room, Ray made sure he gave me his personal attention. "May I help you?" he asked, displaying an ingratiating smile.

My cleavage had certainly caught his attention. I'd practiced twirling my long, blond locks with my finger, then tossing my head, and I did it now. "I was just looking," I said in an itsy-bitsy, know-nothing voice. I paused, then said, "Actually I was looking for a job." I gazed up at him through my lengthened eyelashes, my voice changing to a little more businesslike timbre.

"My boyfriend just dumped me and well, mister … I really need a job." I threw my shoulders back even more, hoisting my cleavage higher under his nose. I saw the twinkle in his eyes. "My friends call me Brandi," I cooed.

"Do you have any sales experience, Brandi?"

"I worked at a lingerie boutique before my boyfriend made me quit. He said he didn't want me to work." I continued the dumb blond routine. I twisted another curl and pouted my lips. His smile spread wider.

"I never said it would be easy; I only said it would be worth it," Mae said. "I think you just sold yourself."

"I can start paying you minimum wage as well as a commission on each vehicle that you sell. Is that okay?" Ray asked.

When I nodded, Ray said, "Follow me."

We neared his office and he pointed to an empty cubicle, saying, "Have a seat and I'll be right back." Even though I disliked wearing this blonde persona, I found out that it did come in handy at times.

He stepped up into his office. Pulling a sheaf of papers from his desk, he returned and handed them to me. "Please fill these out and return them to me in my office."

As I filled out the application, I would frequently glance around. I could see Ray looking down at me and at my cleavage, which I made sure peeked from the opening of my blouse.

Even though there were no customers at present, the saleswomen were busy wiping down the various cars with thick polishing cloths. I finished the forms and handed them back to Ray. He put them on his desk without giving them a second glance.

"Tomorrow, come in at nine a.m." He motioned to a petite brunette to come over. "This is Gracie. She's the gal you'll be replacing. She's pregnant and will soon be showing. Obviously, she can't wear the uniform." He turned to Gracie, saying, "This is Brandi."

Gracie shook hands, then handed me a folder that she picked up from a nearby desk. It contained an inventory list and the stats on each vehicle. She gave me a quick walk-through, then said, "Ray expects us to know all of this information on each of the cars," tapping the folder. "He wants us to be able to talk shop with the customers when they ask. I'll help you to learn the paperwork tomorrow." I thanked her and headed for home.

My dad was an exotic car aficionado, and that certainly helped me now. I thanked my dad silently as I leafed through the inventory list and the specs. Only the newest automobiles caused me to do some extra studying; most of the others were merely a review. I knew engines and suspensions. With a little more research, I knew I could hold my own with any of the saleswomen.

"A cute gal like you, I'd never have guessed you would know your way under the hood of a car. I would have thought a good-looking woman like you would know more about the backseat of a car," Mae snickered. I half expected her to jab me with an elbow.

"I didn't have to know how my Deusy worked; I just had to know my way around men," she continued, the raciness oozing from her voice. "I've only liked two kinds of men: domestic and imported."

Needless to say, Ray and Gracie were impressed with the

way I talked to the customers and what I knew about the cars that the potential buyers showed interest in. Ray seemed to be impressed with the way I filled out the halter top too.

As I learned the ropes from Gracie, she filled me in on her life. "I am so happy that I'm pregnant and I can quit. I needed the job long enough to raise Jack's bail money. I got him out of prison. He's very jealous. He assaulted another guy for buying me a drink and ended up in the slammer. When he found out what I was wearing to work here, he blew up. But he went to jail and I needed a job. I got pregnant by him before he went to jail, but he seems to have trouble believing that I've been faithful to him."

I don't particularly like wearing the costume for the theme of "Tooters" either.

"So, what's it like working here?" I asked Gracie while she was being open.

"It's okay."

"Only okay? What's Mrs. D'Amato like as a boss?" I asked.

"He's fair and honest. He pays the full commission, but he expects you to be busy, even when there are no customers: cleaning, polishing the cars to a shine, or keeping up on paperwork."

Jack certainly proved that he was jealous by stopping in frequently to check on her. He was out of jail because Gracie had paid the bail money. When he came to Tooters, she would pull him aside and have a quietly heated argument and he would leave. Before he would go, he would transfix Ray with a stare that could kill.

We had a small surprise going-away party and baby shower for Gracie on her last day. I hadn't known her for that long, but she seemed to be an all-right person. We each chipped in a few bucks and bought her some baby clothes and a baby blanket. She broke down and cried, giving us each a hug before she left carrying her gifts. Ray had bought the kid a savings bond.

She wisely chose to shake his hand and say, "Thanks" and skip giving him a hug. I was sure that Jack was lurking somewhere around, waiting to give her a ride home.

Arriving early, I walked onto the sales floor. Ray and Mack Hannick were arguing. Mack was the man who did the repairs and inspections in the separate service garage behind the display arena for all of Ray's purchases. Mack wanted more say in which vehicles Ray was buying.

"I'm the one who has to fix them, Ray. Sometimes it costs you almost as much to repair the cars and bring them into tip-top shape, as the amount that you can sell them. Please, Ray, let me review and help you decide which ones will be a better buy and which one can give us a better profit margin."

Ray was adamant. "It is my business and I will run it any way I damned well see fit." Mack walked away after shaking a large wrench at Ray, his greasy rag squeezed tightly in his oil-stained fist. Ray had Mack's work area in a separate building because he didn't want potential customers to have their shopping experience marred by the noise of air impact wrenches, air compressors, or tools dropping in the repair shop.

Gracie was gone and I had been there for nearly a week. Selling the Denali, I earned a small commission and some respect from Ray. I figured that I was still being evaluated and on probation.

I was to the point in my investigation where I couldn't do much more. I called Florine to set up a meeting. I wanted to report the things that I had found out. "Florine, everything seems to be on the up and up from what I can see. Ray may look at beautiful women, but I haven't found a reason to believe that he is unfaithful.

"To investigate anything more, you'll need to hire an independent accountant to go over the books. You need to have the figures checked to be sure the business is earning money and not losing it."

Mae said, "A man I once knew told me to follow the money, but more often than not, he followed beauty, me." Mae gave a throaty chuckle. "I always had the money following me. You know, when women go wrong, men go right after them."

Florine said, "I want you to stay at the business until the audit is done. I did an investigation of you. I found out that you have a sharp brain and several business credits under your belt. I need someone like you on the inside to watch over my money."

"As long as she's paying for your time, honey, there's no need to get your knickers in a twist," Mae said, so I stayed.

Ray enjoyed looking at his cars and his saleswomen, but he didn't stray. His advice to me on the day I started set the tone. He said, "The customer can take the vehicle out for a test drive, but the customer can't take my salesgirls out for a test drive. This is a legitimate business and I intend to keep it that way.

Any extracurricular activities will be cause for immediate dismissal." As salespeople, we were still required to accompany clients on test drives, but Ray made it perfectly clear that nothing further was expected or permitted.

In my mind, that early warning alone went a long way toward clearing Ray of charges of hanky-panky, although there was a lingering rumor in the dealership about Gracie and whether she was pregnant by her boyfriend or by someone else, Ray included, but I didn't see that as something that was very likely.

Gracie seemed truthful when we talked and Ray was straightforward about his business. I had done all that I could without looking at the books. That was something that Florine would have to do.

Florine notified Cal, Ray's accountant, to turn over the books for review as I had suggested.

I came in to work for several more days before something seemed amiss. I arrived early, as usual. I planned on telling Ray that I would be quitting at the end of the week.

Something was wrong here. There was no way that Ray was going to leave the front door unlocked and the lights off. There was only a small desk lamp lighted in Ray's office.

"Be careful, Brandi," Mae warned. "You aren't packing anything other than your 38s."

"Mr. D'Amato," I called. "Are you here?"

I got no answer. It was so quiet I could hear the door ease shut behind me.

I called his name again before moving to the bank of light switches just inside the door and snapping them on. The overhead mercury lamps hummed as they warmed. The spots of brightness bloomed. Light streamed down and sparkled on the individual cars. I walked past Ray's office and saw that the safe where he stored the car keys was still locked.

I made rounds on the inside of the sales floor, checking the pools of duskiness between autos. I thought perhaps Ray was down, sick or injured, on the floor, but I came up empty.

I had checked everything other than the garage out back. I'd never been inside the mechanic's workspace since I had started working, but it was the only place left that I hadn't checked.

The lights inside the garage were already turned on. I stepped onto the workshop floor and called, "Mr. D'Amato? Are you here?" As I waited for an answer, I looked around.

The building had two service bays and several workbenches. Tools and machinery lined all of the walls that weren't doors. One bay held a lift to raise cars to be serviced, and the other bay contained a deep grease pit. I moved farther inside and started to make a circuit of the room. In the lift area was a white Audi on a jack, with one wheel removed.

I noticed a retractable light cord stretched taut from the ceiling. It was then that I saw him. Ray was hanging at its end. His lifeless form dangled near the bottom of the grease pit with the thick, black electrical cord wrapped around his neck. His hands had been taped behind his back. His feet were several inches from the pit floor. His head and neck were visible just above the shop floor. I moved to his side, knelt, and felt for a pulse. But from his skin color, I knew what I would find. Ray was dead. I hurried to the wall phone in the shop and dialed 911.

"Allegheny County 911. What is your emergency?"

"There's been a death. I need the police and coroner," I explained to the voice on the phone and then gave the address. "He's in the building behind Tooters auto sales."

It wasn't long before the cavalry arrived. A police car and an ambulance with lights flashing soon pulled up. I stood just inside the door waiting for the first responders to come in. Two officers entered to be sure the scene was secure. I pointed to the grease pit. One cop strode over to where Ray was hanging, while the other began to question me.

I still had my purse in my hand and held it out to him. There was no way I was going to reach inside my purse for my I. D. in front of a cop at a murder investigation. "I'm Mary Brandon, a private eye, here on an investigation for Mr. D'Amato's wife," I said, trying to explain the reason I was at the crime scene.

I saw the officer look over my attire. He raised an eyebrow in disbelief. I'm sure he thought, "A private eye? Yeah, right."

This was the first murder in which I'd been involved. I was too shaken to give the full response that I wanted to give him.

Sharing what I knew with the officer, Davis, I explained, "I didn't touch a thing other than the shop's doorknob, Mr. D'Amato's neck, and the telephone on the wall." I gave him the telephone number to notify Florine.

The coroner finally arrived and managed to wind his way

between the crime scene investigators. He examined Ray, pronounced him dead, and had his crew load Ray's body into the station wagon, which took it to the morgue for an autopsy later.

The crowd of police personnel slowly diminished. The shop emptied and I was escorted to the police station to give my statement and for questioning.

The police secluded me inside a small, private interrogation chamber with nothing but a table and several folding chairs. I told them all that I knew about exactly what was happening at the dealership.

I laid out the reason that I was at the shop. "Mrs. D'Amato hired me to be sure that her money wasn't being wasted and that her husband wasn't cheating with the saleswomen once she saw the seductive attire her husband had chosen. She'd heard rumors about a pregnant worker and was worried.

"The sales stats for the cars seemed to be fairly strong, and Ray should be making money with his business. Many of the male customers were drawn in to see the women and many were enticed to buy cars."

"Were there any disgruntled employees or customers?" Detective Waverly asked.

"Not that I am aware of," I replied. "Even Gracie seemed to leave on good terms." I wasn't going to point a finger at Jack, Cal, or Mack when I didn't know anything for sure.

I wanted to leave the rest of the investigation to the police, but my curious nature wouldn't let it alone. I needed to do background checks for myself.

"You weren't hired because you're easy; you were hired because you have brains. Your beauty was just the lace on the garter," Mae said. "Florine hired the right person when she hired you."

I went to Ray's funeral service at the church and then to the graveside. The police were there, too, watching to see who showed up. A few family members surrounded Florine for comfort and support.

Every person there would be considered a suspect, and there was a plethora of them who had showed up: Florine, me, Gracie and her ever-present boyfriend Jack, Ray's CPA Cal, Mack, and most of the other employees from Tooters. I noticed several customers I had met in the short time I'd been there. Jack stood behind Gracie, his hands on her shoulders, wearing what passed for a smile on his face.

Mae was there, but she was unusually quiet and subdued. I could smell her perfume and feel her presence at my elbow. Maybe she was thinking about the passing of her close friends and relatives, or even her own death.

Apparently Ray had been impressed with my knowledge of cars and my business acumen and had shared it with Florine, because she begged, "Mary Alice, please stay on as temporary manager, at least until I can find someone to either take over or buy the company. Ray told me he had never seen a woman who loved automobiles and knew about them like you. You do know more about business than you let on.

"Before you say no, let me say you don't have to wear the halter tops, nor do any of the salespeople. They can wear business casual."

I was still under contract to Florine as a P.I. Because I had no other cases or income at the present, I accepted, but with a one-month term limit.

"I want you to continue as though Ray was still alive." She gave a small sob before she went on. "You'll need to have a checking account set up with monies available that you will need to make new purchases. I'll have my attorney, Lee, write the contract so you will have the power to act in Ray's stead. Mack has PennDOT certification and should be able to deal with the titles and legal paperwork."

Once the police released the crime scene, I reopened the business. I asked Gracie to come back to fill my old spot on the team, telling her and the other saleswomen, "I got the okay for you not to wear the revealing clothing. I don't think you want to put more on display than the autos." They laughed at my banter.

I heard a huge sigh in my ear. "It's such a shame to cover up all of those lovely assets," Mae purred. "You know, a curve is the loveliest distance between two points."

I felt anxious and unsure why Ray had been killed, but I was determined not to let Florine down. I needed to watch my back. I picked up my insurance from my office and now carried a trio of 38s. I wore it carefully camouflaged. I didn't want anyone to know that I was carrying a piece.

From the first day I was in charge, I started my own set of books, marking all of the expenses and profits. I wanted to have an account of every cent that was spent and each penny that I took in. I wanted to know everything about the business. I wanted be sure that nothing was being withheld from Florine. I rehired Gracie because I needed an experienced sales clerk and I wanted to put things back as much as possible the way they were just before Ray's murder.

A tall, handsome man in his mid-fifties entered the sales area. He strode purposefully to Ray's office and extended a hand to shake. "Florine sent me. I'm her attorney, Lee Galletri." His grip was firm and filled with confidence.

"I have a few papers for you to sign," he said. "They make you the legal representative for Ray's company and make your signature valid."

I called Florine and told her, "I'm now legal and I'll start to search ads and the Internet for additions to the car stock. It's a solid business from what I can see. I can't let the supplies and inventories dwindle. I'll have Mack sit down with me and go over possible buys." I recalled that he'd wanted more input and thought this would be the perfect time to have him help me.

"Thanks for keeping Ray's dream alive," Florine said before hanging up.

I was still in the P.I. mode and felt a personal responsibility to solve Ray's murder for my own peace of mind. The coroner came to the conclusion that Ray's death was a murder, which I already knew. The police had found the roll of tape that had bound his wrists tossed on a workbench, and there was a hematoma on the back of his head.

The wrench with Ray's hair and blood on it had been found on the same bench. The police hadn't found any fingerprints other than Mack's. Either the murderer was Mack or he or she had worn gloves. Mack was a prime suspect, but there wasn't enough to charge him.

Once Gracie arrived, I began inviting Mack in to review any autos that I thought might be worthy of the Tooters standards for vintage and quality cars. For some reason, I couldn't see Gracie as a murderer and wanted her there most of the hours that I was in the sales area.

As Mack and I reviewed some ads, Mack said, "Ray and I grew up together. He was always headstrong, but a great guy." Emotion choked him. That put him way down on my suspects list and I felt more comfortable having him at my side.

After a minute I said, "I'm keeping an eye on expenses for Florine. Please let me know about any supplies that you buy."

A thought hit me. I placed a telephone call and I asked, "Florine, did you ever have the books audited?"

"No. I told Cal that he would need to have Ray's books available for independent review. Ray's death put that on hold."

Florine added, "Ray had Cal as his partner earlier. A few years ago they had a men's haberdashery selling expensive shirts and ties. They did quite well for a while. Then the bottom dropped out, and finally they went out of business."

That made me even more determined to keep my own set of books. I needed to know this business from top to bottom.

The reopening of the car repair shop for business after Ray's death was hard for Mack Hannick. He didn't want to go back to work in his area of the garage, but a small raise and a reminder of how much I needed his help tempted him to stay. It was Mack's loyalty to Ray and his desire to see Ray's dream continue that tipped the scales.

Every day I would scour newspaper ads and the Internet for specialty cars. I would print out hard copies, sit down, and review them with Mack before we'd make a bid. Mack became an integral part of the business. After all, he would be the one who would have to be sure that the cars were brought up to the high standards of Tooters.

"Mack, look at this. I found a 1934 Lincoln KH with 72,000 miles on it. It's cream colored and they're asking $50,000. It's local if you want to check it out."

Sorry it's not a Duesenberg, Mae. It's the closest vehicle that I could find. When we get it, I want to take you for a ride for old time's sake.

"Too much of a good thing can be wonderful, honey. Thanks." Mae said.

Now that we had reopened, more people than usual poured through the doors and onto the sales floor. Most were drawn by curiosity about Ray's murder, but a few came because of the increased coverage of the business in the news.

And we didn't need to wear breast-revealing costumes to get customers to come in.

It had been an extremely profitable week. We sold a Porsche and a Land Rover, and Gracie sold the Lotus Europa. I felt strongly that the increase in sales deserved a celebration and ordered several pizzas; even Mack joined us. It looked as though Ray's dream was becoming a reality. Mack made a bid on the Lincoln and we'd acquired an Aston Martin. All in all, I thought it was a very good week.

Now a beautiful, bright-red 2011 Mustang Shelby gt1500 super snake sat in the place of honor just inside the door to fill the spot of the Lotus.

Gracie's boyfriend still hovered around the shop. Gracie told me, "Jack's a really jealous guy. Even with Ray out of the picture, he still doesn't trust me. I'm glad I don't have to wear those halter tops that just about drove Jack crazy. But we need the money again. He got fired for fighting once more."

I contacted Florine. I wanted to share the great news with her. After paying bills and salaries, the shop had cleared nearly $30,000. I was proud of myself. This was my first managerial position, other than my few business classes and my own minimally successful private eye company. The second week Mack and I cleared almost the same amount.

Florine asked Cal for the books at the end of my second week as manager. She needed to see the CPA's accounting of the business. When I shared my figures with Florine, there was nearly $2,000 difference between my books and Cal's. Of course, Cal hadn't known that I was keeping a separate account of the finances.

"A little here and a little there; it all adds up to some real money," May said. And if $2,000 per week was what Cal is charging as a CPA, it was time for Florine to hire a new one.

I told Florine, "You need to notify the police. From what I can see, I think that Cal is embezzling your money. Ray may have reviewed Cal's books and discovered the discrepancy in the finances, or possibly the threat of you wanting to see the records set Cal off. Ray may have confronted him about the collapse of his men's shop and the missing car money. I think that Cal may have killed Ray."

When the police investigated the accountant, they found that Cal had set up a dummy account in Ray's name. He had planned to feign ignorance if anyone caught on. He used Ray's personal information but gave his own signature. If Florine investigated, it would look like Ray was skimming monies and hiding it from her.

The police detectives' investigation discovered several more dummy accounts from half a dozen of Cal's recent customers and other accounts reaching back to the time he and Ray had the men's store. Cal had managed to embezzle nearly $380,000.

Initially, Cal had embezzled $6,000 from the haberdashery he and Ray had started. In only three years since then, he'd managed to amass the rest of the money from unsuspecting clients. He planned to disappear after two or three more years.

Cal was arrested and charged with embezzlement and was under suspicion for Ray's murder.

Florine became more and more involved in Tooters. I came in twice a week to help her scan the ads, get the books in order, and work with her and Mack to select which cars to purchase and finally to set the prices. She was great with the employees, especially Mack.

"A hard man is good to find," Mae observed

Florine could run the business by now, but she kept me on as an hourly employee for a bit longer. I said yes because my pay kept my private eye enterprise afloat, and I think she knew that. We became friends and were thankful for each other.

Mack soon took over Ray's position at the auto sales at Florine's side. They did have to hire a new mechanic. My visits diminished over several months and I went back to my old job of being a private investigator, but I was now driving a 2011 Mustang Shelby gt500 super snake, bright red.

Thanks for the car, Florine. And thanks for the help, Mae.

Mae replied, "Honey, when I'm good I'm very, very good, but when I'm bad, I'm even better."

Enjoy Thomas Beck

Character Bio from Michele Jones

Merris Ferris is a fifty-something, overweight owner of Memory Lane, an antique shop in the heart of town. Her vivid blue eyes are framed by short brown hair (usually messy) and large ears. She is always in jeans and a T-shirt with a coffee in hand. She blends in effortlessly and has many friends. Her love of coffee and friends led to a small coffee area next to her messy desk in the back of the shop.

She loves dabbling at mystery and paranormal fiction writing. When she needs inspiration, she turns to her Wicked Witch bobblehead for answers. She has been practicing martial arts since her early thirties and holds a black belt in hapkido, along with various belts in tae kwon do, maui thai, kali, and Brazilian jiu jitsu.

Ding Dong the Witch Is Dead

Michele Jones

The Ferrises were sitting at the kitchen table having a cup of coffee and browsing the Internet. Merris turned to her husband and said, "Harris, I just got the Raystown Lake email reminding all slipholders of the end-of-summer annual sock burn. It says this year they have more than fifty vendors scheduled. Even Sweet Treats candy shop has a tent. We should go up early and check it out."

"I got that same email. I see that they're moving the bonfire time back to two o'clock in the afternoon. Must be to accommodate all the vendors. Too bad they can't have it at night. That would make it more fun."

"I guess that if they had it at night, it would make quiet time impossible."

Harris asked, "Don't you have your writing group meeting this weekend?"

"The writing group won't be meeting for a while. They found mold in our meeting room and it won't be available for at least a month. So I called Eunice and she said she would watch the store, and we always go up for the sock burn —"

Harris interrupted her. "Really? We're going to the lake only because there is no writing group? I know how I rate."

"Harris, don't be silly, we always go to the annual sock burn. Now we can spend the week. I'm sure we can find something to keep us occupied at the lake. You grab the laptops and I'll grab my Wicked Witch bobblehead."

"Honestly, Merris, I don't know why you refuse to go anywhere without that silly witch."

"Are you kidding me? Do I tell you not to travel with your lucky rabbit's foot? No. She's my lucky charm and I'm taking her!"

Heh heh heh heh heh heh heh! The Wicked Witch appeared in a burst of green smoke and fire and a clap of thunder that only Merris could see and hear. So your Harris was trying to leave me behind. I'll get him, my pretty!

"It's not like that; he just doesn't know how valuable you

are," Merris said to the Wicked Witch of the West, or WWW, as she liked to refer to her.

"Who are you talking to?" Harris asked as he reentered the room.

"Just going over what we need for our trip. Didn't realize I was talking out loud. Call Paris and tell her we're going to the lake. She may want to come."

"Doubtful," Harris muttered under his breath.

After a few phone calls they were packing the car. Harris got behind the wheel as Merris Velcroed her Wicked Witch bobblehead in place. Oh, what a world! What a world! Be gentle! WWW remarked.

The drive was uneventful. When they arrived at the lake they discovered that Gertrude Knoall's black Lexus SUV was in their assigned space. Several expletives came out of Merris's mouth as Harris drove to the visitor lot. Merris yanked her witch from the dash. "I've had it. I am going to have her car towed. This is the last time she is going to take our space." She stuffed WWW into her bag and stalked off before Harris could stop her.

On her way, she ran into Gerty. "You. You took our parking spot again."

Gerty brushed Merris off. "If I had my way, I'd be the only one with an assigned space."

"I'll have you towed."

"Just try it," Gerty said. She turned her back to Merris and went down the path to the marina.

Merris continued on toward the office, complaining out loud. "That woman infuriates me." The walk and the music playing on the speaker system started to calm her.

"Hey, detective!" Merris approached a man carrying fishing poles. "Are you here on business or pleasure?" Merris asked.

"Pleasure. Mary and I are taking the boat out later and need a few things," Detective Lawless replied. "And please call me Tony."

"I was hoping that you were here to do something about Gerty. She's getting worse. Today she took our parking spot. Can't you fine her or tow her car?"

"Sorry, Merris. The marina is private property. Unless

she's actually committed a crime, you're on your own." He started walking toward the docks.

"Hey, detective — er, Tony. We're meeting friends at Pirate's Cove later. Why don't you and Mary meet us there around three?" Merris said.

"We'll try. Later!"

Merris entered the Oar House to voice her complaint and found others were doing the same. Poof. Green smoke, fire, thunder, and laughter. Merris knew WWW wanted her attention.

I'll bide my time, Gerty Knoall. You're tangling with the wrong witch. I can't attend to you here and now, but you'd better stay out of my way!

"This is not a working vacation." Merris muttered so no one else could hear her. "We're here to relax and work on my book, not to look for trouble."

Obviously we aren't the only ones who have issues with her. I'm here if you need me. WWW spun around and disappeared in her signature poof of green smoke, fire, thunder, and wicked laughter. "I wonder where she's off to now?" Merris muttered.

Merris waited her turn to voice her complaint, and, feeling vindicated, she left the Oar House, strolling leisurely to their boat. Passing the Princess Tour boat, she ran into Charles Knoall, Gerty's husband, and a woman.

"Good morning, Charles. How are you and — your friend today?" Merris asked.

"Good morning, Merris," he replied. "This is my business partner, Veronica."

"Nice to meet you," Merris said.

"Nice to meet you, too," Veronica replied. "Are you staying for the sock burn?"

"Yes, I wouldn't miss it."

"Maybe we'll see you there," Veronica said.

Charles said, "I'm sorry, but we must go now. Veronica and I have business to attend to."

"Goodbye." Merris started walking to the docks.

On her way up E-Dock, she waved and chatted to her fellow boaters and friends as she passed by: Ben "the mayor" and Amy, Fabio the "stud" and his latest conquest, Ted and Judy, Derrick and Teresa. Before she got to her slip, Butch and

Nancy passed her, complaining about Gerty. Seemed that Gerty was in rare form that day, and no one was happy. The real kicker — Gerty was docked in the slip next to theirs and was already making waves. Waves, no pun intended! That made her chuckle.

Merris turned around. Dang. I left our sunblock at home. She texted Harris. "Forgot sun block. Running to get some. Be there shortly."

As she neared the store, she could hear arguing coming from the woods. "Veronica, you can't go around telling people that you hope we'll see them later," Charles hissed.

"Why? What's wrong with that?" Veronica asked.

"We can't be seen together as a couple."

"But I thought we were a couple."

"Of course we're a couple. But if my wife finds —"

"I'm sorry. I was only trying to be nice." Veronica began sobbing. "You said that you didn't care what your wife —"

"It's not like that, baby. I don't want to ruin things for us," Charles said.

"You promised me that you were leaving her. I thought you loved me," Veronica said, still sobbing.

"I do love you. And I am going to leave her when the time is right. We just need to be careful right now. Remember, our current relationship is that of business partners. We can't be seen as a couple or I'll lose everything."

"Okay, Charles, I understand."

"I'll pick you up later for dinner. Right now, we need to separate. We can't chance it," Charles said.

"Okay, you can pick me up later for our 'business dinner,' but things had better change soon." Veronica walked away.

Keep an eye on that one. She can't be trusted. Heh heh heh heh heh heh heh!

"What?" Merris asked, but WWW had vanished.

Merris ran into the store, bought the sunblock, and headed toward the boat. She saw Veronica on the phone. Remembering what WWW had told her, she moved into listening range.

"It's V… Played the 'I thought you loved me' card… Yeah, he considers us a couple. … Told me to lay low, doesn't want her to find out about us. … We're supposed to have dinner tonight… I'm going to play on his sympathy to get more …"

Harris had just finished taking the cockpit cover off the boat as Merris returned. He declared, "Time to take our La Bella Vita out on the lake."

The ride was exhilarating. Merris loved the wind blowing through her hair, the fine mist spraying her face, and Harris's smile as they cruised down the lake. Merris was tuning the land radio while Harris radioed their friends that they were on their way and would meet them in Pirates Cove.

They pulled in and dropped anchor next to Donny, Steve, and James. Minutes later, Dane drifted in, followed by Larry. They all tied up and were putting their rafts in the lake when Detective Lawless coasted in. Harris quickly helped him tie on. Ten minutes later, Gerty showed up. Groans could be heard throughout the group. Even though Gerty annoyed everyone, they all helped her tie on — an unwritten lake rule.

Thought you wanted to relax. No way with that buzzard hanging around. Heh heh heh heh heh heh heh.

Merris grabbed WWW and took her below deck. "Behave or I'm locking you up." After the mini lecture, Merris returned to the deck and Velcroed WWW in her usual place.

Gerty certainly didn't do anything to help her cause or change her neighbors' minds. She was just as annoying and rude as ever.

Why so rude, Gerty? I won't stand for it. Why, my little party's about to begin. I'll get you, Gerty Knoall, and your oversized boat too!

"Enough. This is not a working vacation," Merris reminded her. WWW vanished in her usual fashion, leaving Merris to watch her head bobble as she secured her below deck.

The sun started to set and it was time to dock for the evening. Gerty was the first to head out, to everyone's delight. Pleasantries were exchanged before people headed to their respective docks.

Harris was putting La Bella Vita through her paces until they reached the no-wake zone. Most seasoned boaters respected the zone, although the novices and holiday boaters seemed to ignore it. Harris slowly cruised to their spot — E-Dock: Slip 31. While he was backing her in, Gerty blew through the no-wake zone and down the dock so fast that the waves crashed their boat into the side of their slip and into the back of the dock.

Harris cut the engine and jumped off the back to assess the damage. Butch, Derrick, Mayor Ben, and Fabio the stud all came running to help. Luckily there was no damage. E-Dock mates are great. They helped moor the boat and clean her up. Before long they were having their usual E-Dock evening get-together. It was like a family picnic: eating, drinking, talking, and laughing until ten o'clock, marina-mandated quiet time.

Merris ran below deck, shut everything down, and grabbed WWW. About time you release me. I felt as if I was melting ... melting!

"You're such a drama queen," Merris said.

Oh, what a world! What a world! Why would you want to destroy my beautiful wickedness?

Harris quickly covered the boat and they headed for their car. They could have stayed on the boat overnight, but Merris preferred the comfort of their camper, and as much as Harris loved the water, he found it difficult to sleep well below deck.

Wicked Witch Velcroed in, they headed for Happy Days Campground. As they started their right turn into the campground, a black SUV raced up the other side and turned onto the driveway in front of them. Instinctively both Harris and Merris tried to protect each other when he slammed on the brakes. They were fortunate to stop inches from the SUV.

"Gerty!" Merris screamed. "Oh, that woman infuriates me!"

I'll get you, Gerty. Heh heh heh heh heh heh heh! WWW cursed.

After a good night's rest and two pots of coffee, they headed back to the lake for the annual sock burn.

"Someone must have spoken to Gerty," Merris said. "Our parking spot is open. I can't wait for them to light the bonfire so we can burn our socks. They've been busy since yesterday. The tables are up under tents, the grills are out, and the bonfire is built and ready to be lit."

"Hey, neighbor!" Mayor Ben said. "Let's do breakfast at Anchors Away."

"We're in! Hey, let's invite the entire dock," Merris replied.

"Great idea. You call your side, and I'll call mine." He pulled out his cell.

Several phone calls and twenty minutes later, they were all entering the restaurant and waiting at the podium to be seated. As they waited, they could hear the staff talking about Charles Knoall and his mistress, who were seated in a cozy booth in the center of the restaurant, near the fountain.

"I'll bet Gerty doesn't know that her husband has been coming in every day for the past month with that woman," Patty said.

"Serves her right," Arnold the waiter said. "I can't believe Charles has put up with her for as long as he has, in fact."

"Arnold, that's not nice. No one deserves to be cheated on," Patty said. "Wow, this place filled up fast, we need to stop gossiping and start taking orders."

After everyone was seated, the only table left was a small two-seater near the restrooms. Everyone was having a great time until Gerty showed up. Billy the busboy, always pleasant, was the only one in the entire restaurant to greet her. "Good morning, Ms. Knoall." She ignored him and walked to the hostess stand, phone to her ear.

"I don't care what you say, Rudolph. I am the majority stockholder and I want him fired. He hasn't done anything but collect a paycheck for months. ... This is my company. I own it and I own you. You sold to me because you needed money. I don't care if you don't like it. I make the rules. Are we clear? ... Good." Gerty hung up the phone.

"Is everything okay, Ms. Knoall? Can I get you anything?" Billy asked.

"Get me the manager."

Gerty turned and addressed her husband. "Charles, what's going on?" she asked. "Who is that woman?"

"Calm down, Gerty. Nothing's going on. Ms. Minx and I are here on business," Charles replied.

"Looks like more than business to me," Arnold whispered to Patty.

Gerty continued berating Charles. After her tirade, she strutted around barking orders to the staff. "I want that booth, near the fountain. Move my husband and his 'business associate' to the table by the restroom."

"I'm sorry, Mrs. Knoall, that isn't possible. But I'd be happy to seat you there," Arnold replied.

"You'll do as I tell you. I make the rules here."

"Sorry, but I —"

Jackie, the restaurant manager, rushed in. "Ms. Knoall, you know that your number one rule is that the customer is our number one priority. Let them keep their table. Come with me and I'll have the cook whip up your favorite."

"Not only am I the owner, but I'm a customer. Not just a customer, but your most important customer."

"Ms. Knoall, please, this is bad for business."

"Bad for business? And having clientele like these people is good for business? Butch is only a plumber, Teresa is a cashier, Jed works at a mini mart, Merris and Harris own a stupid antique store, studman lives off his daddy's money, and our mayor? He is nothing but a truck driver. You want customers like this? Fine. I wouldn't lower myself to dine with such riffraff anyway. And you, dish boy? Don't just stand there gawking. Get me a cup of coffee: three creams and four sugars."

"Ms. Knoall, please," Jackie begged. "Think about the customers. They're the reason we're so successful."

"You mean I'm so successful."

Billy handed her the coffee she'd demanded. "Here's your coffee. Three creams, four sugars."

"Finally, someone with half a brain. At least one of you can take direction." She took the coffee, pushed Billy aside, turned toward Arnold, and poked him on the head. "And you. You're nothing but an idiot."

"Get your hands off me. And I'm no idiot. I'm working two minimum-wage jobs because you bought the lab I worked in and fired me and almost everyone else. And we were working on something really big. You probably lost millions. Who's the idiot now?"

"I'm in business to make money, and I stand by my decision. You mustn't be too smart, or you wouldn't have been terminated. Besides, not everyone lost their jobs, only the ones who were incompetent. You certainly could have found a better job than this." Gerty tried to poke him again, but he grabbed her wrist and twisted it behind her back, causing her to drop her coffee.

"I told you not to touch me!"

"Arnold, let her go!" Merris rushed to split them up, but Gerty tripped her and she fell, taking them all to the ground.

Arnold released Gerty's wrist. Then he turned to help

Merris up.

"You've messed with the wrong person, mister. I'll have you arrested for assault," Gerty shouted. She turned toward Merris. "And you. You'll pay for this, you meddling fool."

"I'm not afraid of you," Merris said. Through green swirling smoke, she heard, I'll get you, my pretty.

Gerty turned toward Arnold and screamed, "I'll have your job for this," thus drawing even more attention to herself. "This is an outrage. My money pays your salary. You should be grateful for that."

Gerty turned to Merris. "And you, you meddlesome old biddy. Don't you dare interfere in my business ever again." She stormed toward the restaurant entrance, rubbing her wrist, bumping into patrons, and knocking food and beverages off the tables as she passed them.

"There's nothing wrong with that table. Besides, the bathroom has several thrones to choose from for royalty like you!" Nancy yelled as she passed her.

Before Gerty was even out the door, everyone started complaining about her.

"I can't believe she said that about me. I never thought she would stoop so low. I could just strangle her," Butch said.

"I know what you mean," Teresa added. "She rubs me the wrong way too. I'll hold her down for you."

"I hope she chokes on her words, and if not, I'd like to do it myself," Jed commented.

"I do not live off my dad's money," Fabio shouted in his Italian accent. "I have a job. She's just angry because I'm better looking than she is. I'd like to shut her up permanently."

"Gerty is really pushing it. I hate to be threatened. I'd like nothing better than if she disappeared for good," Merris said.

"Let's forget about her and have some fun. We came here for the sock burn, not for Gerty," Harris replied.

"She's not so bad," Billy said, trying to keep the peace.

"I feel sorry for her," Patty said. "She's very lonely. That's the reason she acts the way she does. Maybe if she would lighten up, just a little —"

"Please don't defend her," Sis, the marina manager, replied. "She's evil. I wish I could make her go away permanently."

"You just don't understand her," Billy said.

"She's the most obnoxious woman here and doesn't care who she hurts to get what she wants!" Arnold yelled. "She's always insulting me, telling me I'm stupid. That witch bought my lab and fired almost everyone. I could kill her."

"I'm sorry, everyone. Breakfast is on the house," Jackie said, trying to calm things down.

Things went along swimmingly for the next few hours. Everyone went outside walking from tent to tent, shopping, looking for that perfect something.

Then Gerty turned up. "Do you have any idea what you're doing?" she yelled. "Have you ever cooked on a grill before? They're supposed to be hot dogs, not burnt dogs. Get out of my way, you little brat, and take the mangy mutt with you!"

She turned toward Sis. "I thought you're supposed to be were the marina manager. Why aren't you supervising? Your staff is incompetent."

"Gerty, please, calm down. Everyone's here to have a good time and you don't want to ruin it for them." Sis lowered her voice. "Getting upset will keep them from spending money."

Billy interrupted. "Mrs. Knoall, this really large box of candy from Sweet Treats just arrived for you."

"Don't just stand there, dish boy. Read me the card."

"That was one sweet deal. Congratulations on another successful merger. And it's signed Mergers and Acquisitions."

And now dear Gerty, Candy. Candy. Candy will put you to sleep. Heh heh heh heh heh heh heh!

Gerty had a smug look on her face. She snatched the candy from Billy and turned to Sis. "You should be happy that I'm so successful. Without my contributions, there would be no marina or bonfire. Hate me all you want. You need me!"

"Of course we need you, but we have to be aware of our guests' needs too." Sis balled her fists at her sides.

"I'm leaving now, but I'll be back for the bonfire. You're worried about their money? My money pays for it and everything else around here, and I expect to have a front-row seat for it. I suggest you save that table in the front for me." Gerty turned and calmly walked away.

I believe she is more wicked than I. Heh heh heh heh heh heh heh!

"Harris, I'm running to the car. I forgot our socks," Merris said.

"Want me to come with you?"

"I think I can manage."

Merris dashed to the car, grabbed the socks, and started back toward the marina. Then she heard arguing.

"You listen to me, you little vixen. The Resorts Marina belongs to me. You have no authority there," Gerty said in a menacing tone.

"I don't need to listen to anything you have to say," Veronica retorted.

"Knoall Industries and all its holdings belong to me."

"Well, Charles put the Resorts in my name. I have the paperwork."

"Impossible. The Resorts isn't Charles's to give. My attorney will be in touch."

"Don't you dare threaten me!"

"My dear Veronica, that's not a threat. It's a fact."

"Charles loves me. He's going to divorce you so he can marry me."

Gerty laughed. "Charles would never have anything to do with a tramp like you. He would lose everything if he divorced me. He signed a prenup. Charles had nothing before me, and he would get nothing if he left me."

"You're lying."

"You really are a blonde bimbo. The only way Charles would get anything is if I were dead."

"That can be arranged."

Gerty laughed again. "This conversation is over. Vacate my property immediately, or you'll be hearing from my attorney."

Gerty left, and Veronica pulled out her phone. "It's V... Yeah, she thinks I'm his mistress. ... He's starting to confide in me. ... Don't worry. I know what I'm doing. ... I'll be fine... Gotta go..."

Merris returned to the bonfire and told Harris what she had heard.

"Sounds like trouble in paradise. Guess the grass isn't always greener. Let's forget about Gerty and Veronica and check out the vendor tents. I'm sure there's a pair of shoes out there calling your name."

"It's almost time for the bonfire to be lit, and no Gerty," Merris said.

I doubt that anyone cares that she isn't here. "Be nice," Merris said to WWW. "Are you talking to me?" Harris asked.

"Just thinking aloud. Guess nobody noticed that Gerty isn't here."

"I'm sure they noticed, but nobody cares," Harris countered.

Well, Merris, why don't you try and find her! Heh heh heh heh heh heh heh!

Merris just shook her head. The green smoke still swirled. Veronica is up to something. WWW cackled and disappeared. Merris saw Veronica slipping away without Charles again and decided to follow her.

"Harris, I'm going back to the shoe tent. I decided I really want that pair of Crocs," she said. "I'll be back in a few. Get us a good spot near the fire."

Veronica stopped, sat on a bench, and pulled out her cell. Merris went to the nearest tent to listen to her conversation. I wish I could hear more, she thought. I'm only getting bits and pieces.

"Got him to sign over his bearer bonds. ... I'm still working on getting his stock holdings. ... Yeah, yeah. I know she has more assets. ... That is going to be a bit more difficult. ... If she would leave him, that would change everything. ... I've got him right where I want him. ..." She ended the call and headed off toward the parking lot, where the crowd was much thinner.

Merris saw the swirling green smoke. You'd better buy your ruby slippers and get back to the party. And WWW was gone.

Merris bought her Crocs and decided to continue shopping. "There are so many great vendors, I might be able to find something for the shop, or maybe something else for me," Merris said. Looking for something, my pretty?

"Just spending Harris's money," she said before ducking into the craft tent. As she emerged with her new treasures, she saw Billy heading toward Anchors Away with an empty cart. "I see they're keeping you busy, Billy."

He turned toward her and she could see he was multitasking, talking on the phone and pushing the cart. "They sure are, Mrs. Ferris," he replied. Then he returned his attention to his call and the cart.

Merris heard cackling and saw green smoke swirling. It's so peaceful here without that wicked witch hanging around.

"Seriously?"

Heh heh heh heh heh heh heh! Too bad she'll cause you more trouble later. WWW exited in her usual fashion.

"I think I've spent enough money for now. Time to take my bargains back to the car."

Merris was putting her new treasures in the car when she saw Veronica on the phone, again. She ducked behind the car to listen.

"I'm being careful. ... I have a plan that I think might work for us. ... I gotta go. This place is becoming Grand Central."

When Merris returned, the bonfire was in full swing. Harris had gotten them a great table with a couple of their friends. They took turns going for food and drinks, and the conversation centered on boating and the marina's latest improvements. Soon it would be time for everyone to grab their socks and throw them in the fire.

Merris excused herself and headed to the Oar House to use the ladies' room. She saw one of the stalls was out of order, leaving only two, which were both taken. As she waited for a stall to empty, she decided to check her email. Both women left before she finished responding to an inquiry. She opened the first stall and noticed that there was no toilet paper. She moved to the second stall and noticed the same. She went to the third stall, hoping she could get some toilet paper. She opened the door and gasped.

WWW appeared in her trademark smoke, fire, and clap of thunder to comment. Someone killed her. Someone killed Gerty. Fitting end for someone so nasty. Heh heh heh heh heh heh heh!

"She's dead!" Merris exclaimed. As she turned to leave, she saw three women standing behind her. Why must they always come to the ladies' room in groups?

"You killed her!" one of the ladies exclaimed.

"No, I didn't. I just found her in that stall. She was already dead."

"That stall is out of order. There is no reason to be in there unless you killed her," remarked the second woman.

"I'm calling the police," cried the third woman.

WWW whirled in. Who killed Gerty? Who killed that evil witch of Raystown? Almost everyone wanted to do it. Poof, she was gone as quickly as she came.

Word quickly spread of Gerty's demise

Security arrived and escorted Merris, along with the group of women who had reported the crime, to their office. They placed them in separate rooms. After locking the doors, they went to help keep the bonfire attendees from leaving. Merris called Harris to let him know what was happening and told him she would meet him on their boat once she finished speaking with the police. As she was filling him in, she could hear the local police arriving.

Wicked, where are you? I need your help.

Heh heh heh heh heh heh heh! In a bit of trouble, are we, my pretty?

Merris looked out the window. She needed to see and hear what was happening. WWW wouldn't tell her everything; experience had taught her that. It would be difficult, but if she concentrated, she would be able to hear the conversations relating to the investigation and what would happen next.

Outside, several police officers were securing the crime scene. Caution tape was used to block the entrance to the Oar House restrooms, and an armed police officer was stationed outside. Marina security was instructed to close the gate at the exit to keep people from leaving, but that would only deter vehicles. Anyone could leave by boat or walk down the docks to the park. Several officers were working on securing those areas as well.

"Send Records and Investigation to the scene. We need forensic investigation here," Detective Lawless said. "And bring the husband and Ms. Minx in for questioning."

"I called the medical examiner. He's on his way," Officer O'Ryan replied. "The ME said to me, and I quote, 'Don't move the body.' You know, this is not my first crime scene. I know what I'm doing."

"Calm down, O'Ryan, he's just doing his job. When he arrives you can escort him to the scene," Detective Lawless bellowed.

Merris watched Records and Investigation arrive. The officers got out of the truck and started processing the scene. From her window she saw one officer snapping several photos and another using a fingerprint kit. Several members of R & I started canvassing the ground surrounding the restroom, then began working their way farther out, gathering evidence.

After some time, Lawless said, "Pick up everything and send it back to the lab. We have access to one of the best forensic specialists in the state, and we need to take advantage of him."

"Already bagging and tagging, Detective," an officer from R & I grumbled.

"O'Ryan, take over. I'm going to question the women who found the body."

"On it, Detective," O'Ryan replied.

"And have security let our ME in, damn it! I hate rent-a-cops," he muttered as he walked away.

"Let Dr. Carcass in," O'Ryan radioed the gate as he walked to the parking lot to escort the ME to the scene.

"Lead me to her, O'Ryan."

O'Ryan escorted the doctor to Oar House while his assistant followed, toting his gear. "She's all yours."

Merris had the perfect view. The security building window allowed her to both listen to and watch the investigation.

"Any idea what killed her, Doc?"

"It's a bit too early to determine. I don't see any ligature marks, no stab wounds, no bullet holes," Dr. Carcass remarked. "Once we get her back to the morgue and do the autopsy, we will have the cause of death."

"Can you give me a time of death?" O'Ryan asked.

"Based on body temperature and skin color, I would place the time of death approximately an hour ago, around 1:00."

After R&I confirmed that they had finished processing Gerty's body, Dr. Carcass and his assistant transported her to the morgue. Dr. Mortimer Cutright, world renowned forensic pathologist, would be helping with the case at the family's request.

Get ready, my pretty, he's about to come in, WWW cackled as she disappeared in her signature style. Merris was sitting down when Detective Lawless entered the room.

"Really, Merris, how do you always manage to get in the

middle of everything? Tell me what happened," the detective said.

"I guess I'm just lucky. Always in the wrong place at the wrong time." Merris paused and took a deep breath. "I went to the restroom and of the three stalls, two were occupied and one was out of order. So I sat on one of the changing benches and checked my email while I waited. When the two girls left, I went to take my turn, but the functioning stalls had no paper. So I opened the door to the out-of-order stall and there she was, face down in the toilet, not moving. That was when the girls came in and heard me say she was dead and called security."

"Can you describe the girls who left?"

"I've never seen them before, and I really didn't pay much attention. Sorry."

"Is there anything else you can tell me? Do you know who would want to kill her?"

"Well, who do you think? Gerty rubbed everyone the wrong way or pushed them to their limit. She made quite a scene at breakfast this morning and got everyone riled up. She even tripped me as I tried to defend one of the servers. I wish I could be more help, but that suspect list is a mile long."

He sighed and ran his fingers through his thick salt-and-pepper hair. "Okay, that's all for now. If you think of anything, let me know."

"Of course," Merris said.

As Detective Lawless held the door for her, his cell rang. "Excuse me, I need to take this."

Merris left the room but stayed behind to listen. She grabbed a notepad and pen from her purse.

"Lawless. I'm gonna put you on speaker so I can take notes."

I shouldn't be listening, but I need to know what he knows since I'll be conducting my own investigation, Merris thought.

"Detective, it seems that Ms. Knoall was not well liked by anyone at the lake. I have a list of names here of the people she argued with at Anchors Away just this morning. When I questioned Billy Driftwood, a busboy at the restaurant, he reluctantly provided suspect names and possible motives. He said he didn't want to get anyone in trouble. Seems that Ms. Knoall had some harsh words with Arnold Keene, one of the wait staff, and he threatened her and grabbed her wrist. Ms. Ferris tried to break it up, but she got into an altercation with Ms. Knoall as well. Driftwood said everyone hated the vic because she had money and flaunted it."

"Anything else?"

"He also reported that she threatened the management, telling them that she would withdraw her financial support if she didn't get her way. He said he overheard her arguing with Veronica Minx, the new owner of the Resort marina. Said Minx threatened her. He remembered her arguing with someone named Rudolph on her cell about business, but he didn't know anything else."

"Check into Knoall's business and finances. Make sure you freeze her family and company assets. Get her cell records. See if she received any death threats. Let's try to rule out potential suspects. Anything from the ME yet?"

"He estimates the time of death was approximately 1:00. No apparent cause. Dr. Carcass was told that the family is bringing in, in his words, 'the great forensic pathologist' Dr. Mortimer Cutright and his forensic team. He didn't seem too happy, but her niece insisted. Seems the family doesn't trust us hicks. They even got the governor involved."

"The niece? Why not the husband?" Lawless asked.

"Good question, Detective," O'Ryan replied.

"Better get eyes on the husband."

"On it, Detective."

"Get that findings report to my desk ASAP."

"It will be hours before we get any forensic information," O'Ryan said.

"I want it as soon as you have it. I have a feeling about this one. Definitely a homicide."

Veronica Minx requires further investigation. I heard her threaten Gerty, WWW said.

On the way to the boat, Merris called her daughter. "Paris, I'm working on something at the lake."

"Gee, Mom, I'm shocked. What're you working on?"

"Stop interrupting. I need to pick your brain regarding Veronica Minx."

"Is it a case? You said Manelli told you to take a vacation. Guess he called you for help anyway."

"No, Manelli didn't call. This is personal."

"What've you got?" Paris asked.

"Veronica Minx is having an affair with Gerty's husband. She's the new owner of the Resorts Marina, and she doesn't like Gerty."

"Everyone knows about the affair, but I heard that she has a boyfriend as well," said Paris.

"Really? Interesting. Get me a name. Thanks, Paris. Talk to you later. Love ya."

"Love ya too, Mom."

Veronica has an accomplice. She was going after Gerty. Heh heh heh heh heh heh heh!

Merris went back to the boat to meet Harris and filled him in on the investigation before they left for the camper.

Early the next morning Harris said, "I have a few things that I need to do for work. I know it's an hour's drive, but would you mind giving me a ride home? I hate leaving you here without a car, especially if you want to go to the lake. I'll meet you at the boat later."

Reluctantly Merris agreed and headed for the car. After dropping Harris at home and unloading all her purchases, she returned to the lake. "I need to check out my own list of suspects. WWW, I think the police need my help."

Charles is meeting his mistress at the restaurant. He had the most to gain by her death, WWW said.

Merris pulled out her cell, "Harris, can you meet me for lunch at Anchors Away? We can get dessert to go and eat in the cove."

"Sorry, Merris, this is taking longer than I thought. You're on your own today. I have to go. Love you," he said, and the line went dead.

Merris walked into Anchors Away and waited to be seated.

"Sit wherever you like," the hostess said as she walked by.

WWW swirled in. Sit near the lovebirds.

Merris chose a table near the fountain, across from Charles and Veronica.

"Charles, now that Gerty is gone, we need to plan our future," Veronica said.

"We need to give it some time. We don't want to arouse suspicion," he replied.

"Don't make me wait too long." She leaned in and

whispered something in his ear. Charles threw money on the table and the two of them left the restaurant in a hurry.

"Those two are up to something, I just know it."

Don't forget about Arnold, WWW reminded her.

Merris pulled out her notebook and jotted down several notes. While she was still eating, her cell rang. "Mom, what's going on up at the lake? The news cut into programming because of old Gerty's death. They said the cause of death was unknown but foul play is suspected. Is it true you found the body? Your picture was up there and a picture of the store and —"

"Paris, calm down. It's not as bad as it looks."

"Really? Because it sure looks bad from where I'm sitting."

Merris explained, "It's all a misunderstanding. The police interviewed everyone and someone told them about the fight Gerty had with Arnold the waiter, someone named Rudolph that she was arguing with on the phone, and Veronica Minx, her husband's mistress. Besides, they don't even know for sure if she was murdered. Right now they're just speculating."

She was murdered. I know. Heh heh heh heh heh heh heh!

"Well, the news also said she had several enemies in the business world. She was a ruthless businesswoman. She downsized or closed many of the companies she acquired. And they did say they were looking at possible family motives as well."

"That list must be a mile long."

"Mom, please. This isn't a joke. You need to be careful. I'm on my way to help you investigate."

"I'm touched by your concern, Paris. But what I really need is for you to stay home and help your aunt run the store. I'm sure she didn't expect to have to be there this long."

Enemies? Gerty had plenty. Look into Arnold and Rudolph, or as you know him, Dane. Heh heh heh heh heh heh heh!

"What? Dane is Rudolph?"

"What did you say, Mom?"

"Nothing, honey. Talk to you later."

Merris needed answers. She was headed toward Anchors

Away when she saw Arnold and called out to him. "Arnold, do you have a minute to talk with me?"

"Sure. What can I do for you?" he asked.

"I'm just curious after what happened the other day. Why did Gerty acquire your lab, and what you were working on that would have made millions?"

"Well, Merriweather Scientific was a small, privately funded lab with several research doctors that she wanted to work for her. They were loyal to Dr. Merriweather and wouldn't leave our lab, so she made him an offer he couldn't refuse. Since he needed money, he sold. At the time of the merger, we were working to test a vaccine that prevented rats from getting cancer. She came in and cleaned house. She only kept Dr. Merriweather, the research doctors she wanted, and two lab techs, Bob and James Merriweather. They were Dr. Merriweather's cousins and an unconditional part of the deal."

"I'm very sorry, Arnold. What happened next?"

"We tried reasoning with her, but she just wouldn't listen. One of the techs even threatened to kill her."

"So when she was found dead yesterday, I guess you weren't too upset. Do you think someone killed her?"

"I don't know if she was murdered, but if she was, whoever did it did the world a favor. I'm sorry, Mrs. Ferris. I really need to get to work."

"I'm sorry, Arnold. I didn't mean to keep you this long. Thanks for talking with me."

I don't think Arnold killed Gerty, Merris thought. He may have hated her, but he didn't kill her. I need to go a different direction. "A little help would sure be nice," she said out loud.

Her phone beeped. It was a text from Paris. The police had officially ruled Gerty's death a murder. She was way ahead of the police, but she needed to see what they had to say. The marina WiFi was spotty and she barely had phone coverage. Merris needed to go back to the camper to do some research. Whatever did she do before Google?

Googling Gerty's death brought up several results. She decided to start with the article "Police Forensic Evidence Indicates Murder." She learned that Dr. Carcass had originally thought Gerty died from a heart attack. After a thorough forensic examination, he determined that she was poisoned, but the poison wasn't named.

The answer is complicated, and Gerty is the key. You need to check out the candy. Heh heh heh.

"It would be so much easier if you would just tell me who the killer was."

That wouldn't be any fun. Green smoke and cackling, and WWW disappeared.

Merris went to her closet and took out her red suit and a crisp white blouse. She rooted through her dresser drawers to find the right pair of pantyhose. Before dressing, she grabbed a pair of heels from her closet. Pulling her hair into a stylish knot, she dressed quickly and headed out. She was going to Sweet Treats because WWW had hinted at the candy. She needed to find out who had sent that box of candy to Gerty.

"Hi, welcome to Sweet Treats. Can I help you?"

"Yes, thank you. I'm with Knoall Industries, the mergers and acquisitions department. We ordered a very large box of candy for our boss that was supposed to be delivered last Saturday, but she never received it. Would it be possible for you to check your delivery records to see why it wasn't delivered?" Merris asked.

"What is your boss's name and where was the candy supposed to be delivered to?"

"Gertrude Knoall, and the candy was to be delivered to the Seven Points Marina."

After a minute, the young clerk replied, "There was no delivery scheduled for Gertrude Knoall, and there was no a delivery scheduled for the Marina."

"There must be some mistake. We ordered that specifically to be delivered during the sock burn at the marina. Would you mind checking your order log?"

The clerk was pulling up the recent orders on the computer when a customer came through the door. "Excuse me," she said. "I'll be right back."

While the clerk worked to fill the customer's order, Merris started scrolling through the orders on the screen, Smith, Carter, Lane, Sharek, Waugaman, Driftwood. Oh my goodness. Billy? But why? I certainly didn't expect it to be Billy.

"Thanks for waiting," the clerk said as she picked up where she left off. She mumbled "Smith, Carter, Lane, Sharek,

Waugaman, Driftwood, Daily, Griffin, Hamm, Merriweather, Gould, Scott," and then she trailed off.

Merris thought she had her answer, but she was startled when the clerk said Merriweather.

"I'm very sorry, I can't find any order. Are you sure an order was placed with us?"

Merris recovered quickly. "My supervisor said it was, but perhaps the order was never placed. Thank you for your time." Before leaving, she stuffed a few dollars into the counter tip jar and asked for a five-pound box of dark chocolate-covered nuts.

Merriweather. Arnold had mentioned Dr. Merriweather. Merris knew that her friend Dane's first name started with an R, but he always went by Dane. Could his first name be Rudolph and if so, was he on the other end of that phone call from Gerty? Dane did have money, or at least he appeared to. Time to pay Dane a visit. Could he really have killed Gerty? He was a doctor. He would know all about poison — especially what poison would make her death look like a heart attack. What would Merris ask him when she got there?

Merris stopped to change her clothes before going to see Dane. As long as she'd known Dane, he'd been a marina bum. He'd never worked, and now she suspected why. After registering with the Resorts Marina security, she started the long trek from the visitor parking lot to Dane's boat.

Arriving at his boat, she called out to him. The radio was playing, the cockpit cover was off, the door leading below deck was open, but there was no sign of Dane. Something must be wrong. Dane would never leave his boat like this. Merris boarded and made her way below deck. She checked the cabin and the V-berth, but no Dane.

Not wanting to waste this opportunity, she started going through his cabin, not sure if she wanted to find anything or not. She didn't see a laptop, but on the table were several clippings about Knoall Industries, the acquisition of Merriweather Scientific, and Gerty's death. One clipping had the word poison circled. The notebook next to it had several scribbles. The most notable: poison and heart attack.

As she continued going through his things, she felt someone boarding his boat. She headed up the steps to the deck. On deck was Veronica.

"Mary, what are you doing here?" Veronica asked.

"It's Merris, and I came to visit Dane. His boat was open, but he didn't answer when I called out, so I went below deck to see if he was okay. He must be okay, because he isn't on board. I was just coming up to close his boat when you boarded," Merris replied. "Why are you here?"

"Not that it's any of your business, but I got a complaint about loud music coming from Mr. Merriweather's boat. Annnnd, as the new Marina owner and manager, I came to ask him to turn it down." Silence.

Veronica continued, "Since Mr. Merriweather isn't here, I think it would be best if you leave. I'll have marina security close up his boat. Good day, Merris."

"Good day, Veronica," Merris said as she left. She was just out of earshot when her phone rang again. "Hi, Paris."

"Mom, I just heard on the news that they arrested your friend Dane for Gerty's murder."

"What? Are you sure?"

"Yes, Mom, the police had a press conference. They wouldn't give any details, just that they were given an anonymous tip. I wonder who gave them that tip."

"I have no idea. After they found Gerty, they interviewed everyone at the marina. Billy, Arnold, Sis, Patty from the restaurant—"

"Are you talking about Billy Driftwood?"

"Yes, Billy the busboy. He really took Gerty's death hard," Merris mused.

"Are you kidding me? No way."

"What? Why do you say that?"

"Knoall Industries cut funding to the agriculture department at our school. Everyone in that department is scrambling to pay their tuition."

"What does that have to do with Billy?"

"Billy doesn't have the money for his tuition, that's what."

"And your point?"

"Billy took a second job as part of the landscaping crew at the marina," Paris said.

"That doesn't mean he hated Gerty."

"Really, Mom? He needed that money."

"Working two jobs isn't so bad," Merris said.

"He works three jobs. That's the only way he can pay his tuition," Paris said.

"Not possible. He's at the marina all the time."

"Because his third job is as a stockboy at Help-Mart, graveyard shift. I'm pretty sure he hates her-hated her-and he could have been the one who called the police to lead them astray."

"I think you're reaching," protested Merris. "He never gave me any indication that he hated her."

"If Billy or Dane killed Gerty, it was well planned. Using the annual bonfire to stage her murder gave the police many suspects," Merris pondered.

Green smoke swirled. Yes, but only one of them killed her. Heh heh heh heh heh heh heh!

"You're really no help today," Merris mumbled. She continued walking.

She couldn't stop thinking about Paris saying that Billy hated Gerty. What if Paris was right? If Billy was working three jobs for tuition money, he was worth checking out.

And now, my dear Merris, something with poison in it, I think. With poison in it, but attractive to the eye and pleasing to the palate. Poppies … poppies … poppies will make them sleep. As quickly as she came, WWW left.

Was it really possible that Billy could be the killer? He had been at Sweet Treats the week before the murder. "Think, Merris. You can do this," she mumbled. "I need a coffee. That will help. Anchors Away it is. Best coffee at the marina."

Only coffee at the marina, she heard WWW cackle.

No, it couldn't be Billy. He'd always been nice to Gerty. But Paris was convinced he hated her.

Merris entered the restaurant and waited at the register to order her coffee. She was digging through her bag for money when Billy ran into her.

"I'm sorry, Mrs. Ferris. I wasn't paying attention." He quickly hung up his phone.

"It's okay, Billy. No harm done. Would you mind getting me a large black coffee to go?"

His cell phone rang. "Sorry, I have to get this," he said. "Bye, Mrs. Ferris."

"Goodbye, Billy."

Merris ordered a large black coffee to go. Billy was leaving the restaurant as she got her drink. Merris threw a five-dollar bill on the counter and called over her shoulder, "Keep the change!" as she darted out the door. She looked around until she spotted Billy heading toward the woods. She followed him, ducking behind trees to keep out of sight.

Poppies ... poppies ... poppies ... will make her sleep. Billy came to a halt in front of a beautiful flowerbed. He walked over to a rundown shed and grabbed a shovel while talking on the phone.

"Damn, Ronnie. This isn't what we talked about. ... Well, maybe if you let me get off the phone I'll have it taken care of before the storm hits."

Billy ended the call and started destroying the beautiful flowerbed, alternating between glancing at the dark clouds rolling in and glancing behind him to be sure he was alone.

When it started raining, he swore and stopped looking around. He hacked at the flowers even faster as the rain pelted him. Then lightning lit the sky.

"Forget this," he said, throwing down the shovel and running.

Once Billy was out of sight, Merris took pictures and samples for evidence.

Back in the trailer, Merris grabbed her computer and searched poisonous plants that cause heart attacks. After reviewing several sites and comparing the pictures to the plant, she found a match: actaea pachypoda, commonly known as white baneberry or doll's eyes because the fruits of the plant look like eyes. The plant fruit is sweet tasting and extremely carcinogenic. It can affect heart muscles immediately, and it will cause a quick death if consumed.

If the fruit were dipped in chocolate and given to someone, she would never know that it was poisonous. I'm almost positive that's how he killed her, Merris thought. She called Detective Lawless, filled him in, and promised to drop off the plant at the lab.

She drove to the lab and then to the marina. Getting out of her car, she saw Billy walking into the woods and called out to him. He waited for her to catch up.

"What can I do for you, Mrs. Ferris?" Billy asked.

Merris fiddled with the pepper spray in her pocket. "Billy, I know you used those plants in the woods to kill Gerty. I even know why. What I don't know is why you would throw your life away to get revenge."

"You are way off the mark. I didn't kill her."

"I found your plant and gave it to the police as evidence. They'll be here shortly to arrest you."

"I'm innocent. I didn't have anything to do with her death." Billy told Merris everything. He said the plan was to make Gerty sick, not to kill her.

"I met Ronnie when I went to the bank to apply for a loan. I talked about losing my scholarship when Gerty cut all funding to my school for my major. Even working three jobs, I'm still short. The questions kept coming and I answered them. I was given paperwork to fill out. Before I left, Ronnie handed me a card and told me to call the number on the back, told me we have more in common than I think."

"Then what happened?"

"Ronnie was very bitter toward Gerty. They lost their family business to Gerty because Dane couldn't manage money. Gerty eliminated all of the top level management positions at Merriweather Scientific, and Ronnie was the senior VP of finance. Knoall Industries has several top financial VPs, so well-compensated Ronnie was disposable. After learning that Gerty kept all the other Merriweather family members, Ronnie came up with a plan to get back at her. I had no idea the plan was to kill Gerty. You have to believe me."

"Let's go. You need to tell Detective Lawless everything."

Billy caught Merris off guard, pushed her down, and ran. She knew she would never catch him. She reached for her phone as WWW swirled in. Billy is meeting Ronnie at the Bistro Grill Gazebo tonight at seven. Protect Billy before he ends up like Gerty.

Merris called Detective Lawless but beat him to the Gazebo. She hoped he would get there in time.

Don't let the pretty table fool you; you need to scratch the surface. Heh heh heh heh heh heh heh.

Merris examined the table. WWW didn't give clues for no reason, but there was nothing out of the ordinary. That can't be what WWW was trying to tell me, she thought. There must be something more. Merris began to pace. What am I not getting? I checked the table. Then she remembered the entire clue. WWW said you need to scratch the surface. Merris went back to the table and looked carefully at the surface.

You're too high. WWW cackled. Merris dropped to the ground and looked under the table. Well, isn't he the sneaky one.

She grabbed the gun that was taped to the table, removed the bullets and the one in the chamber, and replaced it. Once she rendered the gun useless, she took cover in the nearby bushes.

Merris checked her watch. Billy arrived first. Shortly after he sat down, Veronica arrived.

I assumed that Ronnie was a male. That'll teach me.

"This was a great idea, Ronnie," Billy said. "Let's —" Veronica interrupted him with a kiss.

Merris sat there while they made small talk about duping Charles and spending his money.

"You know, Ronnie, killing Gerty wasn't part of our plan," Billy said.

Veronica put both of her hands under the table. "It was always part of my plan. She ruined my life. She got what she deserved."

Veronica pulled her hands out from under the table and pointed the gun at Billy.

"What are you doing?"

"My dear Billy, I'm tying up a loose end," Veronica said as she aimed the gun at his heart.

"Please don't shoot. I won't tell anyone you killed Gerty. I promise," Billy begged.

"I know you won't," she said.

Merris jumped out from her hiding place and yelled, "Veronica!"

"You've interfered for the last time," Veronica said. She turned to Merris and took aim. Then she pulled the trigger.

"What's the matter, Veronica?" Merris asked as she moved closer.

Veronica tried again, but nothing happened. Merris was a foot from her face. Veronica took a wild swing, but Merris was much quicker. She deflected the punch with her left hand and used it to grab Veronica's wrist. She moved her right hand inside the elbow, forcing the woman's arm up and twisting it behind her back into a painful joint lock.

Veronica squirmed, but Merris tightened her grip. It didn't

matter how much she struggled, Merris just moved with her, guiding her where she wanted her and causing her more pain. Veronica tried one last move, but Merris flowed effortlessly into a Z-lock by grabbing Veronica's right hand just below the pinky and placing her left hand in the crook of her arm, forming a Z, before sweeping her leg and taking her painfully to the ground. As she was doing this, Detective Lawless and his team came in and took over.

"Merris," Detective Lawless said, "I thought I told you to stay out of this. You could have been killed."

"Er ... um ... well ..."

"Please, enlighten me. I can't wait to hear it. I'm sure you have a good excuse," Detective Lawless replied.

Merris followed Detective Lawless to the station and gave her statement. Then she went home, made a cup of strong coffee, took out her computer, and started typing. This would make a great story for the writing group.

Wicked Witchy

Barb Holliday

Wickedness may have two faces,
It can bobble between right and wrong,
Casting its shadow in places,
Knowing its hold can be strong.
Evil can sometimes surprise us,
Deducing one clue at a time,
Weeding through all of the guises,
Inching toward solving the crime.
Thoroughly checking all bases,
Clearing the name of a friend,
Helping to fill in blank spaces,
Yielding results in the end!

Character bio from Barb Miller

Cassidy (Cassie) Flint Kingston is a blond, forty-five-year-old, militantly nonsmoking romance writer who recently started wearing bifocals. She is tougher than she looks. With a farm to run and her mother, daughter, and granddaughter to look after, she never leaves anything to chance. Recently she married her childhood heartthrob, Sam Kingston, a wildlife photographer and all-around great guy. Cassie's inspiration is Athena, Greek Goddess of Wisdom.

Enjoy this off-beat murder

Barbara Miller

Murder 101

Barb Miller

Cassidy Flint Kingston slammed the Jeep tailgate shut and looked around at her loving family. Her mother's farm was now home to her and her new husband, Sam. They enjoyed living with her mother, grown daughter, and granddaughter so much she had a moment of regret that she and Sam were going on vacation. She didn't like uncertainty. That's what you got when you drove hundreds of miles away.

"Are you sure all of you will be okay for two whole weeks?" she asked.

Her daughter, Diane, came and hugged her. "Of course we'll be okay. No lambs arrive in August and I'm working daylight at the police station."

Cassie bent and kissed her granddaughter, Rachel, then hugged her mom. "We'll call when we get there."

"Forget us," her grey-haired mother advised. "Focus on your honeymoon. Make a baby. It's not too late."

Sam, who had been standing patiently by the door of his Jeep, bent double laughing in his deep voice at Cassie's red face. "I think we'd better go before she gets rolling," he said.

Cassie hopped in and Sam gave her a kiss, his mustache caressing her cheek, before he started the vehicle and drove toward Falls Bend. "Are you sure you're okay with this strange interrupted honeymoon, me dropping you off in Nashville for your writers' conference and then you joining me later in the swamp, hoping I'll have taken pictures of the elusive cranes by then? That part will be a camping trip."

"Of course I'm okay with it. I could just opt out of the conference. I only signed up because my arch-nemesis Katherine Devlin isn't going to be there."

"Katherine Devlin. What does she have against you anyway?" Sam sent Cassie an amused look, his eyes crinkling at the corners.

"Years ago she verbally attacked me in the lobby of the conference hotel about stealing her plot, but my book had just come out and hers got delayed for some reason."

"That's ridiculous," Sam said. "Aren't there, like, only a

dozen plots?"

"I never got to read her book because it never came out. I based mine on a real murder. She never considered possibly she'd read the same newspapers articles, only I had finished and sold the story faster. After that you called to tell me Mom needed me. I moved here and all that seemed frivolous."

"You've done fine with your ebooks at your new publisher and now the ones you publish yourself. How did you come up with the name Old Stand?"

"For that stand of trees on top of the hill. That place is ... inspiring." She had never shared with Sam exactly who inspired her there. Athena, the goddess of wisdom, visited the grove if Cassie brought the right offering of wine and cheese.

"I'm probably making as much money without the stress of pursuing contracts. Black Ink loves everything I write. Of course I can do what I want with Old Stand. To tell you the truth, I'm going to the conference more to hunt up cozy mystery authors for my own press than to push my books."

Sam chuckled. "I hope you have fun being on the other side of the desk, so to speak."

"It will be fun since Katherine won't be there. Must be something else going on to keep her and her friend Vivian away."

Cassie sighed as they drove around the Diamond in Falls Bend and waved at a few people, then took Route 711 south. She felt stronger when she was with Sam. He was tall and wiry, with salt-and-pepper hair and a voice deep enough to make your stomach rumble. She wondered what he saw in her, a slight blonde of no particular beauty who already needed bifocals to read. Like many aging romance writers, she had turned to romantic suspense, then mysteries, then thrillers, and now she enjoyed writing cozies the most.

She was forty-eight, so her mother's suggestion to get pregnant wasn't out of the question, but she doubted the wisdom of trying to have a child at her age. She sensed her silence had become awkward. "I haven't been on a trip of any kind in five years."

Sam smiled. "I realize that. You've had your mother and the farm to worry about. But now Diane is able to help there. What I think you need a vacation from most of all is murder."

"What? We have enough crime in Falls Bend to keep me inspired, but I don't think about murder all the time. The problem is getting humor into a cozy about a murder."

"Murder is hardly ever funny. Consider this a much needed vacation from everything. I don't know how you manage the farm business, your writing, and your publishing company, plus your real investigations with the Sleuths and Serpents. Won't they miss you?"

"I forgot to tell you, the library archives room is being remodeled, so we lost our room for the whole of August."

"What will Manelli do without your group solving cold cases? You've reduced him to paperwork."

"Actually he doesn't like it when we get too involved. I think he's looking forward to this month without one of us running in there with a question or even a new case."

"Is he going on vacation himself?" Sam asked.

"He said he might throw a fishing line in the creek, but other than that he plans on having a vacation from us. Except he may read some of our books."

"Just so he doesn't find anything wrong with yours. Yours are all primo, especially the romance parts."

"You've read them all?" She felt herself smiling.

"They're right there on your shelf above the computer. You don't mind, do you?"

"No, I'm flattered. Without realizing it, you were the hero I was looking for in all those books, the man I had left behind in Falls Bend."

He turned his warm gaze on her and made her feel like a princess. "Wow, no one has ever said anything like that to me except you."

"You are a hero, Sam. So don't feel bad about interrupting our vacation because you need to reprise your article on the whooping cranes. You should be glad there's still an interest."

"Yes, they've had a flock in Texas for years. The one at White Lake is just getting established. Have you decided yet how you'll get to Louisiana?"

"I'd prefer a train or bus but since your location is so isolated, I think I'll have to rent a car."

"Just tell me where to meet you. Now catch a nap so you can drive later."

"First some food. I missed breakfast."

It was while she was making herself a Swiss cheese cracker that Cassidy became aware they were not alone in the car. She felt a gaze boring into the back of her head and twitched around to see her paranormal sleuthing partner lounging in the back seat. She blinked her eyes and looked again, but Athena was still there in her chitin, cloak, and elaborate headdress. She gave Cassie a big smile as she held out her hand for the cheese cracker. What was worse, her owl was with her, which was a bit unnerving, especially because Cassie was afraid she'd have to hand crackers to the owl as well.

Cassie had been used to meeting Athena in the sassafras grove that overlooked the farm, the place she called Old Stand. She called on her only when in the throes of an investigation she couldn't solve. What was the goddess of wisdom doing in the backseat of Sam's jeep on the way to Nashville? Moreover, why had she brought her owl?

Cassie handed her the cracker and pulled out the guidebook, flipping it open to the Nashville cultural district. "That's it. There's a full-sized replica of the Parthenon in Nashville."

"Really?" Sam said.

"It's the Athens of the South," Athena said. "Athens of the South," Cassie parroted.

"A lot of U.S. towns have taken foreign names like Athens, Georgia, but the people in Nashville sure know how to grasp culture."

"That must be why..."

"Why what?" Sam asked.

"Nothing. I think I need a drink." She opened a wine cooler but felt Athena's gaze drilling into her, so she put it in the rear-seat cupholder. Odd that the goddess's ability to move physical objects seemed to be limited to food and drink.

"Yeah, have one now, but not when it's your turn to drive."

They changed off every two hours and stopped for a nice lunch that Athena did not interrupt. Cassie drove the last shift before Nashville, which meant Athena's presence in the backseat was even more distracting. The goddess kept asking if they were there yet. Sam couldn't see or hear Athena, thank goodness. Cassie had fed her all the cheese and crackers and given her both wine coolers. For an insubstantial goddess, she consumed a great deal. Cassie did wonder where the food went. She decided to consider the consumables offerings and stop worrying about them, except that she was once again terribly hungry.

"Turn left here," Athena commanded. Cassie wobbled but kept the car on the route Sam had mapped.

"You weren't going to turn there, were you?" Sam asked,

checking the map.

"No."

"It was a shortcut," Athena said. "That's your slang for quicker way."

"You've been here before?" Cassie asked.

"No, I've never been to Nashville," Sam answered.

Cassie was going to have to be careful not to answer Athena, for now anyway. They pulled under the portico of the Oglethorpe Hotel, half a mile from the conference center.

Sam unloaded her suitcase and the empty suitcase destined to hold freebies and books. He came around to take the wheel but when she got out Sam kissed Cassie goodbye in front of the doorman and bellhop, who smiled in appreciation. Damn, that was a good kiss.

"You sure you don't want me to stay?" Sam asked. "It's only three days after today."

She seriously considered it, but three days with Athena haunting their hotel suite was too much to contemplate.

Maybe she could ditch her at the temple. For sure she was not taking her to the swamp with her. "Tempting, but what would you do here? No, hunt your cranes and I'll call you when I'm ready to leave. If all else fails, we meet at the ranger station at White Lake on Monday."

"Okay, you have everything you need: phone, credit cards, bail money?"

Cassie laughed. "I think I'll be okay."

"One good thing about registering late, they didn't tap you to speak or anything."

"True. You be careful. It's a long drive to White Lake. Don't get eaten by alligators."

"I'd stay the night but I can probably get there late tonight and start photographing by dawn."

"I'm going to check on a rental car for Monday."

"Get lots of sleep before you head after me."

"I will."

Sam kissed her again, then slid into the Jeep and waved.

"So where's our room?" Athena asked as Sam drove away. Cassie no longer jumped when her paranormal sidekick addressed her, but she had to resist the urge to answer her in front of people.

The bellhop was picking up her bags and seemed surprised one was heavy and one was light. She resisted the urge to explain as he preceded her into the lobby. She registered and Athena refused to enter the elevator. Now why would she trust it less than a car? "What is the room number?" Cassie asked.

"222," the bellhop said.

Cassie nodded. "We could almost take the stairs to the second floor."

"Might be faster," the boy said as the elevator door slowly chugged shut.

It was a lovely suite overlooking the gardens at the back of the hotel and catching the breeze. It had two four-poster double beds and comforters in the cabbage rose pattern.

"If you want the AC on, I'll close the window."

"Let's leave it for a bit," Cassie said. "The flowers smell lovely."

She handed him a five, then went to the door to look for Athena. No sign of her, but she heard the toilet flush. Her mouth was still open when the goddess emerged from the bathroom. "Too many wine coolers?" Cassie asked.

"Just seeing how things work in this century. Leave that window open for Minerva. She decided to eat out tonight."

"Isn't that your Roman name?" Cassie asked.

"That's why I gave it to my owl. She could have flown on her own. Now she needs to stretch her wings."

Once again Cassie gaped. "You made an owl ride cramped up in the backseat of our Jeep when she could have flown?" Even to her this sounded ridiculous and she burst out laughing.

"I could have flown on my own for that matter, but I thought a road trip together would be fun. That's the right term, isn't it? Road trip?"

"Yes. So happy to add slang to your knowledge base about our times. You can teleport?"

"Wish myself to be where I want? Yes."

"I'm curious. Why didn't you just wish yourself to the Parthenon here in Nashville?"

"I found the drive pleasant and I liked the company." Cassie smiled and plopped on the bed. "You know, if you weren't a goddess I might hug you."

"Sam's an attractive mate for you." Athena was walking around the room fiddling with the TV, the flower arrangements, and the venetian blinds.

Cassie nodded, wondering if the fiddling was an illusion. But that toilet had flushed and it didn't do that by itself, unless it was just a sound effect. "Everyone thinks so. Besides that, Sam's a really nice guy."

"Are you going to take your mother's advice?"

"About what?" Cassie unzipped her full suitcase and pulled out slacks and a shirt.

"Making another child, of course."

Cassie felt a little wistful for a moment. "I think I'm a bit past the age."

"Forty-eight? 'It isn't over until it's over,' to quote one of your movies."

"Thank you so much for that reminder. It seems you spend more time with me than I realized." But she was glad for the reminder about her family. She took a moment to call home and let them know she had arrived safely. She'd only just finished when her cell phone buzzed. It was Gretchen, her friend from her days writing for Mandalay Press.

"Hi, Gretch, I'm at the Oglethorpe. Where are you?"

"I'm at the Bellefonte. Cassie, don't come to the conference."

"Why not? You're the one who invited me. You know, as part of your tourist bureau duties. We're going to do the town in the evenings."

"As soon as your name went on the list of registrants, Katherine Devlin and her evil twin, Vivian Hunt, registered as well."

"That could be a coincidence."

"Or she might be here to cause trouble again."

Cassie thought back to the lobby scene, which was still vivid in her memory. "That incident was five years ago. Probably she's forgotten all about it."

"I don't think Katherine Devlin forgets any insult."

"She started it." Cassie hated sounding juvenile.

So I can't talk you out of this?" Gretchen asked. "Not that I don't appreciate a good catfight."

"It takes two. Nothing is going to happen. Is it too early to check in and get my goodie bag?"

"No, they just set up the table. I'll meet you in the lobby."

"I need time to shower. Say, half an hour counting the walk." Cassie became aware of Athena staring at her like a roomie who was going to be deserted.

"I guess you're not coming to the temple with me today," Athena said. "You'll spend the whole four days with your little conference friends."

"I'll come after I talk to Gretchen. I won't go to the cocktail party tonight. Come with me. After we meet Gretchen we'll walk to the temple, then go out for a nice dinner, my treat."

Athena smiled at her. "I should come with you now since it sounds like you're in some kind of danger. If this Katherine attacks you, I can defend you."

"How, with a thunderbolt or something?"

"You're thinking of my father. No, I can make her see reason. I'm good at that."

Cassie tossed over in her mind the implications of taking her goddess muse with her. What could go wrong? "Would you mind coming? I'm not afraid of Katherine and her lackey, but I have to admit if I'd known she would be here I would never have registered."

"Go, rinse off the dust of the road. We can talk on the way to the conference."

"What about Minerva?"

"We'll leave the window open."

It took Cassie twenty minutes to shower, blow-dry her shoulder-length blond hair, and decide on a casual pair of slacks and blouse. She grabbed a denim jacket in case the air cooled down later.

Gretchen was sitting tensely in the lobby of the Bellefonte, looking stylish in a white suit and a new bob to her dark straight hair. When Cassie came in, Gretchen made a tiny pointing motion to a mountain of luggage being wheeled through the lobby. Cassie ducked behind a palm tree until Katherine's train had passed. Besides Vivian there was a young guy with her. Too young.

"So that's her," Athena said, "your arch-nemesis."

"In the flesh. You're not going to, like, kill her or anything?"

"Not if you don't want me to."

"No, I don't want you to."

Gretchen sneaked to Cassie's side. "Here, sign in and get your ID tag." Gretchen felt her own ID and then swiped it off her jacket just as Cassie read Press on it.

She must be volunteering to help with publicity at the conference, thought Cassie. After all, she was local and would have contacts. This meant she was going off duty.

Cassie signed up, got a packet and yet another tote bag,

then pinned her tag to her shirt and hugged her friend. "Where's the bar?"

"This way. You are so brave."

"When are you going to come visit the farm?" Cassie asked as they made their way to a table in a dark corner.

"I don't know. I'm still struggling with my career. You can afford to retire since you've made it."

"I haven't retired," Cassie said. "I'm writing more than ever."

"You don't write romance anymore."

Cassie grabbed a handful of pretzels from the dish on the table and looked at the wine list. "I'm trying the chardonnay. What about you?"

"That sounds fine."

She ordered and turned to the woman she hadn't seen for five years. Gretch looked thinner and more stylish with her dark hair cut in a twenties bob, shorter in back. Maybe she looked less happy than the last time they had parted in D.C. "That's because I have enough romance in my real life now. I always did write romantic suspense. Now I'm writing cozy mysteries and thrillers as well."

"I've read your three most recent books and they're very edgy, almost like real crime fiction."

"That's because ... of my new writing group." She didn't want to admit the books were based on real murders. Why freak Gretchen out already?

"Which is? I mean I did notice when you dropped out of all the professional organizations."

"The Sleuths and Serpents. It's a local group."

"May I join?"

"Sure. You are hereby a member. We have no officers or dues, just meetings and a wonderful mentor, Detective Manelli. You can meet him if you come to visit."

"Sounds like it might be worth a trip to the farm to jump-start my writing."

"Your writing is wonderful. You just need more time to produce more books."

The waiter brought their wine order, poured a glass, and waited for Cassie to try a sip before he served them.

"Could you leave the bottle?" Cassie asked, knowing Athena's appetite and wanting a little for herself. She poured some into the water glass on the table.

Gretchen blinked. "You seem to have two glasses of wine now."

"Silly me. So, Katherine just decided at the last minute, as I did?"

"She must have wedged herself onto the marketing panel. I saw they just stickered the programs." Gretchen bent down to pull the program out of her bag.

"Surely you don't expect her to attack me publicly, do you?"

"I don't know what to expect, after she stole your contract. But I guess that was in retaliation for you stealing her plot, not that you did. Anyway, I think she'd be capable of — did you drink that whole glass of wine already?"

"Oops. I guess I did." Athena had emptied the wine glass. Cassie got a grip on the water glass. "She didn't steal anything. I mean, Katherine didn't steal anything from me."

Gretchen twitched. "I was there, remember. She sat down with the Mandalay editor and when she got up, she had a three-book contract and you got dumped."

"Okay, so maybe she got the contract that I might have had."

"She got a better one, a bigger advance."

"Jeez, Gretchen. You're depressing me. I came here to have fun."

"Sorry, but it's true. She took such a big advance that after three books they dropped the historical romance line just to get rid of her, and now Mandalay is merging with another publisher."

"You're kidding." Cassie gulped her wine. "Where do you hear this stuff?"

"I keep my ear to the Internet."

"They can do what they want. I don't care."

"You may." Gretchen gave her a warning look.

"Come on, they're not merging with Black Ink. Why would they?"

"Just what I've heard." Gretchen fluttered the fingers of one hand.

"Even if they were, what has that got to do with me?"

"She could steal your publisher again."

"Black Ink is electronic," Cassie said. "I know they print books too, but the big money is in ebooks, so it's a different world. I'm not worried."

"What if she tries to move in on your other publisher, Old Stand Press?"

Cassie choked on a pretzel crumb. "Small potatoes — and they don't take submissions from just anybody."

They have an open submission period."

"Why don't you send in a book?"

"I don't have anything cozy written. Look who just walked in. I hope they don't sit by us."

"Who's the guy?" Cassie asked, assessing the golden-boy tennis-player type who guided Katherine by her elbow.

"Her boy toy." Gretch was staring at him as well, but in resentment.

"He looks expensive." Cassie wrinkled her nose at the drift of sweet cologne and perfume that came their way. "What a burden."

"You are getting old." Gretch turned back to her and looked surprised. "You haven't acquired a drinking problem, have you?"

Cassie looked at both her empty glasses. How did Athena do that? "Not yet."

Katherine looked shocked when she saw Cassie. She turned down the table next to theirs and said something to her longtime writing buddy, Vivian Hunt. She and the guy laughed. Katherine looked good for her age. A cap of blond hair hugged her head, and her jawline was clear of wrinkles. She looked remote and unapproachable, so scary that no one tried to get her autograph. Vivian almost mimicked Katherine's makeup and hairstyle, but her hair was nut brown. Though she was younger than Katherine, she looked brittle.

"Are you going to let her get away with that?" Gretchen asked.

"With what? You don't even know what she said. Listen, I have to go somewhere tonight."

Gretchen stared at her. "You're not coming to the cocktail party?"

"Not after that. Are you free for breakfast?"

"Sure, the continental breakfast is free. What time?"

"Before the first session, say, 8:30." Cassie gave her another hug, flagged the waiter, and asked for the check. He produced it from his vest pocket and she gave him a generous tip. Then she dumped the dregs of the bottle into her glass and walked out with it before she realized she'd be stealing the glass.

"I'll take it," Athena said. "We can bring it back tomorrow."

"I saved it for you anyway." Cassie left the hotel, reaching for her guidebook.

Athena pointed up West End Avenue. "I know the way."

"That's right. You've been here before."

"I've been known to fly down for a long weekend. It's the Athens of the South, remember?"

"Right."

It was less than a mile and gave Athena a chance to finish the wine. Cassie stowed the glass in her tote. When they finally came to the Parthenon, it was more impressive than Cassie could have thought.

"No wonder you like it here."

"It's one place where I come to feel revered."

"Oh, Athena, haven't I shown you the proper respect all this time?"

"Yes, but helping you with your cases falls under the category of what you'd call slumming."

Cassie blinked. "You've picked up a lot of slang. I hope you enjoyed the wine."

"It was primo. I got that word from Sam."

"What about the dedications I put in the three books I've written because of your hints? Mind you, they aren't solutions, but you always point me in the right direction."

Athena nodded. "The dedications were just and of a good length."

"Aha, you did read my books."

"Of course. Don't I sit on your shoulder while you're writing?"

"You do? Ew."

"Do you think I always want to be revered?"

"I guess not. What do you think of the statue? It's a good likeness." It had Athena's strong, honest face, her ornate headdress, and her stately gown. In fact, it was the same gown right down to the sandals.

"Someone must have guided the sculptor's hand."

Cassie sent her an accusing look. "I think it must have been you."

"I like the flowers as well. It's an art museum, you know."

"I should have looked at the guidebook earlier. They're just closing. We can come back tomorrow. So where do you want to have dinner?"

"That place with the bell."

Cassie nodded. "That should keep us both up all night."

When they got back to the room, the window was closed. "What about Minerva?"

"She's in the bathroom drinking out of the sink," Athena reported.

"That's a relief, I think." Cassie opened her phone and dialed Sam, but the call went to message. Possibly he was out of cell area or else still stalking the cranes. Then she noticed she had a message from him telling her as much. He would drive out to get supplies once a day and try to call her. It was comforting that he would contact her, but she wouldn't be able to get hold of him any time she wanted to. She would miss his strength. But at least she had Athena.

The goddess came away from the window with her majestic headdress in her hand. "Something's wrong, isn't it?"

"You mean something beyond my arch-nemesis showing up here?"

"Yes. All these women bunch together and buzz like bees, but no one comes up to you except your special friend."

"You noticed that?" Cassie asked.

"The males stand around and drink and watch you. The women whisper and look at you. Did you let any other friends know you were coming?"

"I'm not sure I have many friends any more in the publishing business, if I ever had any. You get into a mode when you meet people at events and you fake closeness. Moving back to the farm showed me who I really am. I wonder why I wanted to come."

"Because Gretchen invited you." Athena took off her outer cloak and tossed it on the bed. "Your books are better now, full of real people with real problems."

"That's quite a compliment coming from you." Cassie was glad Athena had not gotten the jest about being real. She hung her ordinary clothes in the closet. No shimmering gowns for her.

"And you look better without face paint. They are the ones who look like fakes."

"I don't think about putting on a show anymore. I guess I'm a different person. Coming to the conference was a mistake."

Athena pursed her lips. "A realization is never a mistake."

"You're right. I like the person I've become more than the one I was. Maybe I should join Sam early."

"But what about the Parthenon?"

"Don't worry. We'll go back there. There are only two sessions I'm really interested in: Evidence and Murder 101, the crime scene reenactment. Those are both tomorrow. After that I'm yours."

Athena beamed, then looked puzzled. "Why didn't you tell Gretchen not to worry about Old Stand Press dumping you? You are Old Stand."

"I wanted to remain anonymous."

"You are Cassidy Flint. You could never be merely anonymous." Athena stretched out on the bed and composed herself for sleep. Minerva flew to the window, so Cassie opened it for her. The owl couldn't possibly get into trouble. She wasn't real.

As she crawled into bed in her sweatpants and T-shirt, Cassie pondered whether Athena was just a figment of her writer's imagination. But if that were true, she would not hold so many surprises or bring Cassie to such startling revelations about herself. She'd rather think of Athena as a supernatural entity than as a part of herself that was inaccessible to her except after being wined and dined. Best to leave things as they were.

She was writing well and writing what she liked. Sales of Old Stand ebooks were soaring. She still printed them for readers who demanded to have the physical book in hand. Black Ink did the same. She should have had more of a plan when she came here, maybe even revealed she was a publisher, but she feared getting too big too fast. She didn't want Old Stand to take over her life.

Friday, August 23

The morning was actually chilly when Cassie got up. Both Athena and Minerva were gone, so she had the place to herself for showering and getting ready. She made a cup of coffee the way she liked it just in case the stuff at the buffet tables stank. Then she went down the stairs and out into the morning in her buff cargo pants and Hawaiian shirt. West End Avenue was already busy but the hotels were on the same side of the street, so she wasn't worried. Time to find Gretchen and the goodie room. She carried a folded tote inside her small one.

When she got to the hotel, Gretchen was waiting for her in the part of the lobby partitioned off for their continental breakfast. "Have you heard?" Gretchen grabbed her satchel and followed Cassie through the clumps of early risers. She was wearing a stylish gray pantsuit.

Cassie helped herself to a couple of mini-muffins, a slice of melon, and some Earl Grey tea, wondering if she had underdressed for the conference. "Let's find a place to sit."

"Right, privacy."

There were two cushy floral-print armchairs and a table in one corner. Cassie arranged her snack and noticed Gretchen wasn't eating.

"Katherine went ballistic when she found out you were here. She thinks you're trying to get Mandalay back."

Now that's just silly. I don't even write romance anymore."

"Because of the merger with Black Ink, she's really worried you may try to push her out."

Cassie blinked and shook her head. "Are you making this up? Because it sounds bizarre."

"The cocktail party was abuzz with rumors."

"Was either of the editors there?" Cassie asked.

"No. They were probably in top-secret meetings," Gretchen whispered.

"Or maybe eating a quiet dinner before the insanity."

"So what are you going to do?" Gretchen asked.

"Go to the session on evidence gathering." Cassie checked her watch.

"You are so brave to carry on alone." Gretchen said it dramatically, almost like a character in one of her books.

Alone? Yes, Cassie did feel the absence of Athena. But the goddess would just be bored hearing a police detective speak about preserving fiber and hair samples. "I'd better get to my session."

Gretchen jumped up. "I'm coming with you."

"Are you interested in crime and mystery writing?" Cassie shouldered her bag and left her dishes on a tray.

"No, but somebody should be there to support you."

The session wasn't full by any means, but Cassie chose a seat in the back row so she wouldn't feel people staring at her. The padded rose-colored banquet chair was even comfortable. Detective Morrissey knew his stuff, but she had heard all this many times from Detective Manelli. Morrissey wasn't as young or fit as Manelli, but he spoke with the same authority. Before the session was over, Cassie discreetly slipped out.

"I thought you wanted to listen to that person," Athena said.

Cassie didn't jump but checked the hallway and then turned to her invisible companion. "Athena, you have to understand conference timing. When faced with limited ladies' room facilities, we cut the question portion of a session for more important tasks."

Athena nodded knowingly. "I'll come with you."

Cassie blinked, unaware the goddess had any such need. But then she had not been aware Athena slept. "Okay, but not into the stall."

"Minerva has found a shortcut to the temple."

A burst of talk silenced them both as they went into the spacious restroom and chose companion stalls. The other ladies hurried out.

"I heard Black Ink was courting Katherine," Athena whispered.

"I know the Black Ink editor. It's more likely Katherine was thrusting herself on her. Besides, she doesn't write dark."

"Maybe she could. Her personal life is pretty rocky." Athena quoted from someone. "First the divorce, now this cover model."

Athena was picking up too much contemporary jargon and far too much gossip. Cassie refused to take the bait. A good thing, too. When she emerged to wash her hands, a group of women rushed in and ducked around her. At least she had not been caught talking to thin air or gossiping about Katherine.

She made her way outside with Athena at her elbow and zipped through the goodie room, picking up pens, bookmarks, and freebie books. She had to admit she was actually shopping for more authors for her own publishing company. She had drafted several of the Sleuths and Serpents who wrote novel length, but she wanted a bigger group of cozy authors for Old Stand, and this was a painless way to sample work. When her spare tote was full, Cassie hunted up the next room. To her surprise when she opened the door, it had crime scene tape around the speaker area. She took a seat up front.

"The corpse looks realistic," Athena said.

"It's not a mannequin. They must have talked one of the

husbands into playing victim."

Athena stepped over the yellow tape. "But it seems uncomfortable for him to lie on the floor like that."

Cassie went as far as the tape, amazed at the stillness of the actor. She couldn't even detect him breathing. Then she saw the blood and it was good. How on earth were they going to get that up? The carpet would be ruined. It looked ... too good. She dumped her totes and ducked under the tape for a better look.

"Cassie, I think he's really dead," Athena said.

Cassie felt the blood drain from her face as she recognized the man who had come in with Katherine. She had seen a few corpses in her time, and this was one. She turned and swayed a little as she stumbled toward the chairs and in the process broke the tape.

"Cassie, are you unwell?" Athena asked.

"Hey, no one is supposed to be in here for ten more minutes." Morrissey ducked under the tape himself and plopped a pile of handouts on the lecture table.

"You'd better get security," Cassie said and leaned against the wall.

"No big deal, just close your eyes while I set up the rest of the clues."

"But he's dead. You have to call the police. What am I saying? You are the police."

"I haven't even gotten the mannequin out yet." When he turned and saw the body, he jumped and made his way to it. Morrissey dropped to one knee and searched for a pulse. "Crap, he is dead."

"How could this happen at a conference?"

"Murder is never convenient," Morrissey said.

"Murder?"

"His throat's been cut with this broken wine glass. You didn't touch anything, did you?"

"No, of course not. I'm not an idiot. He just looked so realistic. I'd better go."

"No, sit back there. You're the closest thing to a witness we have."

Cassie moved her totes to the very last row and slumped in a chair.

"Can I get you anything?" Athena asked.

"No I'll be okay. Not much has gone right so far, has it?

Gretchen turns out to be a paranoid lunatic, everyone is gossiping about me, and I find a body. I should never have come."

"Are you talking to yourself?" Morrissey asked as he tapped the keypad of his phone.

"It's a bad habit under stress. I'll try to be quiet."

"You look familiar."

"I was in your last session."

"She's Cassidy Flint," Athena said.

"I know. You're Cassidy Flint. I read one of your books."

"That's right. I'm ... flattered."

"Do you know who he is?"

"I saw him with Katherine Devlin last night."

"I'd better lock the door." He almost got the door barricaded while he talked on his phone to someone, but Katherine barged in and screamed. She fainted, then woke up and cried. Vivian was there to help her through the hysteria — which was a good thing, since Morrissey pretty much ignored her.

"Horrible dramatics," Athena said. "This isn't the theater. This would kill Aristotle if he weren't dead already."

"Is she faking?" Cassie asked.

Suddenly Vivian turned and saw her. "She did it. She'd do anything to hurt Katherine."

"Me?" Cassie almost fell off her chair. Bad enough finding the body. Now she was a suspect?

"Yes! You must have killed Jerome." Vivian's dark gaze felt like a rifle bead homing in on Cassie.

"But I didn't even know him."

"Check the fingerprints on the glass." Vivian pointed at Cassie. "I bet they're hers."

Morrissey finally finished on the phone. "Of course we'll print the glass. You don't have to tell me that. What are you doing in here anyway?"

Vivian gaped, unable to answer.

Athena looked at Cassie. "Why would she think that's your glass? You took it with you."

"But yours was left on the table," Cassie whispered. "I know this is a strange question, but do you leave fingerprints?"

Athena seemed puzzled by the question. "Even if I do, they won't be yours, so she has no grounds on which to accuse you."

"Gretchen could have taken your glass from the table."

"I thought she was your friend. Besides, after Gretchen left, Katherine or this termagant could have taken your glass."

"Did you touch anything?" Morrissey asked, looming over Cassie.

Cassie shook her head. Clues were so much easier to grasp when you were not a suspect.

Four hours later she was allowed to leave the hotel with a warning to not leave town.

She'd done nothing but sit in a plastic chair in a small office and answer questions for those four hours while they tried not to listen to Katherine's hysterics from the conference room. "I feel a little dizzy," she confided to Athena as they began the short walk to their hotel.

"No wonder. You missed lunch. Want me to carry your bags?"

"You're kidding, right? The only things I've ever seen you move are consumables."

"I was joking, if that's what kidding means. And I don't consume things, it just looks like I do to you."

"I hope you enjoy all the wine and cheese you are not actually consuming."

"Of course I do. I take them in as offerings."

"Oh, we were supposed to go to the temple."

"We can do that tomorrow. Let's go back to your hotel and try room service."

"Good idea. Then we can get some rest. I've had it with the conference, so we can spend all day at the Parthenon tomorrow-unless the police have other ideas."

Some soup and a baguette did much to settle Cassie to the notion that she had to figure out who had killed Katherine's latest so that the gossips would not blame her forever. She had his name now, Jerome Lacey. She powered up her laptop for the first time in days and began researching him and Katherine. Athena looked over her shoulder as she killed the bottle of wine from dinner and munched on cheese and crackers.

"This is fun."

Cassie stared at her dubiously.

Athena dipped her head. "Well, except for the unfortunate murder part."

"I just have a feeling I had better find the killer so they

don't take Vivian seriously. Huh, he was a cover model. Katherine met him three years ago at a conference, and they seem to have been tripping the light fantastic ever since."

"Vivian is in most of the pictures as well. A third wheel, or is it fifth wheel?"

"Depends on whether you're used to chariots or cars. I wonder what the connection is."

"Is Vivian published?" Athena asked.

"Yes, with Mandalay. Funny, Katherine had only three books with them. I thought she would have written more in five years."

"Just because you do two a year doesn't mean everyone does."

"Mine are shorter. Huh, there's Gretchen sitting behind the group and not looking happy. That was at the last MurderCon, in Detroit. I wonder why Katherine was there."

"Why does Gretchen go to so many conferences?" Athena scrutinized the photo on the laptop screen. "It must be expensive."

Cassie shrugged. "I think to inspire her."

"Is Gretchen published?"

"One with Mandalay."

"You should have taken her with you to Black Ink."

"I don't own Gretchen and have no in with Black Ink. Maybe she did submit to them, but she never said."

"Would a word from you help her?"

"No, book contracts are business decisions. I could publish her at Old Stand, but I'd rather not solicit a book from her."

"Because she'd know you're the publisher then?"

"Maybe she'll submit on her own. That's the bad side of being an editor. If the book couldn't be fixed, I'd have to turn it down." The phone rang and Cassie was so glad to hear Sam's voice she started to cry.

"I heard something about a murder at the conference," Sam said.

"That's right, and no, don't cut your trip short. I'm fine and yes, I will stay out of it. In fact, I may be leaving Sunday instead of Monday."

"You sure you're all right? I hate to think of you there alone."

Cassie glanced at Athena. "I'm not as alone as you think."

"Okay. See you when you get here. I'll try to call every

day around this time. There's a pretty nice fish shack here with the best food ever."

"I'll look forward to it." Cassie ended the call and sighed. "You didn't exactly tell him the truth."

"I have you and Minerva. You won't desert me."

"No, we won't."

Saturday, August 24

When Cassie got up, she was alone again. She decided to order a real breakfast from room service. Unfortunately the bacon, eggs, and grits came with a copy of the Nashville Herald, which covered the murder at the conference.

She was prominently listed as a person of interest. The police had never used that term. And the newspaper had quoted her, erroneously of course, since she hadn't even talked to a reporter.

She finished her coffee, then made a scathing call to the editor of the paper. She had to threaten a lawsuit to get past the palace guard. She demanded to know who the reporter was who had claimed to quote her without ever speaking to her.

The editor said he didn't know which reporter it was.

"Really? You don't even know who works for you, yet leave yourself open to lawsuits? I would never speak the words, 'It was only a matter of time before something like this happened.'"

He cleared his throat. "Are you sure in the heat of the moment—"

"Besides being judgmental, that's a horrible cliché. That alone should have made the editor suspicious. Now either you print a retraction or I call my lawyer."

He agreed to find out who had written the article and demand their tape of the interview.

Athena and Minerva were still not back, but Cassie decided it would be a good idea to go to the conference and put in an appearance just so people wouldn't think she was under suspicion. She did wonder if they would cancel the rest of the conference, but apparently not. When she got there, the door to the murder scene was locked, and she saw Morrissey bustling around.

She went and got hot tea. No sign of Gretchen, but they hadn't made plans. Maybe this latest notoriety had scared her away? It wouldn't help Gretchen's career to be associated with a murder suspect.

Still no Athena. Cassie was feeling just a little abandoned, especially after her companion had sworn to stick by her. She decided to go to the marketing panel. What could it hurt? Katherine wouldn't be there, since she seemed to be in deep mourning. To Cassie's utter shock, Vivian Hunt was sitting in front of the room, looking bereft but courageous.

After the usual nonsense about agents versus self-submissions, someone asked about electronic publishing. It was Gretchen, in fact, at a front seat. She was taking notes and looking serious in her beige linen suit. Vivian talked about it as though it were a passing fad.

To Cassie's surprise, the Black Ink editor on the panel called on her.

"Well, it's green?" Cassie said. "By that I mean it saves a lot of trees. And there is always the print option for those who love to hold a book."

"E-publishing will kill the industry," Vivian declared, "by undercutting print book prices."

Cassie blinked. "It's been going on for years and we're not dead yet."

A titter of laughter stilled.

Vivian drew herself up and glowered. "That remark is in very bad taste."

Athena slipped in beside her. "She was the one who mentioned killing. Wait till you hear what I found out."

"Maybe later," Cassie mumbled. She raised her voice. "The value of a book should be in the writing and editing, not just in printing and distribution. Print books will always have a place and will have to cost a little more, but electronic ones aren't going to be given away."

"Thank you," the editor said.

"Time for a bathroom break while they sum up?" Athena asked.

"Good thinking." When Cassie entered the bathroom the four women there shut up, a good indicator of the subject of their gossip. She and Athena went to the luncheon and found a table near the back.

"Am I going to be taking someone's seat?" Athena asked her.

"Do you really think anyone will sit with me besides you, under the circumstances?"

"Probably not." Athena looked at the menu card. "What's chicken cordon bleu?"

"Chicken with cheese sauce." Cassie put on her bifocals to scrutinize the menu herself. Tiramisu for dessert. Athena would like that. Overall, being shadowed by a hungry goddess was good for her diet.

Betts Albright from Black Ink saw Cassie and waved, then dropped into the chair on her other side, heaving her tote onto the table. "Can you believe this gossip?"

"I wish I'd never come. In fact, I only signed up because Katherine hadn't, but she came anyway."

"Word is she came only because you signed up. It's not true that you quit writing, is it?"

"No! Who told you that?" Cassie could now see that the gossip wasn't harmless.

"A dozen people. We want to keep going with your still-life series. You sure you don't want to distribute your Old Stand books through us?"

"I hadn't thought about it. I started that venue for the local authors who like to write cozy stories. What royalty would they get?" Cassie asked.

"Forty percent, same as you. I'll send you a sample contract. You have an idea for your next book for us?"

"Yeah, a cover model gets murdered at a writer's convention. But I'd probably get accused of stealing Katherine's plot again."

"Actually I like that idea, but why don't you make it an agent who gets killed? A couple of them are giving me fits."

"Done, but it does mean I have to solve this thing."

"Well, count me out. I just print 'em; I don't write 'em. Get something to me when you get home. We need to slot a book for February."

"This is August already."

"I know, but somebody let us down." Betts looked at Katherine when she said it, or else at Vivian. Cassie couldn't be sure which. They were both wearing black and looking bereft. So at least one of them had sold to Black Ink, then not delivered.

"I know you can produce a book in three months. That leaves us two months to edit."

The servers brought salads then. Cassie was so grateful that Betts had the courage to be seen with her and actually stayed and ate. She barely heard the keynote speaker as she went over what little they knew. She needed to talk to Morrissey. When she parted with Betts outside the room, he was waiting for her.

"I need some of your time," he said.

"Again?" It wouldn't hurt to play hard to get. "I'm scheduled to tour the Parthenon this afternoon."

"That big temple?"

"Walk along with me."

"How far?" Morrissey checked his watch.

"Less than a mile."

He puffed out his cheeks. "Let's take my car."

Though it was pleasant to be whisked away, several writers saw her crawl into the detective's car. The next rumor would be that she'd been arrested.

"Well, were my fingerprints on the glass?"

"No. There were fingerprints, but not yours or any of the waitstaff who might have handled it."

"Why did Vivian think my prints were on it? For that matter, why does she think I'd have a reason to kill that man? And why did she bring Katherine into that session? It's not as if Katherine writes murder mysteries."

"Miss Hunt wasn't coherent about those things. We've asked her to stay in town also."

After Morrissey parked, they entered the temple and paid their fee. Cassie looked at Athena grinning for getting in free.

"Why are you so interested in this place?" Detective Morrissey asked.

"Athena, goddess of wisdom," she said, staring up at the forty-foot statue. "I consult her often in my work. You might consider it."

"If I thought burning incense and praying would help, I'd be the first one on my knees. But that isn't how solving a murder works."

"No, what usually happens is the murderer makes a mistake," Cassie said.

Morrissey turned to her. "Who do you think did it?"

"I have a limited cast of suspects because I don't know anyone who had a reason to commit the crime unless they could blame it on me. Either Katherine or her lackey Vivian, but they're almost too obvious."

"We've talked to Vivian Hunt. She can't account for her

whereabouts yesterday morning."

"When was he killed?"

"After 8:00 a.m., when I set up the room, and before 10:30, when you sneaked in early."

"I was in your evidence session that whole time."

"You did slip out early."

"To the bathroom. I gave you the names of the women who were in there."

"Okay, I believe you."

"Where was Katherine?"

"Sleeping in, and the maid confirms that. She didn't come downstairs until 10:36."

"Something's wrong."

"What?" He stared at her much the way Manelli did when she wasn't making sense.

"It's not complex enough, and we don't have a motive except maybe for Vivian."

"What do you mean?"

"Vivian would hardly kill someone close to Katherine even if she did want rid of him. There's something we don't know. I should call Detective Manelli."

"Who?"

"My mentor back in Falls Bend. He might have an idea. Oh, I'm supposed to join my husband in Louisiana on Sunday. What about not leaving town?"

"Okay, you can leave town. I don't believe half the stuff I'm hearing about you."

"I don't even want to know." She slumped onto the bench in front of the statue.

"So you don't really have a huge grudge against Katherine Devlin?"

"I'm too busy for juvenile stuff like that. I have a family to take care of, a farm to run, and now a publishing house to manage. I am not Katherine's competitor."

"That's all I wanted to hear. It checks out with what I learned from the police in Falls Bend."

"I must thank them for vouching for me when I get home. You do know that my daughter is the desk sergeant, right?"

"I'd have been disappointed if you hadn't mentioned that. Yes, she told me before forwarding my call. You've been forthright with me. Now I want to ask you a difficult question. Is there any reason someone would want to frame you for murder?"

"I've been giving that some thought and I can't think of any motive that seems strong enough. Yes, Katherine got mad at me a couple years ago because I sold a novel similar to the one she was plotting, but it really wasn't that big a deal."

"To you." Morrissey tapped his foot and jingled the change in his pants pocket.

"Okay, maybe I minimize spats." Cassie sat up straight on the bench and stared at the statue. "I think you have to look for someone who had a real motive for killing Jerome. Pinning the crime on me may have been secondary."

"Oh, right, two birds with one stone. Okay. Can I give you a ride back to your hotel?"

"No, I think I'll linger. I need to feel some peace."

Morrissey left and Athena reappeared on the padded bench beside her.

"Did you notice I left you alone so that I wouldn't distract you?"

"Yes, and I appreciate that. Let's sit and look at the statue a while."

"It's peaceful here." Athena sighed. She looked no less regal in quiet repose than when she was being statuesque.

Cassie leaned back against the wall and almost drifted off until she remembered what Athena had said before. "What did you find out?"

Athena turned her head and smiled as though she had been expecting the question. "Katherine doesn't write her books, not totally."

Cassie sat up straight, jolted from her meditative mood. "What do you mean?"

Athena ducked her head to whisper to her even though no one else could hear or see her. "She and Vivian write them together and divide the money. You said Jerome was expensive. What if he didn't think Katherine should be splitting with Vivian?"

"He didn't know they were writing partners?"

"Most of the people at the conference don't know it. I tracked down the Mandalay editor and stalked her and her assistant. They just found out about the writing duo. They might have been okay with it if they'd known, but I think they dumped Katherine because she violated her contract. The publisher has to do the split of money between writing partners."

"I wonder who told them." Of all the gossip Cassie had heard whispered, this was not among the absurd tales making the rounds.

"It's some of what you call gossip and it's just getting started, but it's not like a fire where you can track it to its origin by looking for hot spots." Athena was quoting from the Evidence lecture.

"No, it would take forever, and mostly people don't remember where they heard things, though they are all too willing to believe what they hear and repeat it."

"Especially if the gossip discredits someone," Athena observed. "Why is that?"

"Makes them feel more powerful, sort of like movie critics. It's easier to tear someone else down than make yourself better."

Athena frowned. "I've certainly known some gods and goddesses like that. But why do people listen?"

"I'm not sure. It's like staring at a car wreck. I think writers listen because they are always looking for a plot, and gossip is stuff that didn't happen to them so they can enjoy the disaster from afar and then possibly even write about it."

"You wouldn't do that."

Cassie thought for a moment. "Not unless I could get a lesson out of it. That's what's wrong with this case. There is no lesson to be learned from it. The problem with this crime is that it seems to have no motive."

"None that we know of yet." Athena tilted her head. "What about my theory that Jerome came between Katherine and Vivian?"

"Would that really provoke a murder? And look how it was done. Almost as though it was an accident."

"What do you mean?" Athena asked. "May I remind you someone stole a glass from our table and then Vivian insisted they check it for your fingerprints?"

"Okay, maybe there was some planning, but a glass to the throat? Can a woman actually count on killing a man that way?"

"Maybe she was throwing wine in his face and she missed."

"Highly unlikely. I need to talk to Manelli, but I won't tie up the phone until I hear from Sam."

No longer feeling meditative, they walked back to the hotel and went to the gardens, but the heat by now was so intense that they couldn't stay for long under the bougainvillea arbor. They climbed the stairs to the suite, turned on the AC, and stood in front of it with their arms spread like birds drying their feathers after a nasty plunge into water.

When Sam called, Cassie could report that she planned to rent a car Saturday and start out Sunday morning.

"Solved it yet?" he asked with his deep drawl.

"No, but I've got a few ideas."

"Don't be a hero."

"Who, me?"

As soon as he hung up, the phone rang. It was Gretchen. "What about dinner?" she asked. "We hardly got to talk."

"Sure. You want to come here?" Cassie asked.

"Let's go out. I hear the Top of the Mark has wonderful food."

Cassie almost dropped the phone. "I hear the wine is a hundred dollars a bottle and the entrées fifty. I'd rather go somewhere else."

"What about the Oglethorpe? I'll buy."

"Okay. Say 6:00. I want to hear about your writing." She hoped Gretchen was still writing.

Athena stared at her as Cassie pulled out some slinky black slacks and a lemon silk top. "I'm glad I opted for a modest place now that she's treating. Besides, I'm not focusing on food enough right now to do the Top of the Mark justice."

"Are you going to offer to consider her work for Old Stand?"

"I think I will. Her writing used to have something."

"You want me to come with you?"

"Yes, because you are very observant. I have time to shower before I change. Let's see if I can raise Manelli."

When he finally picked up and grunted a response she asked, "Am I interrupting? ... What do you mean, did I find a body again? ... No, that is not the only time I call you but yes, there was this crime-scene tape at one of the sessions and I ducked under it. ... Yes, it was real tape, but it wasn't supposed to be a real crime scene. I was the unlucky person to discover the dead male cover model. ... No, he wasn't nude ... What do you mean, writers are funny birds? I don't see any reason why their motives for murder would be any different from those of the average murderer. ... Ego? Now see here, Manelli. I have practically none, and most writers are very helpful and empathetic. … Aristotle?"

"Did he hang up on you?" Athena asked. "That is the right phrase, isn't it?"

"Yes. He thought it was ironic that I found a body at a murder mystery conference. Did Aristotle say something famous about writing?"

"He said many things about writing. Let me ponder while we get ready for dinner."

Cassie went in to shower, wondering how long it would take a magical entity to freshen up and whether she would need time in the bathroom. When she came out, the goddess had put on a more elaborate cloak over the chitin and there was an owl ornament on her breast, a multipieced pendant that was hooked together with gold links so the owl's body actually flexed and twinkled. The eyes shone like topaz gems. Too bad only Cassie would appreciate it.

When they got to the restaurant at the Oglethorpe, Gretchen hadn't arrived, so they got a table and ordered wine. After a glass, Cassie began to wonder where her friend was. "Any thoughts on Aristotle?"

"His most famous quote is 'A likely impossibility is always preferable to an unconvincing possibility.'"

"So that's where Sherlock Holmes got it. I'll ponder that. You changed your cloak."

"Why not? I have a mythical wardrobe. Notice the jewels."

"Beautiful." Cassie gave a nod of approval.

"You didn't ask if they're real."

"That would be gauche—besides being difficult to answer."

"They're real and so am I."

"Yet no one else sees you. What amazes me more, no one else sees you drinking and eating. Half the bottle is gone."

"It's particularly good wine. I don't have to lift a fork or glass to consume food."

"But you do," Cassie said. "I see you."

"A conventionalization for your benefit, though it wouldn't be possible if you were less empathetic."

"I've always thought empathy was important for a writer to be able to create characters."

"It's important in any walk of life. That's why it's surprising so few people have the skill," Athena said.

"Are we talking about Gretchen?"

"And Katherine and Vivian."

"What about Jerome? Do self-focused people tend to hurt each other more than empathetic people?" Cassie asked.

"Without a doubt." Athena poured herself more wine and raised the glass to her lips.

Now that was just showing off. "You think one of them killed him and tried to pin it on me."

"And if they'd grabbed your wine glass instead of mine, they might have been successful."

"Dodged that bullet." Cassie took her napkin and wiped her glass, then pushed it away from her.

"It may not be the only bullet coming your way," Athena said.

Cassie swallowed, amazed at how quickly her goddess picked up on such expressions. "You don't suspect Gretchen, do you?"

"The fact that you ask makes me think there may be reason to."

"She's always been jealous of Katherine's success. I keep saying everyone has to seek their own rewards, but she just stares at me. Here she comes now."

Gretchen scooted into their booth in a black sheath dress that pulled and twisted as she slid. Once she righted her clothing she said, "Sorry I'm late. I just wanted to say I'm glad you stood up to Vivian at the panel."

"You think she was expressing Katherine's views about ebooks?"

"Oh, yes. She hates not having them in her hands."

"I like a good book, but when it comes to distributing them, electronic makes sense."

Gretchen scrunched her nose. "Not sure how I feel about them myself."

"Would you sell to an epublisher if there was a print option?"

"Sure."

"Send something to Old Stand. Here's the email address." Cassie handed her a card.

"Do I have to mention your name?"

"No. They don't have any romance yet and might be interested."

"I'll think about it." Gretchen looked at the card and slid

it into her purse.

Katherine came in with Vivian and glared at Cassie. Then she said something to the maître d', who frowned and shook his head.

Gretchen helped herself to some wine. "Probably trying to get you tossed out."

Cassie opened the menu. "What looks good to you?"

Athena leaned over Cassie's shoulder. "Get the lamb dish," she said.

"I'll have the steak," Gretchen said when the waiter appeared.

Cassie had no intention of eating lamb chops but ordered them anyway.

Gretchen looked intense for a moment, as though she was making some decision. "You know, Vivian and Jerome were having an affair."

Cassie choked on a breadstick.

Gretchen nodded. "Katherine must not know, or she wouldn't still be speaking to Viv."

"Where did you hear all this? You think Katherine killed Jerome?"

"I heard Katherine say she wanted to get rid of him."

"Maybe he was just annoying," Cassie said. "That's no reason to kill someone."

"What do you think of her writing?" Gretchen asked.

"Katherine's? It's changed a lot." Cassie re-evaluated it in her mind now that she knew Vivian had a hand in it. She actually liked it better now.

"That's because she's co-writing with Viv. But I think Vivian writes them and they just put Katherine's name on them and split the money."

"Why would they do that? Vivian Hunt could publish under her own name if she's that good."

Gretchen was staring at the women, who had settled on a faraway table. "She wouldn't make as much."

"I guess not, but you can't keep stuff like that secret — not with a cover model living with you."

"Exactly." Gretchen nodded. "I think Jerome started putting the squeeze on Katherine, so he had to go."

"Extortion? The stakes aren't high enough for murder. They could have just come out as writing partners."

Gretchen stared at her as their food was delivered. "It's

not always just a matter of money."

"What, then?" Cassie asked. "Pride? I don't get it. I don't see why either one of them would kill him."

"To frame you, of course." Gretchen cut into her steak and it bled onto the white china plate.

So did the lamb chops when Cassie cut a bite for Athena. Cassie ate a brussels sprout. "You think they're in it together? That's so dangerous. And I don't think they hate me that badly."

"Why else would they take your wine glass from the table?"

"How did you know about that? And my prints were not on it."

Gretchen swallowed a mouthful and Cassie hoped she would not have to remember the Heimlich. "Oh, that's why you haven't—"

"Been arrested? Correct. The police have some prints, but they aren't mine. Maybe they're yours." Cassie watched as Gretchen rearranged the case in her mind. Morrissey hadn't said not to tell anyone. "Did you notice Katherine and Vivian haven't ordered yet, and they seem to be arguing."

Gretchen smiled. "I'm glad the maître d' stood his ground. Everyone's watching you. You're kind of a celebrity."

Cassie glanced down at her vanishing dinner and snagged another brussels sprout. "That's not the kind of fame I want."

Cassie was relieved when Gretchen excused herself to go to the ladies' room. That way Athena could enjoy the rest of the lamb chops and wine fully. "So other diners notice the food disappearing, but they don't see you take a bite or a drink."

"They see what I want them to see, which is nothing. That was good. You sure you don't want a nibble? You're probably hungry."

"I'm no fan of lamb on the plate. Remember, I raise these little guys. I'll just finish the salad." When she was done, she quietly wiped her prints off the plate and silverware.

"You should call Manelli again and ask him what he meant."

"I have too much pride. I want to figure it out on my own. Wait. Let's turn on our empathy. Morrissey said he locked the door after he set up for the Murder 101 workshop, so how did Jerome get in there? There's your impossibility; now where's the likely part? And why was he there? Let's pretend we're

Jerome."

Athena frowned at her. "I'll try, but I don't channel males well. I guess someone could have asked to meet him and he could have broken into the room."

"There are plenty of other places to meet."

"In private?"

Cassie shrugged. "Maybe not. What if he was there because of the workshop? It would have been a feather in Katherine's cap to solve the workshop since she wants to break into crime writing. Maybe he was there to scope it out like—"

"As you were trying to do," Athena pointed out.

"And someone followed him in."

"That's an unconvincing possibility," Athena said. "If you plan to kill someone, you don't leave the location to chance."

"The location is rather ironic when you think about it." Cassie used air quotes for imaginary headlines. "Heartthrob of famous writer turned into corpse at crime-scene workshop where all her peers witness her grief. I'm thinking Katherine would never have set that up."

"Could it have been Viv? And why is Gretchen suddenly calling Vivian Viv, as though they are bosom friends?"

"Good point. I thought they hardly knew each other. Athena, what if Vivian heard Katherine ask him to break into the room?"

"And Vivian could have stolen the glass to try to incriminate you. That gets rid of the fly in their co-writing ointment and eliminates—"

"The competition," Cassie finished.

Athena shook her head as she downed the last of the wine. "I don't like it much."

Cassie sighed. "It's the best we've got so far."

Gretchen came back and finished her steak, then ordered a dessert sampler to go. She seemed to want to end the dinner, though they hadn't really talked about writing. Then one of the waiters brought Cassie a note she knew she shouldn't open, but she wanted to see what effect it would have on Gretchen.

"Well?" her friend asked.

"Katherine wants to meet with me at the Parthenon to bury the hatchet."

"Probably in your back," Gretchen said.

"Who knows?"

"Are you going to go?" Gretchen was almost salivating.

"I haven't decided yet." As they were leaving, they had to pass the table where Katherine and Vivian sat, and the gaze Katherine sent her way did not speak of peace-making. Cassie couldn't reconcile it to the note. But then maybe Katherine had not really sent the note.

Back at the hotel Cassie waited for Sam's call before she decided if she should contact Manelli. Reassurance from her husband was more important to her than any case. As always, Sam made her feel that everything would work out. He was so excited over his pictures, she didn't even tell him about the case. When she punched in the familiar number, a gravelly voice answered, "Manelli here."

"I know it's late and I hate to interrupt your vacation again, but I need your advice. There's been a new development." She told him about the note. "How much trouble am I in?"

"None at all if you don't meet with her. It's a setup, and you might even get killed. Give the note to the police now and let them decide if they want to act on it."

Cassie tried to call Morrissey, but of course, she could only leave a message at that time of night. She had handled the note by the edges as much as possible and now had it in a plastic bag.

She then dumped the tote from the goodie room onto the bed and began sorting through its contents. She saved to one side business cards and bookmarks of authors she wanted to contact and even dipped into some of the freebie books. A few were on CDs. One she meant to offer a contract to since it looked to be a homemade CD and the story was good. When she came to Katherine's book, she leafed through hoping for a signature, but it wasn't autographed. Under the author's ten-year-old picture was a printed signature. Cassie got her tweezers out and opened the note.

"Not the same," Athena said over her shoulder. "Not even close."

"Could Vivian have sent the note?"

"Why would she?"

"Duh. So she can kill you." Modern slang out of Athena's mouth was unsettling.

Cassie shook her head. "I've never even spoken to Vivian."

"Remind me what that fight was about so long ago? I was half asleep in the car."

"Katherine accused me of stealing one of her plots. But my book came out first, so I pointed out that wasn't possible. Besides, a similarity in plots isn't unusual. She was just being paranoid and accused me of lifting it off her website, where she posts sample chapters."

"That seems unwise, giving away sample chapters."

"I pointed out that I based my story on a real-life crime and maybe she read the same newspaper accounts." Cassie hesitated, recalling the moment. "Now that I look back, Katherine went blank, as though she had no idea what I was talking about. That might go along with that writing partnership you found out about."

Athena's eyes lit up. "If Katherine didn't write the chapters, she might not have known the inspiration."

"Right. Vivian might have written that part. Anyway, there was a shouting match in the lobby, mostly on Katherine's part, and someone called the doorman to drag her away. I went back to my room, and after that the rumors started."

"And that's when Mandalay dumped you," Athena concluded.

"Oh, right. It was the next day. I didn't connect the two events at the time because..."

"You're not paranoid."

"I wasn't then. I have to get some sleep. Maybe I can get hold of Morrissey tomorrow."

Sunday, August 25

Sometime during the night Athena and Minerva both left and Cassie doubted her opinion about who had sent the note. She had tied it to opportunity and assumed Gretchen had done it while in the ladies' room, but it was so much more likely that Athena had done it because of where the meeting was to be. Of course, she could never tell Morrissey that. She had a hard enough time admitting to Manelli where her solutions came from. If Morrissey didn't get back to her, she was not going to the Parthenon. Athena could handle this herself. The phone rang and it was Morrissey asking if he could drop by.

"Room 222 at the Oglethorpe. Please do. I know the note was not written by Katherine."

When he got there, Morrissey looked at the two signatures and shook his head. "We got some toxicology back on Jerome."

"I was wondering if maybe he was drunk enough to fall on

the glass, but it was early in the morning. Most drunks are still in bed."

"Which is why we did the tests. He wasn't drunk. Someone slipped him a roofie."

"So did he fall on the glass?"

"No. If that had been the case, we'd have found all the glass shards next to the body. Some of the pieces were by the podium, some in the wastebasket."

"So someone drugged him and tried to make it look like an accident."

He looked at her. "Such an optimist. No they tried to make it look like what it was, murder, only with you as the perp."

"But I didn't even know him."

"And now that someone is trying to lure you to the Parthenon museum at 9:00 in the morning."

"Doesn't seem that sinister a time," Cassie said. "Possibly Vivian wrote the note and is trying to engineer a reconciliation."

"You don't really believe that, do you? You could have even written the note and invited Katherine to draw out the murderer."

Cassie shook her head. "I didn't, and I'm sure the murderer isn't Katherine."

Morrissey gave her a speculative look. "Her grief seemed theatrical to me."

"She would never have staged something like that. Too much pride."

"Why the Parthenon, and not the hotel or any other place?" he asked.

"That's been puzzling me. It's impressive. And it's handy."

"Are you going?" he asked.

"I called my mentor, Manelli, and he said not without protection."

"I agree." He checked his watch. "I've arranged for some backup to meet us there."

"This could be stupid. I mean, it's a public place. No one would try anything."

"Murder can happen anywhere, anytime. Even in broad daylight people may not notice."

Cassie grabbed her jacket. Jeans and a T-shirt seemed a

better outfit for getting shot or stabbed in than her new linen suit, but the jacket made her feel secure. Cassie was bereft that Athena had left her.

Possibly the goddess was doing some investigating on her own. She had always wondered why Athena couldn't just find out the truth and hand it to her, but the goddess had to be invited into a room or onto property, somewhat like a vampire. Well, nothing like a vampire, but her abilities were not unlimited.

Perhaps in Athena's own temple that would be different. She was certainly welcome there. As they drove to the Parthenon, something Morrissey had said stuck in her mind. "Murder can happen anywhere, anytime."

"Wait. I just remembered the temple doesn't open until 12:30 on Sundays. It said so on their website."

"We'll check it out anyway." Morrissey parked out of sight of the main door and let her go ahead of him. Her loafer heels sounded cold and hollow on the floor. Why was the door open? Not a coincidence. Now she really was wondering if Athena had set this trap.

She crept into the area with the statue and looked around. She saw what looked like a dummy laid out on a bench in front of the statue. It was wrapped in the kind of floral gauze dress that—

"Katherine? No!" Cassie screamed. There was an ornate dagger protruding from the writer's stomach.

"Put your hand on the dagger," Vivian said, cocking the pistol she held.

Cassie spun to face her.

"You killed them both? Why?"

"Can you believe it? When Jerome found out we were co-authors, he wanted her to exclude me and let him take my place."

"Could he even write?" It was a stupid question when someone was about to kill you, but Cassie actually felt outrage for the injustice of a nonwriter trying to take Vivian's place.

"Put the gun down," Morrissey said from the doorway. "There are two officers behind you." Vivian slowly knelt and laid the gun beside her knee.

Athena glided down from the head of the statue and whispered to Cassie, "She isn't dead."

Cassie ran to Katherine and felt for a pulse. While the

other officers cuffed Vivian and read her her rights, Morrissey called for an ambulance.

"I can feel a pulse," Cassie whispered. "Her breathing is shallow, but it's there. Maybe she was drugged as well and that slowed the bleeding."

"Did you drug her?" Morrissey shouted at Vivian.

"I didn't want to hurt her, but I'm the one with the talent. They were getting rid of me? Even after Jerome was dead, she said we had to stop. She was going to write by herself. What gratitude."

"How did you even get in here?" Cassie asked

"You arranged it. Katherine came here for a showdown, not a peace conference. I thought, what a golden opportunity."

"But I didn't. How could I have gotten this place to open early?"

Athena motioned Cassie to the window, where she could see Gretchen running for her car. "Stop that woman," Cassie yelled.

When a policewoman brought Gretchen back in, Cassie said, "You live in Nashville and work for the tourist bureau."

"I used to." Gretchen shrugged.

Cassie tried to suppress her anger. "I wouldn't be surprised to find out you're a docent here."

"What if I am?"

"What did you hope to gain by setting up a confrontation?"

"A story. I work for the Nashville Herald now."

"You wrote that story that misquoted me so badly?"

"You said yourself, she's a competitor." Gretchen nodded toward the supine Katherine. Morrissey still knelt beside her.

"But competition is a good thing," Cassie said.

The sound of ambulance sirens did nothing to break the tension. Morrissey motioned for the male officer to take Vivian to the squad car.

Probably he wanted to question these two separately so they could implicate each other. Surely Vivian would not take the fall for everything.

Gretchen looked past Cassie to the unconscious Katherine. "You were thinking she was getting what she deserved by losing him. Admit it."

"No," Cassie said. "Why kill someone over books? They're supposed to be for fun."

"You get all your inspiration from real murders. I thought

I could help you write a great one about this case." Gretchen sounded confident and rational.

Cassie felt as though she had never known her. "I don't think I could stand to write about this. So you sent the note."

"I was hoping for a great picture." Gretchen held up her camera. "I didn't realize I might push old Vivian over the edge. So why did you have me dragged back here? I didn't commit a crime."

Morrissey opened the door for the paramedics, then turned to Gretchen. "She's right. We can't even get her for breaking and entering. She has a key. But there are some latent prints on the rim of that broken glass. There may be a charge of evidence tampering."

"Oh, but it wasn't evidence before the murder," Gretchen said.

Morrissey blew out a tired breath as they wheeled Katherine out. "But handing it over to Vivian Hunt, knowing what she planned to do with it, could make you an accessory to murder. Certainly letting them in here when you knew what Vivian planned makes you an accessory."

"I had no idea what she planned. I came in for my camera. I can't help it if others entered."

"We'll know more once we interview Ms. Hunt. For now you're free to go. I'll contact the director and arrange to have the building secured."

Gretchen yanked her arm out of the hands of the policewoman holding her. Her cell phone chimed "Dixie" and she grabbed it and flipped it open. "Fired? You're firing me by phone?" She turned to Cassie and glared at her. "I could have made you look good."

"You can't stage the news like a novel. You could have broken the story about their writing partnership and had a real scoop. Why did you have to push Vivian into murder?"

"She was going to do it anyway."

"You supplied the weapon, maybe even the plot. If you're a reporter now, you should have stayed an observer."

"Guess it's just the fiction writer in me." Gretchen tilted her head. "This whole thing might make a good story for the Enquirer."

"If you're free to write it," Morrissey said. "By the way. Don't leave town."

Cassie was back at the hotel packing when Morrissey called to let her know Katherine would recover.

"That's a relief. I wonder if I should send flowers."

"Maybe just sign the card from fellow writers or something. Otherwise you might just raise her blood pressure."

"Right. Thanks for saving my life."

"No problem. It was nice working with you. If you're ever in town again, let's have lunch."

Sam called then. "Did you leave the hotel yet?"

"No, and I just realized I may not be able to rent a car on Sunday."

"Good. Can you get the room for another night?"

"I guess so. The birds eluding you?"

"No. I've got lots of footage and the article mostly written. I should be there by midnight. You'll miss the swamp and fish shack, but the mosquitoes aren't much fun and temps have been over a hundred. Then we can head east and north, that romantic Blue Ridge drive."

"Great. First there are a few inspiring places I want to show you in Nashville."

Athena and Minerva flitted in through the window then. This was only the second time Cassie had seen Athena fly. She was graceful. "I missed you two this morning. I'm just glad you showed up for the finale."

"I would have told you about my hunch, but I didn't want to wake you. So I went through the records at the temple and finally figured out Gretchen was a docent there."

"You didn't come and tell me."

"By then I realized Katherine was in danger."

"How awful not to be able to do anything about it," Cassie said.

"Minerva managed to stir the air enough around Vivian to make her miss. And then you and Detective Morrissey arrived."

"So you two saved Katherine's life."

Athena nodded. "That's what you wanted, right?"

"Of course. She was a victim of the same jealousy that prompted Gretchen to run off the rails."

"Is that another of your metaphors or just slang?"

"Both," said Cassie. "It means to become dangerous and unpredictable, like a train derailing."

Athena watched Cassie unpack. "Gretchen was the one

who invited you into this chaos."

"Then she said not to come to the conference." Cassie stopped and thought about it.

"Which made you insist on coming." Athena smiled.

"She wasn't really interested in Old Stand as a publisher."

"So you almost insisted she submit a book. You never told her you are Old Stand."

"Salt in the wound for her. She knows what I'm like and she used that. Not exactly empathy. More like manipulation."

Athena looked pensive as she perched on the bed. "I always thought writers all wove stories for the fun of it. When you get your pride tangled up in the success or failure of the books, then it can become a matter of life and death."

Cassie nodded. "I used to be more invested in my books when I had nothing else. I was just wondering: Were you watching over me even then?"

"I visited you because you seemed to have promise as someone who could deliver good messages. But you were not as open to advice then."

Cassie smiled. "Perhaps all we humans grow wiser with age, wise enough to listen. So Sam is coming to spend a day and a couple of nights. I plan to show him the Parthenon. You and Minerva are welcome to drive back home with us. We'll be taking a different route."

"Oh, I think we may hang about here for a bit. My temple needs some cleansing."

Character Bio from Judith Gallagher

Colleen McKiernan has long brown hair, blue eyes, and Irish skin that blushes far too easily. She is a fiftyish, overweight, nearsighted night owl who works as a freelance writer and editor. She has edited books on subjects ranging from banking to basketball, from math to mythology. She recently broke free of her addiction to *Jeopardy!*, which she won regularly in the privacy of her living room.

Years ago she moved from Chicago back to western Pennsylvania and built her house on land that has been in her family for two hundred years. She lives on her hilltop in the woods with four cats, all of whom see phantoms regularly. Her detective inspiration is Harriet Vane from the Lord Peter Wimsey novels by Dorothy L. Sayers.

The Fourth Treasure of Ireland

Judith Gallagher

Colleen McKiernan got off the plane and looked for a chauffeur holding a sign with her name, as promised by the administrator of the Ella Young Literary Prize. The people she'd flown with were scooped up by family or friends until she was the only one left. Had she misunderstood? She hauled her suitcase down the hallway of Dublin Airport, painted in one of the few shades of green she found ugly, but she was afraid to get out of sight of the gate where her ride was supposed to meet her.

Take a deep breath, she told herself. At least they speak English. She tried to call the number she'd been given by Professor Murphy when he called to tell her she'd won the prize and it included a trip to Meath College, but she couldn't get her phone to work. Finally she walked over to an airline employee and asked him for help.

His voice lilted in such unusual patterns that she wondered at first if he was speaking Gaelic, but when she replayed his words in her head, she realized he'd said, "You'll need a new SIM card for your mobile."

"Okay," she said slowly.

He laughed and got out a map of the airport. "There's a mobile store in B concourse. Or I can call someone for you, if you like."

He was getting easier to understand. "Yes," she said. "Thank you." As she looked for Professor Murphy's number, a strange man ran up to the counter, hugged her, and said, "Colleen, is it?"

Colleen looked him up and down, trying to ignore his handsome face and thick black hair. "And you are?"

"Dermot," he said, shaking her hand vigorously. "Dermot O'Hara. Professor Murphy asked me to pick you up and take you to the college."

"Did he now?" Hey, she was starting to pick up the speech pattern. She could practically pass for Irish. "Did he ask you to pick me up at 4:15?"

"He did." Dermot grabbed her suitcase and began rolling

it down the hall. "I'm parked over this way." No apology for being half an hour late.

Colleen followed, mentally chastising this tornado of a man. He was about six feet tall and looked quite fit for his age, which she estimated at about forty. He was wearing lived-in jeans and a rumpled royal-blue polo shirt. A piece of paper fell out of his jeans pocket. Colleen picked it up.

Then she had to run to catch up with him. "Hey, you dropped this!" As she held it out, she noticed her own name and "4:15, Gate 12." Clouds were sketched in above her name. Written sideways was the phrase "4 Treasures of Eire."

He saw her looking and said, "I've read your books."

"Really? You mean my Tales from Tirnanog series?"

"Yes, the ones you won the prize for."

She tried not to ask, she really did. "So what did you think?"

He looked serious for the first time and said, "You've got the gift. But you muddled the Four Treasures."

"What do you mean?"

"Nuada's treasure was a sword, not a crystal."

"Well, of course I know that. Consider it poetic license."

He shook his head and started walking again. "I consider it taking liberties. Why?"

"Why what?" she asked, glad she'd worn flats so she could keep up with him.

"Why'd you change it? What's wrong with the real treasures, whose legends have come down to us over the centuries?"

"Well — too many weapons."

"What?" He raised an eyebrow, but she saw a small smile.

"Think about it. The Four Treasures are supposed to be Dagda's cauldron, the spear of Lugh, Nuada's sword of light, and the stone of destiny, right? A spear and a sword struck me as, well, overkill. Too much violence."

"Those were violent times," Dermot said.

"I understand, but I wasn't writing history. I was writing fantasy. That's why I made the cauldron the goddess Brigid's instead of Dagda's. Those were sexist times, too, but I didn't want to glorify either the sexism or the violence."

"So you made the sword into a healing crystal." He looked

thoughtful.

"That's right." By now they were in the parking lot. It was a breezy summer day. Ireland at last! The bustle of Dublin reminded Colleen of Chicago. So did the sunlight glinting off the water: surprising but welcome. She pinned up her long, chestnut-brown hair in a twist and turned her already ruddy face up to the sun.

"Enjoy it while you can," he said. "It'll be raining soon." He gave her a huge grin and pointed at a white Mini. "There's my car."

He unlocked the trunk (boot, she corrected herself) and stowed her suitcase. She remembered to get in on the left side.

As he pulled out of the parking lot, Dermot said, "I'd love to give you a tour of the city, but Professor Murphy and his wife are giving a small dinner for you tonight at 7:00. And you are the guest of honor."

Colleen felt butterflies in her stomach. Guest of honor! "Am I the only visiting writer here?" she asked.

Dermot flashed that grin again. "Nope. You're just the star of the show."

"Gulp. What does that mean?"

"You won first prize in our most prestigious award. You're the only writer the college is flying in all the way from America. But there are a second and a third prize in the Ella Young Award, plus a couple of smaller awards. Prepare for some resentment from Stan Bishop at the banquet tomorrow."

"Who's he?"

"The third-prize winner, who thinks he should have won first for a book that Ella Young wouldn't even have read. Just because he teaches at the college, he expects the moon."

"What did he write?"

"Unlike you, he seems to think the ancient Celts weren't violent enough. His novel is called *The Blood-Soaked Sword of Cúchulainn*."

"Seriously? That sounds like a parody."

Dermot shrugged. "Stan is usually dead serious."

"Tell me who else will be at tonight's dinner," Colleen suggested.

Dermot passed another car. She liked the way he drove: assertively but not aggressively.

"Professor Covert and his wife; he's the second in

command in the folklore department. Kelly O' Bannion, the second-prize winner. The Murphys' daughter Delia, who is in town briefly on her way to Sumatra. She's an anthropologist. That's all. Tonight will be cozy," he said.

"And tomorrow night?" Colleen asked.

"Ah, the big bash: A reception, a fancy dinner, the awards presentations, and your speech. The other prize winners will be there, of course, and the whole folklore department, really. Two professors, plus four adjuncts, plus about ten students. Plus various family members who either share their interests or aren't good at saying no. And me." He did a little bow from the waist.

"And what's your status?" Colleen inquired.

"Single," he said quickly.

"In the department, I meant."

"I'm being groomed to take over Professor Covert's spot when Professor Murphy retires and Covert becomes head of the department."

"You don't sound very excited about it. If Ireland is anything like the States, full professorships are hard to come by these days."

Dermot cupped his ear. "Was that my mother speaking to me from beyond the grave?" he said. "I like my job fine, but I'm not sure I want to be here for the next twenty years. And once I have tenure, I'll be stuck serving on committees. That won't leave much time for my travels or my own writing."

Colleen sat up straighter. "What do you write?"

Dermot laughed. She thought she heard a note of regret. "These days, mostly scholarly articles. I just had a piece on Yeats and the shamanic fire published in a journal." He looked at her sideways and declaimed dramatically, "But I too feel the siren call of storytelling from the rich source material our Emerald Isle provides."

They spent the rest of the drive discussing Celtic mythology, Ella Young's books, and their respective plans for future projects. Colleen was surprised at how big the town of Meath was. Dermot parked in front of a B&B, a rambling but well-maintained Victorian with the sign "The Bee-Loud Glade."

"Speaking of Yeats," Colleen said as she met him at the boot, where he grabbed her suitcase.

"Wait till you see the room names." He led the way inside

and greeted the young woman at the front desk, who checked Colleen in and handed her an old-fashioned metal key.

"Did you give her the room I requested, Rosalie?"

"Indeed."

They got into a tiny elevator. On the second floor, they walked past two rooms. The sign on one door read "A Crock of Gold," on the other "The Wonder Smith." Dermot led the way to the next room, labeled "The Flowering Dusk."

"See?" he said as she opened the door.

"Ella has two rooms named after her books, and James Stephens has one," Colleen said.

"That's right." He carried her suitcase in and said, "I'll pick you up at 6:45."

"All right." After he left, she locked the door and rushed over to the window, which overlooked a small garden. Then she took a shower and sat in front of the window while she tried to decide how jet-lagged she was. She wouldn't have time for more than a five-minute nap, so instead she dressed and got out her laptop. She had remembered an adapter so she could write while in Europe.

Colleen was deep into her current story when she heard a knock. She opened the door to Dermot, looking exactly as he had earlier.

"I didn't realize tonight was so casual," she said. "Maybe I'm overdressed." She pulled her top down further over her abundant hips, thinking of the ex-boyfriend who had called her an earth mother.

He took in her green-and-purple skirt and purple peplum top and said, "You're dressed just right. I'm the one who will be out of place."

"I gather that doesn't bother you."

"It's the story of my life. May I?" He gestured vaguely at the door."May you what?" Colleen asked.

"May I escort you out and lock up for you?"

"You wear jeans to your department head's dinner, but you think I need help locking a door? In what century are your sensibilities?" She walked out of the room.

Dermot followed her out. "I was just trying to show you that chivalry is not dead."

"That's too bad." Colleen locked the door and tucked the old-fashioned key in her purse. "I'd throttle it myself if it weren't so slippery, always popping up in unexpected places."

They drove a few miles to a neighborhood of stately but new-looking homes. Colleen got out of the car fast enough to forestall any further chivalric impulses. Dermot rang the doorbell, and a tall woman of about sixty, with deep brown eyes, silver hair in a sophisticated twist, and a silk dress that nearly matched her hair, opened the door.

Dermot said, "Deirdre Murphy, may I present Colleen McKiernan?"

"Come in, come in." When Mrs. Murphy smiled, her eyes looked golden. She shook Colleen's hand. "Thomas," she called. "Our guest of honor has arrived."

A distinguished-looking man with white hair and twinkling blue eyes gave her a firm handshake and said, "I'm Professor Murphy. It's lovely to meet you."

"Thank you so much for having me," Colleen said. "I've always wanted to come to Ireland." She realized she was babbling. Nerves.

"Thank you for coming all this way," Mrs. Murphy said. She led the way to a bar. "Have you never been to Ireland before?"

"No, never. My grandparents came over to the States around the turn of the last century. We had relatives here until recently, but I didn't get here in time to meet them."

Mrs. Murphy nodded. "Would you like a cocktail?" she asked.

"What are you having?"

"A strawberry daiquiri, but we can give you something more Irish. Guinness?"

Colleen grimaced. "The daiquiri sounds better." Mrs. Murphy made quick work of mixing one and handing it to her.

"Thank you, Mrs. Murphy."

"Please, call me Deirdre."

"That's a beautiful name. Not Deirdre of the Sorrows, I hope?"

Deirdre smiled, but this time her eyes remained dark. "No more sorrows than anyone else." She turned to Dermot. "The usual?"

"Please."

She handed him a Guinness.

Professor Murphy said to Colleen, "Call me Thomas.

Now, come into the living room and meet the others."

They walked into a room that was painted a rich burgundy and decorated in subtle shades of gold and silver. An older man was sitting on the couch, his hand on the knee of a woman half his age.

"These are the Coverts," said Thomas. "Alfred and Jane. He will be introducing you before your speech tomorrow night."

"How nice to meet you!" Colleen offered her hand. Alfred looked at her and then slowly shook it. "Professor Covert," he said firmly. He looked a lot like Thomas Murphy — same white mane, almost the same age and about the same build, blue eyes — but his eyes definitely did not twinkle when he looked at Colleen.

She turned to his wife, who smiled apologetically as she shook hands. "I'm Jane. How was your flight?"

"Not bad at all. I'm just a little jet-lagged."

"Ah, sleep deprivation," said Jane, running her fingers through her curly black pixie cut. "All too familiar. We have two children. I've been reading them your Tales from Tirnanog. We're all enjoying them."

Colleen tried to ignore the fact that Professor Covert was rolling his eyes. "Thank you. How old are your children?"

"Luke is six and Alfie is nine. I have to define some words for them, but the story has them so engrossed that they're just lapping it up."

"I'm glad to hear that," said Colleen. "My editor was concerned the vocabulary might be too high. I made an effort to provide context clues. I was trying to teach my readers new things without making them feel as though my books are homework assignments."

"A spoonful of sugar, hmm?" said Jane.

Colleen thought she heard Covert say, "More like tripe" just as Dermot came up to them, followed by a baby-faced man with a white stripe through his mop of dark hair. "Hi, Jane," Dermot said. "Colleen, let me introduce you to Kelly O' Bannion. He won second prize in the Ella Young Awards."

"So nice to meet you, Ms. McKiernan," he said. "I love your books!"

"Thank you. Please, call me Colleen."

They chatted for a while. Colleen noticed Dierdre looking at her watch. She relaxed visibly when the front door opened and a young woman walked in. Dierdre smiled. "I'd like you to meet our daughter, Delia."

As Colleen stood to shake her hand, Deirdre said, "Shall we adjourn to the dining room?" Placecards made of scrolled paper nestled among fresh-cut evergreen boughs on the snowy tablecloth. The greenery took up much of the table's center, with just enough gaps for serving dishes. Glass stars, some clear, some in jewel tones, nestled among the boughs.

Thomas was seated at the head of the table, with Colleen to his right. Kelly was to her right, followed by Delia. Colleen was relieved to see that Professor Covert was at the far end. To his right was Deirdre, followed by Dermot, then Jane across from Colleen, who hadn't yet figured out whether Jane was a saint or a fool for marrying such an unpleasant man. Perhaps a bit of both?

Colleen flinched every time Covert opened his mouth, whether it was to denigrate America, fantasy as a genre, or his wife. The rest of the group conspired to politely change the topic after each insult. She wondered whether anyone ever stood up to this bully.

Other than him, it was a congenial gathering. Everyone claimed to have read and liked Colleen's books, and she learned much about Ella Young and the Celtic Renaissance. She had read most of the stories and some of the literary analysis they were discussing.

Dermot asked Delia about her work. She described how she was living in Sumatra to study a matrilineal society.

"Matrilineal!" Covert snorted. "That'll never work! The more power you give women, the more they screw things up."

Delia had her mother's thick, glossy hair, though hers was chestnut brown, and her father's round features, ruddy complexion, and twinkling blue eyes. In fact, she looked a lot like Colleen. Those eyes stopped twinkling when Covert spoke, but she forced a small smile. "Actually, it's pretty well established that most societies, including the ancient Celts, were matrilineal during Neolithic times."

"And they were all conquered by men from patriarchal societies. They couldn't survive."

"They survived for thousands of years in a far more peaceful mode than any that patriarchy has brought," Delia said in measured tones.

Colleen said, "Several American Indian tribes are largely run by women."

Delia shot her a grateful glance as Covert roared, "Run by women! God give me strength."

Colleen ignored him and said to Delia, "I have a friend who's a member of the Lenni Lenape tribe. She's learning her ancient language from her grandmother as part of the tribe's effort to keep it alive."

"That's fascinating," Delia said. "There's nothing like really getting to know someone from another culture to remind us how much we take as gospel is really just arbitrary rules."

Kelly pushed his chair back so the two women could see each other better. By now Delia had her back to Covert, but Colleen had all too clear a view of him as she faced Delia. His face was getting so red that he reminded Colleen of a volcano.

Perhaps Deirdre too feared that Covert would explode. She laid a hand on his arm and said softly, "How are the boys doing, Alfred? Are they playing soccer this year?"

His face relaxed and he turned away from Delia. Colleen half-heard him describing his talented children as she listened to Delia's far more interesting talk of her fieldwork and the people she had met. Everyone else at the table seemed equally riveted, though after a tale in which Delia was almost blown off a cliff by a strong wind, Thomas said, "So when are you coming home to stay, Delia?"

"Oh, Daddy. I'll be back for Christmas. But I have at least three years of fieldwork still to do. And life is no more risky there than here."

"We've finally resolved our religious troubles here, and now you're living in a Muslim society."

Colleen said, "They're both matrilineal and Muslim? That's unusual, isn't it?"

"Yes. They had a war over it, nearly 200 years ago." Delia looked at her father. "I'm living in a much safer place than most Western cities. And I love it! If you could see the mountains, and the rice paddies, and the traditional architecture. And I've made some really good friends. You always told me that people everywhere are more alike than they are different."

Thomas twinkled. "You're right, I did. I didn't know you were paying such close attention when you were a little girl."

By now everyone had finished eating. Deirdre said, "Shall we move into the living room? We have a lovely port I think you'll all like."

She led the way. Colleen dropped her purse and had to retrieve it from under the table, so she was the last one to leave the dining room. As she stood, she saw Covert scoop up one of the glass stars and tuck it in his pocket so quickly that she doubted the evidence of her senses.

As she was trying to decide what to do, Deirdre returned for the shawl she'd left draped over her chair. "Is everything all right?" she asked. "You look as if you've seen a ghost.

Colleen paused. "This is awkward," she began, "but I just saw Professor Covert — um ..."

"Yes?" Then Deirdre said, "Ah. Did you see him remove something?"

"Yes. One of the glass stars from the centerpiece. He put it in his pocket."

Deirdre nodded. "Don't worry about it. He has a little psychological issue."

Little? Colleen thought. If by that you mean he's a blowhard, chauvinistic, sexist pig, then yeah. Then she realized what Deirdre meant. "He's a klepto?" she asked.

Deirdre looked as if she were about to burst out laughing, but she restrained herself. "We prefer to think of it as borrowing. Jane always returns the items when she finds them. And those stars aren't valuable. We're lucky he didn't go after the silver — but he tends to favor glass objects, especially reflective ones."

"Maybe he likes to look at that mug of his," Colleen muttered.

"Maybe. Thank you for telling me, but don't worry about it." Deirdre put an arm around Colleen's shoulder and steered her into the living room. Colleen gathered they must have staff to clean up, at least when they entertained. She hoped no employee had ever been blamed for one of Covert's "borrowing" episodes.

The conversation continued to be fascinating as it swirled around Colleen, but she soon found it hard to keep her eyes open. When she felt a hand on her knee and heard a deep voice say, "Colleen?" her first thought was "What did I miss?" She opened her eyes to see Dermot.

"Looks as if the jet lag caught up with you," he said. "Why don't I take you back to the B&B?"

"B," she muttered. "The Bee-Loud Glade. Hey, I just thought of another interpretation of that name. Maybe they're telling guests to be loud. I hope it's not too noisy for a good night's sleep."

"I don't think you need to worry about that tonight." Dermot helped her stand, which woke her enough that she could voice her thanks to the Murphys.

Professor Murphy said, "You have a free day tomorrow until the awards ceremony. We'll be happy to send you a student guide for sightseeing, or you can just take it easy. Your choice."

"Thank you for the offer, but an afternoon on my own sounds good. I'll see you all tomorrow night." Colleen said her goodnights.

When she got to Delia, the anthropologist said, "I really wish I could be there for the awards, but my plane leaves in the morning."

"Have a good trip," Colleen said. "Your work sounds wonderful."

By the time they walked to Dermot's car, the warm night air had wakened her just enough to function. She took a deep breath as she got in. "What is that gorgeous scent?"

"An Irish garden in high summer," he said. "Honeysuckle, phlox, lavender. Roses, of course. Are you buckled in?"

"Yes, Dad."

"Ah, sarcasm. I feel I know you well enough already to know that means you're fully awake."

When they got to the B&B, Dermot said, "Am I permitted to escort you in?"

Colleen laughed. "I suppose. As long as you recognize that I'm not helpless."

"You? Perish the thought!" He got out of the car and waited on his side until she headed up the path.

He followed her into the building and then into the elevator. Then he leaned against the wall outside her room while she rummaged for her key.

"Well, this is embarrassing," she said. "I know it's in here somewhere."

"I'm sure it is," Dermot said with an excess of politeness.

Colleen continued to rummage as she said, "Hey, that reminds me. Did you know that Professor Covert is a kleptomaniac?"

"Everybody knows. He often reminds me of a very large, colicky baby wailing, 'Mine!' about everything he sees. What caught his eye this time?"

"A glass star from the centerpiece." Colleen finally found her key and unlocked her door. "Would you like to come in for a minute?"

"You're tired. I shouldn't," Dermot said as he quickly followed her in.

Colleen laughed as she turned to face him. "And now that you've behaved appropriately—"

"I can behave inappropriately?" he asked, brushing a strand of her long brown hair from her face with his right hand as his left went around her back.

"Briefly," she said. They leaned toward each other and kissed. Ten minutes later he came up for air sufficiently to say, "I should probably let you get to bed."

She squelched the play on words that came to mind. "Yep." She opened the door.

He paused with his hand on her wrist and said, "Would you like a tour guide tomorrow?"

"No, thanks. I'm staying in Ireland for a week, so I'll have time to sightsee later. Tomorrow I want to just take it easy and get ready for my big speech."

"You'll do great."

"I hope so. Bye."

There was no chance Colleen would get to sleep now. Her body was humming with energy and possibilities. At home she would have cranked up some music and danced until she was tired, but the walls weren't that thick. So instead she settled down with one of the several leather-bound volumes displayed on the desk: *The Golden Bough* by James Frazier. A reference survey of beliefs around the world sounded like a good way to lull herself to sleep.

She crawled into bed with the book. Half an hour later she was muttering, "The Polynesians and their wives, indeed! What were the wives, chopped liver?" Now she remembered the author's annoying style, not to mention his sexism, the reasons she'd never finished the book on an earlier attempt. She'd better try to sleep before she got too riled up.

Colleen woke to birdsong. Her travel alarm read 1:00 p.m. She leaped out of bed before realizing it was only 8:00 a.m. at home, well before her usual waking time. She wasn't a lazy slugabed; she was just in the wrong time zone.

Rosalie was happy to serve her breakfast at lunchtime, lend her a map of downtown Meath, and suggest some good walking areas. "Are you interested in sightseeing? There's a lovely castle and gardens just a few miles away. And then there's the glassmaking tour."

"Castle Dombray?" Colleen asked. "I have my eye on that. But I still have to fine-tune my speech for tonight. I was thinking of going tomorrow after I've met all my obligations."

"How long are you staying in Ireland?"

"A week. I thought I'd head south on Friday and then west. Any pointers?" Rosalie gave some excellent advice about what to see and what not to waste her time on.

Colleen spent about two hours wandering around town, soaking in the sights and sounds. She stopped at a café for the obligatory cup of tea and was diverted by a used bookstore next door. The only thing that tore her away was recalling that she wanted to rehearse her speech a few times.

When she got back to her room, she showered and then read over her speech in her bathrobe. A few moves with her red pen and the title became "Faeries, Goddesses, and Americans: How Far to Tirnanog?" She edited a bit but tried to avoid the temptation to rewrite. At 6:20 she put on makeup. Then she put on the blue-and-green floaty dress she'd bought for the occasion. She didn't know which made her more nervous: dressing up, which she did rarely as a freelancer, or giving a speech. She was fairly confident of its content but worried about her delivery. She was brushing her hair when there was a knock on the door.

She opened it and said, "I just have to put on my necklace."

"Allow me," said Dermot.

Colleen lifted her hair out of the way.

"A silver unicorn," he said as he fastened the necklace. "How appropriate."

"I brought it to honor the woman who wrote *The Unicorn with Silver Shoes*. Without her award, I wouldn't be here."

She grabbed her purse, complete with rolled-up speech, and they headed out. She walked to his car and said, "Ceelian Hall must be close."

He laughed. "So close that we're not taking the car. May I?" He crooked his elbow.

She put her hand through it, and they started walking. The building was across the street.

When they entered the hall, Colleen thought there must be more people there than Dermot had said, judging by the noise levels. She took a deep breath, plastered a smile on her face, and let go of his arm.

She greeted Kelly O' Bannion and exchanged a few words with the Murphys as a crowd gathered. Professor Murphy said, "We'll talk later, after you meet the rest of your fan club."

Dermot nodded at a burly, angry-looking man and whispered, "Stan Bishop. Heads up." Then he introduced her to Mary McConnell, an adjunct professor who said she specialized in Maud Gonne. Mary looked about thirty and resembled Maud, with dark, deep-set eyes and dark, upswept hair.

Mary's husband was staring across the room, perhaps at Professor Covert or his wife. Mary tugged on his arm and introduced him as Fred. He had a handshake like a dead fish, but he seemed nice enough, and he was familiar with her work. As Colleen looked into his brown eyes, he reminded her of her main character's sidekick, Jeffrey.

"It has such resonance that you give the children proxy parents when they arrive in Tirnanog," he was saying to her.

"Proxy parents? I'm not sure what you mean."

"Well, Ranelda is the ideal mother figure, and Conneda is the stern but fair father."

"Uh — well, yes, I see your point." Colleen barely had time to think about his comment before she was introduced to Neva Flaherty.

"Another adjunct," Dermot explained.

With an angelic smile and curly blonde hair, topping out at perhaps five feet two, Neva looked barely old enough to be a college student. "I've been teaching your Tirnanog books in my freshman folklore class," she said. "My students are fascinated by the way you juxtapose Celtic lore with that of other traditions."

"Thank you! That's what I was trying for. That's why I dared to break with the traditional lore in places." Colleen smiled at Neva.

"I love that the cauldron is Brigid's, not Dagda's," Neva said. "It makes so much sense when you consider that she's the goddess of creativity and healing. No wonder she can craft the cauldron and infuse it with the magic to regenerate the sick or wounded."

Colleen had done enough readings and interviews to get used to people talking about her books, but this took it to a whole new level. She mentally saved up the compliments to pull out next time facing the blank screen was a burden. She was experiencing sensory overload even before a bell was rung to announce dinner and Professor Murphy escorted her to the dais. Great; everyone would be watching her eat. Not that she would be able to eat much anyway, what with the butterflies trying to escape through her chest wall.

She nibbled just enough of her dinner to know it was delicious as she chatted with Thomas Murphy on her left and tried to chat with Alfred Covert on her right. The two men might look nearly interchangeable, but while Murphy seemed glad she was there and had actually read her books, Covert could barely conceal his sneer when he spoke dismissively of her American background.

After dinner the awards went quickly. Then Professor Covert gave Colleen an introduction that wandered off topic. He went on and on about the importance of family and the need to pass on the old stories to young children. He talked about his two little boys and how glad he was to have had a second chance at fatherhood late in life and how it was his greatest joy to spend time with them.

Finally he brought it around to the human children in Colleen's books and their adventures in Tirnanog. He couldn't bring himself to praise her books, but he did mention their "unexpectedly good sales both here and in America."

She had never given a talk this long before, and now she had to follow this bore. She started off shakily, but soon she got into the flow and found herself riffing on her material. Examples of the influences of Irish mythology on her fiction appeared as if she could see the words floating in the air. Everything made sense to her, and she felt no fear at all.

When she finished, the applause was sustained. She sank into her seat with a sigh of relief. People approached her to give their perspectives on Tirnanog and goddesses. Mary McConnell told her a story about Flidais, the goddess of beasts, that Colleen had never come across in all her research.

"My grandma used to tell it," Mary said in her lilting voice. "I thought you must know it because of the way you described Flidais, with the small creatures clinging to her as she walked."

"No," said Colleen, "I just made that up. Unless the goddess Flidais was speaking through me." She smiled, but she wondered.

"I'm so glad we found a sitter," Mary said. "For a while today it looked as if I might have to stay home with the kids."

"I'm glad you managed to escape," Colleen said. "I wouldn't have missed your Flidais story for the world."

"I love the relationship between the mother and daughter goddesses, especially when Fand gets miffed," Mary said. "You made me picture a ten-foot-tall water goddess sulking like a child."

"That part was written in a fit of inspiration."

Stan Bishop came lumbering up. "Inspiration!" he shouted. "You don't even know the meaning of the word. You — you American! What gives you the right to usurp our national myths?"

Colleen was stunned. "Well, uh — my grandparents were born here. And the myths have always spoken to me, ever since I was a little girl."

Even as she spoke, Dermot was springing into action. He put his arm around Stan and said, "Let's get you some coffee, shall we?" Colleen could see his arm muscles flex to keep Stan from breaking free as they marched away.

There was a flurry of apologies and assurances that she had done the old myths proud. As she smiled at the people complimenting her, Alfred Covert, still sitting next to her, spoke much more quietly than Stan had, but just as venomously. "He's right. You don't belong here. You never would have won if you weren't a compromise for the judges."

Colleen tore her eyes away and focused on a friendly face, that of Kelly O'Bannion. He stood at an angle as if trying to block Covert, and he leaned forward and spoke up. "Ignore him. You deserve first prize for *The Sea of Summer Stars* alone. Hell, you deserve honorary Irish citizenship for the whole series."

"That's kind of you to say, especially when without me you would have won first prize."

Kelly shrugged. "Ah, my book is doing well enough that my publisher offered me a three-book contract. I can't complain."

"What's your next book about?" Colleen asked. They passed several pleasant minutes in shop talk, with Colleen trying to ignore the increasingly loud Covert.

"Young Alfie just turned nine," he was saying to Deirdre Murphy. "When I was starting my career, I made the mistake of seeing my children as an impediment to my work. You know, the pram in the hall and all that."

She gave a small, insincere smile and looked ready to move on, but he grabbed her arm and kept talking. "This time around, I realize how much my children enrich my work. I see the legends anew through their innocent eyes."

Jeez, thought Colleen. I wouldn't have figured him for the sentimental type. As he spoke ever louder, everyone was staring at him. Kelly had that what-do-we-do-now expression, as did Neva. Dermot was striding across the room looking angry. Fred looked frozen in place, with Mary's hand on his. Professor Murphy was gritting his teeth, but he managed to sound pleasant when he said, "Where is Jane tonight, Alfred?"

That snapped Covert out of it. "She's home with the children," he said, releasing Mrs. Murphy and turning to her husband.

"You'll be wanting to rush home to say goodnight before they go to bed, then. We won't keep you," said Professor Murphy.

Smooth, thought Colleen. Covert stood up and said, "I must be off." He walked — somewhat unsteadily — out of the room.

"Should he be driving?" Colleen said.

"Probably not," Professor Murphy said. He gazed around the room. "Dermot, you live in that direction, don't you? Could you give him a ride?" Dermot looked dismayed, Colleen thought, or maybe angry, but he went after Covert.

Fred McConnell shivered and Mary turned to him.

"Honey, what's wrong?"

"Nothing. Let's get out of here."

"All right." Mary turned back to Colleen. "That was a wonderful — or as Ella Young might say, wonder-filled — talk. I really wish I could see you in action teaching your workshop tomorrow."

"As far as I'm concerned, you're welcome to sit in."

Mary smiled. "Thanks. Maybe I will, if I can grade enough papers first. It runs from 10:00 to noon?"

"Right. Speaking of which, I think the jet lag is hitting. I'd better get to bed early." Colleen waved as Mary piloted her husband to the door. She hoped she could remember how she'd gotten here. Her hotel was only a stone's throw away; surely she could find it.

Deirdre Murphy said, "Why don't Thomas and I walk you back to your room?"

"That would be lovely."

Deirdre turned to her husband. "Thomas?"

"Yes, dear. Just one moment." He clanked a spoon against a glass a few times and said, "Thank you all for coming to celebrate with us the recipients of the Ella Young Award, and we thank the first-prize winner for traveling all the way from America to be with us."

Colleen nodded.

He continued. "My lovely wife and I are escorting Ms. McKiernan back to her hotel. You're all invited to her workshop tomorrow morning: 10:00 a.m. in Finley Hall. There's plenty of food and drink left, so enjoy."

They came upstairs in the elevator, which was barely big enough for three, and waited while Colleen unlocked her door and turned on the light.

"Thank you," she said. "On my own I would have turned the wrong way out of the building and probably wandered around Meath all night."

After the Murphys left, she locked the door and settled down to review her notes for the workshop. She had decided to focus on character motivations; she had several prompts and writing exercises prepared. After reading through them once, she told herself to go to bed, but instead she read them again.

She was sitting in the easy chair, feet up on the bed, when

she heard a knock. When she went to the door, she saw Dermot through the peephole. He whispered, "I saw your light on and thought I'd make sure you're all right."

"Yes, fine," she said.

"Would you like some company?"

"All right." She let him in and said, "I was just going over my notes for tomorrow."

"Too jazzed to sleep? I can help you relax."

Colleen laughed. "Yeah, I'll bet."

Dermot grinned. "Not what I meant, honest. Here, sit in the chair."

"Okay."

He sat on the bed. "Now put your feet up here and I'll give you a foot rub. Close those bright-blue Irish eyes. This is guaranteed to make you sleepy in ten minutes max, leaving plenty of time for me to get home and get six hours of sleep before my first class."

It didn't take ten minutes before her eyes were drooping. "But I wanted to talk more about Ella Young and the Celtic Twilight."

Dermot smiled. "We'll have time for that tomorrow. Do you want to go to bed? Alone, I mean?" He stroked her foot.

She planted her feet on the floor and leaned forward. "First, a kiss. So that I don't stay awake all night thinking about it." She kissed him. Then she crawled into bed, said goodnight, and closed her eyes.

Dermot gently pulled her long brown hair away from her face and kissed her neck. She opened her eyes and he kissed her mouth.

"Do you want me to leave?" he asked

"No. Suddenly I got my second wind."

The next day Colleen was glad she had set two alarms. She dragged herself out of bed and washed her face, which helped. Good thing she had time to sit and stare for a few minutes before she had to get dressed. A knock at her door turned out to be a waiter with tea and scones.

"How civilized!" Colleen said. "Thank you." Caffeine had never been so welcome. By the time she heard another knock, she was dressed.

It was Dermot, grinning from ear to ear. He hugged her.

"I'm so glad you're here."

"Uh — thanks. Let's go."

They were silent in the elevator. As they got into his car, he said, "I gather you're not a morning person."

"I'm not even a noon person. But here we are." She looked at the buildings they were passing. "By the way, where are we?"

"We're here." He pulled in front of a large stone building with "Finley Hall" chiseled into its façade. "I'll drop you off and then park."

In the classroom, she wrote on the board, "Tales from Tirnanog." Then she listed four characters from her first book in the series. Before she was finished, Dermot was there, practically giving off sparks.

"I gather you are a morning person," she said.

He grinned. "I like to think I do pretty well at night, too. Listen, I have to teach a class now, but how about a late lunch?"

"I was planning to snack on crackers as I sightsee. I've heard very good things about the gardens at Castle Dombray, and I can get there by bus."

"That's true. It's only two miles away. But if you wait until tomorrow, I can take you."

She smiled. "Surely you can find some other sights worth showing me tomorrow."

"All right." He thought for a minute. "We could go into Dublin to see the Book of Kells."

"Now you're talking my language."

Magic found her again when she started teaching. Every student had read her books and could discuss her characters' motivations. Several made points she had never thought of that sounded right. They all came up with great characters of their own in response to her prompts, and she was on fire with ideas for improving their writing. Two hours passed in minutes.

After Colleen wrapped everything up and encouraged the students to keep working on the stories they had just created, she said, "Now can anyone tell me where to catch a bus for Castle Dombray?"

She was inundated with directions. One boy, Jamie, insisted on walking with her to the bus stop. "Five stops," he said. "There will be a sign for the castle. When you come back, stay on the bus to the stop beyond this one. You'll be a block from your B&B."

She supposed they all knew where she was staying. Perhaps it was where every visiting writer stayed. Jamie seemed prepared to wait with her, but then the bus arrived and she jumped aboard it. "Thank you! Keep writing," she called out to him.

She drank in the scenery on the way out of town. It was not quite as green as she'd always pictured it, but then it was August. A very hot August. And the brown made the forty shades of green show up that much more. She had pictured all the stone walls. And she'd heard about the narrow roads. They made her glad she wasn't driving.

The bus let her off at the entrance to the grounds. She bought a ticket.

"Would you like the 1:00 house tour?" the elderly ticket taker asked.

"I'd like to look at the gardens first. Is that all right?"

"Certainly. The house tours start every half hour. Just buy your ticket any time before 4:00 and meet your guide over there." He pointed at some benches.

Colleen sat down and studied the map. The Daffodil Walk sounded lovely, in season. Maybe she'd come back in the spring someday. For now, the rock garden appealed. It was through the white garden, past the boxwood maze, and down the primrose path. Someone had a sense of humor.

There were half a dozen people in the white garden, and she could hear people talking as she passed the maze. But the primrose path was peaceful, and the rock garden was blessedly empty. She wandered over to a stone seat in front of a small waterfall to savor the view. When she got up, she followed a wooded path. She was so busy admiring a flowering groundcover that she nearly tripped over something she thought at first was a large ball. On closer inspection, she realized it was a human head. On even closer inspection, she recognized it as the head of Alfred Covert. The attached body was mostly hidden by flourishing foliage.

"Oh, my God!" Colleen gasped. Her heart began to pound so hard that she couldn't hear herself think. She'd seen very few dead bodies before and none of them unexpected. Had this heartless man had a heart attack? He did seem the type. She took a deep breath and forced herself to feel for a pulse in his neck, but somehow she was already sure he was dead. Damn, she hadn't gotten the new SIM card — and she didn't know the Irish equivalent of 911 anyway.

She ran back the way she had come, looking for an employee but finding none until she reached the white garden. A young woman in a Castle Dombrey T-shirt with the nametag "Kathleen" was weeding a quiet corner. Colleen took a deep breath and said quietly, "Excuse me, but there's a dead man in the rock garden."

"What?" Kathleen dropped her trowel. It clinked on the edging stone, and several tourists looked their way.

"No need to alarm anyone. He's beyond help."

"Oh. Right." Kathleen ran toward the front entrance. Colleen didn't know whether to follow her or stand vigil over the body. After a few minutes she headed back to the rock garden. She didn't want to touch Covert again, but she did look closely at him. There was blood on his left temple. A few drops stood out against the green grass.

Maybe it wasn't a heart attack. She looked around for a weapon but saw nothing likely. Finally the police arrived.

"You the one who found the body?" said a short, redhaired man whose nametag said Officer O'Neil.

I wondered where all the redheads were, she thought irrelevantly. "Yes. Alfred Covert."

The officer's eyes narrowed. "You know him?"

"Yes, I met him last night." As she saw the officer's eyebrows rise, she added, "At a dinner at Meath College. He teaches — taught — there."

O'Neil jotted something down. "And you are?"

"Colleen McKiernan."

"Where do you come from?"

"America," she said. "Pennsylvania. I'm here to teach a workshop."

"Can anyone vouch for you?"

"Me? Sure." She thought. "Professor Murphy, the head of the folklore department."

A gray-haired woman officer knelt beside a patch of creeping phlox and picked something up in a gloved hand. Colleen couldn't make out what it was before the officer placed it in an evidence bag.

O'Neil shouted, "O'Toole!"

A young man in uniform came up to them. "Sir?"

O'Neil waved at Colleen. "Take her down to the station. Get her statement and run her bona fides."

"Yes, sir." O'Toole turned to Colleen. "Come with me please, ma'am."

"Is that really necessary?" Colleen asked. "I'm staying at a B&B in Meath — though I am leaving town tomorrow."

O'Neil squinted at her. "I wouldn't count on that."

Colleen yawned. Again. She couldn't remember being this bored since the last time she'd had jury duty. Maybe all municipal buildings suffered from a lack of air circulation. Or slow poisoning. O'Toole had handed her off to a more senior officer, who had walked her through every minute since her arrival in Ireland. Well, nearly every minute. She had not mentioned her interlude with Dermot last night.

Detective Burleigh was studying his notes and rubbing his forehead, which was no more bald than the rest of his head. "Did you know the murder weapon was a solid glass sphere?" he asked in an angry tone.

"How would I know that?"

"You invented it."

Suddenly Colleen was wide awake. "What do you mean?"

"You wrote about a glass sphere that you claimed was one of the four treasures of Ireland."

"In my books, you mean? The whole reason I changed Luada's sword to a crystal — a healing crystal — was so it wouldn't be a weapon. I don't believe in violence."

The skepticism in Burleigh's eyes drove her to go on. "Besides, why would I kill someone I didn't even know?"

"He was rude to you last night."

Colleen realized that by now the police had probably interviewed everyone who had been at the dinner. Several people besides Kelly had doubtless overheard what Covert had hissed at her. She tried to laugh, though she felt more like crying. "If I killed everybody who doesn't like my books, bodies would be stacked like cordwood."

Burleigh shook his massive head and squinted at her with watery blue eyes. "You Americans may find mass murder amusing, but here we take it seriously. How long have you known Dermot O'Hara?"

"What?" The sudden shift in subject confused her so much that she didn't challenge the "mass murder" accusation. "Less than 48 hours. Why?"

"Were you aware that he and Professor Covert had come to blows before?"

"Of course not. How would I know?"

Burleigh looked at her sideways. "Pillow talk?"

Uh-oh. He'd caught her little white lie about her late-night activities. "Mr. O'Hara and I did not discuss Professor Covert," she said. "He said nothing to me about any animosity."

"Mr. O'Hara, is it? He failed to mention that not a week ago, in full view of at least two other teachers, he knocked Alfred Covert to the ground and threatened to kill him?"

"No!" She meant both no, he didn't mention it, and no, I can't believe he did that. If it was true, Dermot was a suspect. Damn, she thought. Is the first man I've been attracted to in five years a murderer?

Finally they let her go with a caution that she remain in town until notified. O'Toole drove her back to the Bee-Loud Glade. When she went inside and found Dermot waiting for her, she was glad that O'Toole had merely dropped her off.

Dermot hugged her and said, "Are you all right?"

Colleen sighed. "Not really. I'm a suspect."

"Yeah, me too."

She stepped back. "You don't seem too concerned about that."

Dermot flashed his trademark grin. "I'm not guilty."

Colleen narrowed her eyes. "They tell me you had a knock-down, drag-out fight with Covert last week."

He frowned. "You can't seriously think I would kill someone, can you? There's a world of difference between throwing a punch at a narcissistic idiot and killing him."

She shrugged. "We've known each other only 48 hours."

"I know you didn't do it."

"Really? How?"

He put his hands out to his sides, palms up, and shrugged. "I just do. The woman who decided to turn a sword into a healing crystal wouldn't kill anyone. Now, let's get some tea."

Colleen decided to reciprocate his trust, at least for now. "That's just what I need," she agreed. "Caffeine and comfort."

They headed into the B&B's dining room. A young man

whom Dermot greeted as Robbie took their order.

"Speaking of the healing crystal," said Colleen, "did the police tell you that was the murder weapon? That appears to be the main reason I'm a suspect."

"They did ask me if I owned a solid glass sphere," Dermot said.

"I wonder if they were able to lift any useful prints from it," Colleen mused. "Do you have any idea who it might belong to? Or what it is, for that matter?"

"It sounds like an objet d'art in the conference room at Finley Hall. There's a metal framework in the shape of a helix that hangs in one of the windows. A solid glass ball in it, about four inches across, rests in one of the spirals and reflects the view in a funhouse mirror sort of way." Dermot gestured with his hands as he talked.

Colleen took a sip of hot, sweet tea and slumped in her chair. "Hmmm." Then she sat up straight as an idea began percolating. "We need to see if that ball is missing. And we need to get all the suspects together in a room."

Dermot shook his head. "Are you planning to solve the murder yourself?"

"If I want to continue my travels tomorrow, I think I have to. The police are wasting their time suspecting you and me. We need to present them with someone likelier. And I have written a few mystery stories in my day. And read a million of 'em." She tapped her fingers on the scarred wooden table. "Means, motive, opportunity. So what was your fight with Covert about?"

When he shook his head, she added, "I could use your help."

"Oh, very well. He had just failed a scholarship student, Eliza Davis, on a paper I knew she had spent weeks researching. I've had her in several classes, and she's one of the best writers I've seen. Yet Covert's unfair grade could get her sent down."

"Huh. Sexual harassment, perhaps, and she wouldn't play along?"

Dermot thought. "I wouldn't have put that past him in his single days, but I doubt that he would cheat on Jane. But he was horribly class-conscious. He didn't think we should even offer scholarships. He truly believed that the more money a person has — preferably old money — the smarter he is."

"Or she. Was Eliza at the dinner last night?"

"Yes. She was the girl with the swept-up brown hair. You talked to her a bit about rainbows as portals."

"Oh, yes, I remember. I liked her." Colleen frowned. "Although losing her scholarship sounds like a motive."

"I don't know," Dermot said. "Covert certainly wasn't popular, but I can't imagine Eliza, or anybody I know, committing murder."

"Well, somebody you know probably did." Colleen thought. "Hey, I saw them taking Stan Bishop into an interview room. Did he and Covert have a beef about something?"

"Not that I know of, but Bishop certainly doesn't like you. Maybe he killed Covert to set you up," Dermot mused.

Colleen shrugged. "Seems too subtle for such a straightforward, blustery guy."

"Then maybe it's the person we least suspect, the nicest person in town."

"And who would that be? Thomas Murphy? Neva Flaherty?" Colleen stood up. "Dermot, I need some time to think."

"Sure. I'll help. I'm a well-known thought provoker."

She shook her head. "I'm sure you are, but I need some alone time."

He nodded. "Okay. Shall I come back in an hour or so to take you to dinner?"

"Thanks, but no. I keep seeing Alfred Covert's dead face. It's hard to imagine myself having an appetite anytime soon."

"Okay." He squeezed her hand and stood up. He leaned in to whisper, "Shall I come back in three or four hours? It would be my pleasure to satisfy whatever appetites you may have."

Colleen gave him a small smile. "I'm tempted, but not tonight." She stood on tiptoes to kiss him. Then she forced herself to let go of his hand and walked toward the tiny elevator. She really was tempted, but she couldn't enjoy anything until she spoke with her muse. She needed some guidance.

In her room, she lit the lavender-scented candle from her nightstand. She placed it on the round table in the corner of her bedroom and gazed into the flames.

"Harriet?" she said in her head. "I need your help." No

reply. She said it again, this time out loud. She mentally pictured Harriet Vane. Dorothy L. Sayers had created her as a sidekick for Lord Peter Wimsey, but Colleen found Harriet a cleverer sleuth than the star of the series. She had helped Colleen figure out the solutions to several problems in the past.

A tall, thin woman with wavy dark hair materialized in the seat across from her. "Harriet! Thank you for coming," she said.

"It's my pleasure, to be sure. How nice to see you in the British Isles." Harriet smiled. "Congratulations on your writing award."

"Thank you very much." Colleen made an effort to stop smiling. "Are you up to speed on the circumstances surrounding this murder?"

"Indeed I am. I believe a line from the Irish poet William Butler Yeats sums up this circumstance. 'The intellect of man is forced to choose: perfection of the life or of the work.'"

"I know the poem, but I'm afraid it sums it up rather obliquely," Colleen said. "What am I missing?"

"Your Professor Covert became a family man late in life. How resentful would his first child, neglected and then cast off, be when he learned how much the good professor cosseted the children of his second family?"

"Very, I suppose. Covert did go on and on about his children. But who ..." Colleen trailed off.

"His firstborn son was a junior," Harriet prompted. "His father abandoned them when the boy was only eight years old. His mother changed his surname to her family name, but he kept his father's Christian name."

"Hmm," Colleen said.

"One thing I'm not sure of," said Harriet, "is if it was in fact murder. The professor had too small a heart."

"Do you mean that metaphorically, like the Grinch? Or medically?"

"The Grinch? Oh, yes, his heart was two sizes too small, wasn't it?"

"So you're familiar with the work of writers after your time?"

"Of course," said Harriet. "We ghosts have plenty of time to read, and I like to keep up."

"But you're not corporeal. How do you turn the pages?"

"Telekinesis." With that, the muse faded away.

"But wait!" Colleen called after her. "Do you know the son's last name?" No reply.

She stood and got her laptop out of her suitcase. When my muse bails, I guess it's time for a search engine, she thought. She googled Alfred Covert and got a list of publications and a very brief biography. Jane and the two boys were mentioned, but there was no reference to their grown-up stepbrother or to Alfred's first wife. Damn! Colleen was sure the information was lurking somewhere on the Web and an expert could find it. She wondered if Dermot knew any hackers.

Meanwhile, she typed up a list of every male she had met through the college who looked to be between 25 and 35. Then she methodically researched each name. She started with Kelly and thought at first she had the luck of the Irish: His middle name, it turned out, was Alfred. But no. None of the faculty or award winners seemed to be Alfred Covert's son. Even if Harriet was wrong about him being an Alfred too, either the age was off or the person she was researching had a biography with no holes in its early years.

She let her mind drift. If Covert were older than he looked and had married very young, she supposed his first child could be as old as 45. Or maybe the child was transgender and had since become female. A couple of her students had looked just barely old enough to be Covert's child. She googled them but found mostly social-network stuff.

She mentally pictured everyone she had met since she arrived in Ireland. Could it be Dermot? Only in a bad movie. Besides, he'd been in her workshop until he'd had to rush off to teach a class. She and her twenty students were his alibi.

What about people not directly connected to the college? Robbie, the waiter at her B&B, might just be old enough, but she didn't know his last name. Kathleen, the gardener at Castle Dombrey? She would have had the opportunity, but the transgender theory was unlikely. Colleen wondered again where the murder weapon had come from. What about Neva Flaherty's boyfriend? She racked her brain for his last name. Or Mary McConnell's husband?

Colleen's scalp tingled as she realized that Mary's husband was named Fred. She'd assumed it was short for Frederick, but what if his name was Alfred? She typed his name into the search engine with shaking fingers and waited. And waited.

Nothing came up. She was about to pound the table when it occurred to her to google Mary McConnell. Wait, wait. Yes! Mary, like so many authors, had a website. Colleen clicked the Bio tab and read about Mary's children and husband: "Fred has illustrated two of Mary's children's books, carrying on the tradition of his mother, noted artist Maeve McConnell."

Not conclusive proof yet. She still had to find evidence that Maeve McConnell had been Covert's first wife. She wondered if Dermot knew.

There was a knock on her door. When Colleen opened it, Rosalie presented a smartphone on a silver tray. "It's Dermot," she said with a giggle.

Ten minutes earlier, Colleen would have been annoyed. She'd told him she wanted to be alone tonight. But now she was eager to move forward with her sleuthing, and he might have some useful knowledge. Not to mention warm lips and a sweet manner. "Hello?' she asked. Rosalie discreetly closed the door as she left.

"Did someone call for a bed warmer?" How familiar his voice had become already.

She had to laugh. "Maybe. I was thinking more of calling for a faculty member whose brain I could pick."

"Then it's your lucky night. I'm very good at multitasking."

"Okay."

"Great! See you in ten minutes."

Colleen opened the door and found Rosalie down the hall, dusting desultorily. She waved the phone and Rosalie walked back to get it. "Expecting company?" she asked. "He's a charmer, isn't he?" She giggled again.

Colleen smiled and then said, "How much of a charmer? Have you ever dated him?"

"Oh, no, he's too old for me." She paused. "I didn't mean—"

"No, that's all right. Very sensible of you. Has he charmed a lot of women my age?"

Rosalie seemed to be looking for an answer in the ceiling. "I don't know. But I can tell you Dermot's nice to everyone. He's just charming by nature. I've known him all my life, and even when I was little he talked to me like I wasn't an idiot. My cat died when I was seven, and almost everybody else tried to tell me I'd be fine when I got a new one. But Dermot found me crying on the swing in the backyard. He just patted my back until I finished. I said, 'I suppose you want me to get over it,' and he said, 'Pangur was a special cat. You grieve as long as you need to.' That was just what I needed to hear."

"Aww. Come on in, Rosalie." They sat at the table and talked about the pros and cons of cats and men.

A few minutes later there was a light knock. When Colleen opened the door, Dermot held up a big paper bag. "I brought sandwiches," he said.

Colleen's stomach growled and she realized that she hadn't consumed anything but tea for hours. "You read my mind. In fact, you read what hadn't entered my mind yet," she said.

Rosalie stood up. "Well, I'll leave you to it. Dinner, I mean."

Colleen put a hand on her arm. "Actually, would you mind staying for just a minute? Dermot, you have a seat too." She leaned back against the radiator. "Did you know Professor Covert?"

"Oh, yes. I babysit the boys sometimes," Rosalie said.

"Anything you can tell us about him?"

"Just that those boys were his life. I never saw a man so tender with his sons." Rosalie paused to think. "Also, I saw the murder weapon at his house last Saturday night."

"The glass sphere?" Colleen asked. She wasn't surprised that the details had spread so quickly. It seemed they wouldn't need to check the conference room.

"Yeah. They keep a bowl near the front door for keys and change and such. It was in there. I didn't know what it was at the time, of course."

"So he stole the weapon that killed him? Huh." Colleen scratched her head.

"Suicide?" Dermot suggested with a short laugh.

"He must have had a great arm to knock himself out." Colleen pondered. "Can you tell me anything about the professor's routine, Rosalie?"

"Let's see. He walked at Castle Dombrey often."

"Really? Who would have known to find him there?"

"Just about everybody. He was always talking about how he had to take good care of himself if he wanted to be here to see Alfie and Luke grow up. He could bore you on the subject of either diet or exercise if you gave him half a chance."

"Alfie?" Colleen said.

"Sure. Alfred Junior."

Alfred Junior the second, Colleen thought. "Well, thanks, Rosalie."

"Glad I could help." Rosalie headed for the door.

After she left, Dermot pulled out of the bag sandwiches, cole slaw, napkins, condiments, plastic glasses, and a bottle of whiskey. He raised it suggestively.

"That's too rich for my blood," Colleen said as she sat down, "but you have at it."

"All right. We have grilled chicken, roast beef, tuna, and — just in case — a veggie burger."

"Grilled chicken, please." There was little talking for a few minutes as they both wolfed down their food.

"How did I work up such an appetite sitting at my computer?" Colleen wondered.

"Creating people and incidents out of whole cloth takes energy," Dermot said.

"Oh, I wasn't writing. I was trying to figure out who killed Alfred Covert."

"Really? Any progress?"

"Rosalie gave me an idea."

"What, Alfred Junior? Surely you don't suspect his nine-year-old son."

"Of course not." Colleen wished she could tell Dermot about her muse, but that was a lot to expect anyone to believe, even an Irishman. "I suspect he already had a son named Alfred Junior, from his first marriage. Do you know Mary and Fred McConnell very well? Do you know who his mother is?"

Dermot sat back. "Fred? As in Alfred Junior? Hmm. His mother's a rather well-known artist. The college threw an author's reception when one of Mary's books was published, and Maeve was quite charming. Quite talented, too. The books are wonderful. I've bought multiple copies for my nieces and nephews."

"Was Maeve McConnell Alfred Covert's first wife?"

"I don't know, but Murphy might. He's known Covert for years."

Colleen said, "Good. Do you think it's too late to call him tonight?"

They both looked at their watches. "Ten o'clock," Dermot said. "Latish."

"It's important."

"Okay. What should I say?"

"First, ask if he knows who Covert's first wife was. Then, ask if we could get everyone back together tomorrow. In the same room, ideally. It wouldn't have to be so fancy this time. We could call it a wake for Professor Covert."

"That might not get a great turnout, but if we mention that you'll be there, everyone will want to come. I'll ask him to set it up."

"And ask him if someone can put together a slideshow of photos of Covert throughout his life. A memento mori kind of thing." Colleen clicked her keyboard and brooded as she listened to Dermot's side of the phone conversation.

"That's right. Low key," said Dermot. Then he ended the call. "Professor Murphy liked the idea of a wake. 8:00 p.m. in Ceelian Hall. His secretary will text everyone on last night's guest list. He's not sure Jane will want to come so soon after her loss — he'll call her — but most everyone else probably will. Especially since the college is providing free drinks."

"I can't say I blame her," said Colleen. "Of course the spouse is always a prime suspect, but I wouldn't think she'd want to raise two kids alone. Covert sounded like a very involved parent, despite his less savory qualities. How about the slideshow?"

"Murphy will ask Deirdre to talk to Jane about family photos. And yes, you were right about Fred McConnell's parentage. Murphy knew the Coverts when Alfred was married to Maeve."

Colleen thrust both arms in the air. "Yes!" Then she became pensive. "What kind of a man would completely abandon his oldest child — even recycle the kid's name?"

Dermot stood up and came to stand behind her. He began massaging her back. "So you really think Fred McConnell murdered Alfred Covert? And he's his son?"

"Well, I'm almost sure Fred's his son. But I'm not sure it was murder."

"Huh?"

"I think Covert may have had a heart attack."

"I thought you saw blood on his face."

"A little. No indentation though, as there would have been if the solid-glass sphere had hit him hard enough to kill him." She tapped her fingers on the table. "I wonder when the autopsy will be done."

"Do you feel brave enough to ask Burleigh?"

"That question might be best coming from a nonsuspect."

Dermot kneaded the muscles at the back of her neck. "These muscles are tight. You must be exhausted."

Colleen laughed.

"What's funny?"

"Sometimes you seem like such a smooth operator. It makes me wonder how many times you've said that, to how many women."

Dermot's hands stilled. "Do you care?"

"Just curious." She thought of Rosalie's story about her childhood cat. "I know there's more to you than that."

"Good." Dermot gently pulled her hair to one side and kissed her neck. She turned so that their lips met.

When Colleen woke on Friday morning, Dermot was still there. He opened his eyes as soon as she turned her head to look at the clock. "Am I early, or are you late?" she murmured.

"My first class isn't until 11:00, so I guess you must be early."

"I never wake up this early at home. Of course, I never go to bed this early, either."

"And you never get such strenuous cardio exercise right before bed?"

She smiled. "Well, rarely." She stretched. "I feel as if I could conquer the world."

"So what are you going to do between now and 8:00 p.m.?" Dermot asked.

"Fine-tune my plan, and maybe get in a little sightseeing."

"What is your plan, exactly?"

Colleen frowned. "To make sure the wake inspires Fred to confess."

"Are you that sure he's guilty, then?"

"I'm pretty sure he thinks he's guilty, and it will help everyone involved, even him, if he speaks up."

Dermot raised his eyebrows but said only, "Shall I meet

you after my last class at 5:00?"

"I'm not sure where I'll be then, but I'll be back here dressing for the wake by 7:00."

"I'll pick you up."

Colleen thought of Dermot's question many times that day. Was Fred guilty? She couldn't help thinking that his father was at least as guilty as he was. She called Deirdre to make some subtle suggestions about the slideshow. She tried to work but found it hard to concentrate. She went back to Castle Dombrey, which provided some distraction. She forced herself to visit the rock garden. It looked untouched by human tragedy.

On the way back, she got off the bus downtown and wandered around, grabbing a bite at a pub. She got back to her room in time for a nap but was far too keyed up to sleep. Instead, she lay thinking about fathers and sons, about Dagda and Aengus, about a new idea for a short story. When she heard a knock, she leaped up off the bed and opened the door.

Dermot swept her up in a big hug. "Ready?" He looked at her robe. "I guess not."

"Give me ten minutes to throw on some clothes and a little makeup."

"May I watch?"

"No. You may go downstairs and use your charms for good. Chat with the employees. See what they know about Alfred Covert." Colleen pushed him out the door. He certainly looked good in a black suit. Eight minutes later, she appeared in the bar wearing black slacks and a black silk jacket. Thank goodness I threw something black in my suitcase at the last minute, she thought.

Dermot was sitting at the bar talking to Robbie. He jumped up when he saw Colleen and gave her a hug. "You look lovely," he whispered.

"Thank you. I was aiming for — funereal, I guess. Somber, at least."

"There's no rule that you can't look both somber and hot. Which you do."

"Thanks." Colleen looked at her watch: 7:30. "Did you pick up any useful information?"

"Robbie has a klepto story about Covert, but it just reinforces what we already know."

"Then let's head over to Ceelian Hall. I do want to get

there early."

Only a couple of waiters were in the dining room, putting cloths on tables and setting out appetizers. Colleen was glad to see there was no dais tonight. She and Dermot staked out a round table halfway down the room and spoke in whispers until Neva Flaherty arrived.

Neva hugged them both. "It's so nice of you to attend the wake, when you barely knew the professor," she said.

"The least I could do," said Colleen. They chatted with everyone who came in. The Murphys brought printed programs, titled "A Celebration of Life," that showed who would speak and in what order. Fortunately Colleen, the near-stranger, was not a speaker. She would have had hardly anything to say about Alfred Covert, much less anything nice.

She asked Deirdre, "Were you able to put together a slideshow?"

"Yes," she said. "Jane had an abundance of current photos and a good many from his past as well. I helped her go through them and arrange them."

"Good."

Deirdre said, "I think it was cathartic for Jane. Sad, of course, but a necessary step."

Detective Burleigh walked in.

By 7:55 everyone from last night was there except for a couple of students and the McConnells. Colleen raised her eyebrows at Dermot and looked at the door. Her plan wouldn't work if Fred didn't come. Was he on the run? What had he told his wife and children?

She took a deep breath and walked over to Burleigh. "Good to see you," she said, forcing a smile.

"Ms. McKiernan," he said flatly.

"I've been talking to people who knew the professor," she began.

Burleigh frowned.

"Did you know that Fred McConnell is Alfred Covert's son?" she asked.

Judging by the look on his face, apparently not. "Is that relevant?" Burleigh asked.

"Maybe. You see, Covert was talking on Wednesday night about how important his younger sons — his second family — are to him and I got the impression Fred was jealous. Thought you might want to keep an eye on him tonight." Colleen began to back away.

"I plan to keep an eye on everyone," Burleigh said coldly.

"Yes, sir." Colleen fled back to her table, but before she could sit down, she heard arguing in the hall.

"But I don't want to!" said a voice that she recognized as Fred's.

"You're here now, so you might as well put in an appearance," said Mary.

The couple walked in hand in hand. To Colleen they looked like a mother leading her rebellious son. They sat at the table next to hers.

Professor Murphy stood, and the wake began. Most of the speakers struggled to say something nice about the dead man. Colleen was glad that his widow wasn't there. She watched a gamut of emotions play across Fred's face: anger, sadness, fear. Even, briefly, happiness.

But then a man she didn't recall from last night stood. According to the program, he was John Dunleavy. She turned to Dermot and tapped the program.

He leaned in close. "Covert's assistant. Out of town yesterday."

Dunleavy looked about thirty-five, though his hair was gray. His head was so large it made even his six-foot-tall body look top-heavy. "Alfred was my mentor, dare I say my father figure," he was declaiming. "Tonight I am bereft." He clasped his right hand over his heart. His stagey gestures and odd pauses reminded Colleen of William Shatner. Of course, the fact that he was emoting like a bad actor didn't mean he wasn't really grieving.

Colleen looked at Fred. His hands were curled into fists. He didn't relax until Dunleavy finished.

Professor Murphy stood to say, "And now we have a slideshow of Professor Covert's life." He narrated the photos of Alfred as a child: sitting on a rocking horse, kicking a ball around, lying on his stomach reading on a dark-blue carpet. The Alfred of the photos grew into a young man. There was a wedding photo that did not feature Jane, followed by one of Covert holding a book up to the camera. The cover read *A Reappraisal of Faerie Courts* by Alfred Covert. "His first major publication," said Professor Murphy.

The next slide showed a five-or six-year-old boy on a bicycle. Next was that boy, about two years older, in a baseball uniform, pitching a ball to his father. At least, Colleen assumed he was Alfred's son. There wasn't much family resemblance, just as the adult Fred didn't look much like the professor. Fred did, however, look very much like the boy.

A sob filled the room. Fred's head was buried in his arms. He raised it and cried out, "It was an accident!"

Detective Burleigh stood immediately. "What's that, Mr. McConnell? Do you want to make a statement?"

"Yes! I just went to talk to him." Fred shook his head. "I knew he walked at Castle Dombrey every Wednesday morning, and I just wanted to tell him who I was and ..."

Colleen saw Burleigh looking at her. "And ask why he left you?" she asked quietly.

"Yes! It was the least he could do to answer." Fred sat up straighter. "I've been working up the courage to ask him for months. Instead, he walked to the other side of the garden. I thought he was just leaving me, with no explanation. Again. Then he reached into his pocket and got out that damn glass ball and threw it at me. I wasn't expecting it. I didn't have time to catch it."

"Then what, Fred?" she prompted.

"It hit me in the stomach and fell to the ground. I picked it up and threw it back. He always used to say I had a lousy arm. I never expected it to hit him at all, let alone in the head. Why didn't he catch it? And why didn't he recognize me? I've met him three times since Mary started working here!"

Burleigh moved closer to Fred. "Do you wish to call your solicitor, Mr. McConnell?"

Fred sighed. He looked ten years older than he had last night. "I don't know," he said.

"He certainly does," said Mary. "It was an accident."

"I'll take him to the station," Detective Burleigh said to her. "You can meet us there." He led Fred out of the room, and Mary followed.

"What do you think?" Dermot whispered. "Was it really an accident?"

Colleen looked at the image up on the screen of the young Fred and his father. "I hope so. If it wasn't, Fred's children will grow up without a father, just like him."

"Either way, Covert's children will."

"Yes. Two tragedies from one treasure of Ireland."

The room was silent for a minute. When conversation resumed, Colleen thought of something. "If Fred had such a bad arm, it's unlikely he could throw that sphere hard enough at that distance to kill his father."

"If the autopsy reveals that the cause of death was a heart attack, would Fred be guilty of causing it?"

"I wouldn't think so." Colleen rubbed her silver unicorn. "He could stay out of jail and be there for his kids. He'll help them grow up, and they'll help him heal."

"Maybe he'll even get to know his half-brothers and help them grow up too."

"Maybe. If Jane can forgive him."

Later that night Colleen half woke from a short snooze. "This is nice, isn't it?" said Dermot, who was lying on his back with his arm around her.

"Uh-huh." One of the nicest nights she'd had in years. She cupped his chin in her hand.

"What would you think about moving here?"

Now she was wide awake. "What?"

"Since you're a freelancer, you can write anywhere, right? You might even find inspiration for more tales from Tirnanog." He added, "You did a great job teaching that workshop. The department might hire you as a part-time adjunct if you need a guaranteed paycheck. And we could spend time together."

Colleen sat up, her mind racing. "That's very flattering, but I have a life back home."

"Okay. Would I like Pennsylvania, do you think?"

She traced a circle on her knee while avoiding eye contact. "It's a nice place to visit."

Dermot sat up too. "Look at me," he said quietly. When she did, he frowned. "I see. You're not looking for a serious relationship."

"Are you?"

He looked surprised. "I wasn't. But now — I don't know. I thought we had chemistry."

Colleen touched his hand. "We do! But we've known each other all of three days. Three rather stressful days. If this is more than a fling, we need to get to know each other better.

There's so much we don't know about each other. You know that's true."

"Ask away," he said, with the first sign of his famous grin. "I've got nothing to hide."

"Oh, I doubt that. Anyway, I meant get to know each other slowly, over time."

"But you're leaving the country in a few days."

"We can Skype. And how romantic would it be to write each other long letters? On paper."

Dermot laughed. "I'm pretty sure the answer's supposed to be very, but—"

He was interrupted by a kiss. When Colleen came up for air, she said, "Just be glad I don't feel the need to take the physical side of our relationship slowly."

"When you're right, you're right."

Character Bios from M. A. Mogus

Jessie Laconia Griffin is five foot six inches tall, with dark-brown hair and gray eyes. She is fifty years old. Her hair is shoulder length and she often wears it up in a french twist with the addition of feathers and specially designed jewelry. In winter she wears a vicuña poncho and a hat (similar to the one Clint Eastwood wore). She is slender but strong and has a black belt in aikido. She has a Ph.D. in forensic archaeology and history, with specialties in both authentication studies and ethno-pharmacology, as well as a background in computer science. She trained with shamans in Mexico and Central America during her graduate studies.

She sometimes aids the police in facial reconstruction. She has many friends in the neo-pagan community but is not active in it. She does freelance work in archaeology and anthropology as well as writing fiction.

The Nittany Needles

M. A. Mogus

"I'll be there by lunchtime," I phoned to tell Barbara Goodwin just after I left State College, Pennsylvania. I knew a bypass around the town and headed for the village of Mountain Brook twelve miles southeast. I hadn't seen Barbara in several years, but we had corresponded by email while I was teaching at the university in New Mexico. Barbara was fifteen years my senior and had been a good friend of my late Aunt Aggie's. She and Aggie were fiber arts buddies, by which I mean they knitted and crocheted together. Fiber art is now the more acceptable title for such handwork.

When I arrived at Mountain Brook, I noticed that Barbara's store was the last one in the village. It was called the Nittany Needle and housed yarns, roving, threads, and notions, crammed into two of three floors of a huge Victorian house. It wasn't long before I saw the parking lot. I'd seen the images she'd sent me, but I wasn't prepared for the tall gingerbread-covered house that contained her business.

"Whoa, Barbara," I called through the open window as I parked my car in the ample parking lot. "This is something."

"Jessie Laconia Griffin, I'm so glad to see you." She tried to open the door of the Honda before I unlocked it.

I shut the window, shut the car, and managed to get out in time to be hugged until I couldn't quite breathe. "Good to see you too," I gasped. She let me go and I stood back to get a real-life look at Barbara. Her hair held a few threads of gray and hung in a braid behind her. Her figure was still what is referred to in polite circles as Rubenesque.

"You've lost weight," she accused. "You need to put more meat on your bones, Jessie, and I have just the recipes that will do it." She stood back and put her hands on her hips. "No gray hairs either, just like Aggie."

"You aren't exactly a little old white-haired lady yourself at seventy."

She laughed and motioned for me to open the hatch. She pulled out my suitcase. I grabbed my briefcase and purse and trotted behind her. We reached the porch and I stood for a moment looking at the flowers in colorful clay pots separating wicker chairs and loungers. The place was a riot of color, just like Barbara in her lime-green slacks and matching tunic with strings of beads and silver charm necklaces as accents.

I followed her into the store and stood amazed at the reality of what I had only seen in email photos. Displays of yarns filled the first room, used as a checkout area. Beyond lay a huge ballroom-sized parlor; I hurried to see what displays it contained. It outdid the entrance, and I felt as if I'd entered a land of eternal yarns.

"Barbara, it's magnificent. Your photos didn't do this justice."

She swung to face me. "It's what I dreamed of after Jacob died. All that work managing a lab for the university paid off." She chuckled. "That and the fact that Jacob left the farm, this land, and a hefty insurance policy for me and the kids."

"How are Beth and Orrin?"

She took a deep breath before answering. "They're both in California pursuing their own dreams. I see them when they visit, or when I visit, but I hate to leave this place. It's the energies, you know. Come, I've even put in an elevator for the time when the stairs become too much for me. I also use it for my students since I hold classes on part of the second floor."

She and Aggie had a lot in common, but Barbara was not a shaman. She was a sensitive, as her husband had been. I'd known that from the first time we met.

We took the small glass-enclosed elevator to the third floor, where Barbara lived, and she showed me to one of the tower rooms.

"I love this place, but the thought of maintenance would drive me nuts."

"It drives me nuts too, but Evan Asher takes care of a lot of it. He lives in the cottage out back and farms eight of the ten acres that came with this house."

This was news to me. But Barbara explained that Evan was taking courses at Penn State in the agriculture program and had established an organic farm on the property. He was also engaged, but Barbara didn't elaborate on his fiancée.

"Take some time to rest and get settled. I'm having a

party tonight and you know some of the guests." Barbara was biting her lower lip. This was not a good sign.

"Who would I still know here? I got my master's years ago; my doctorate's from the University of Penn. Except to visit you before I left for New Mexico, I haven't been back in ages."

Barbara sat on the handmade quilt covering the carved cherry bed. She patted the quilt with her hand. "You'd better sit down. The party was set before I knew you were coming. I would have backed out. But the village merchants are part of it, and the guest of honor is Derrick Hixon."

"Sleazebag Hixon." I began to pace. "I dumped that sociopathic narcissist before I got my degree."

"Jessie, he's running for the state senate and he's brought a lot of money into the area."

I stared at Barbara. "You're kidding, right? Who on earth would vote for that man?"

Barbara sighed and rubbed at the quilt. "Not me. I got roped into this because I have the largest area for a party. I have a second ballroom that opens onto an outside stone patio. I'm closing off the yarn area. The party is a political fundraiser. If I might add, though, he'll get nothing from me except the use of my house."

"Maybe I'd better go to a motel until this is over with." I began gathering the items I had been unpacking.

Barbara took my clothes from me and returned them to the dresser. "You will not go to a motel. Just be civil to the bastard until this is over with. You'll not have to deal with him again. It's just that ..." Barbara continued to place my clothes in the drawers.

"What is it?"

"I owe him some money."

"But you said you had insurance from Jacob's death, and I know you sold the farm."

Barbara drew a deep breath.

"It put the children through college and gave them a start. But there wasn't much left to invest and I hit a rough patch a few months ago. Besides, I actually deeded the farm to the conservancy so it would remain an intact watershed. It has wetlands on it, if you remember?"

"I remember, but if you needed money you could have

called me."

Barbara turned to face me. "I should have called, but you were dealing with Aggie's death and the expenses of a move back to Pennsylvania. I couldn't ask you for money. Besides, I've almost paid back what I owe him."

She didn't know about Aggie's investments and my inheritance. "Barbara, I can—" I began, but we were interrupted by her cell phone.

"I've got to take this," she said and moved to the hallway to answer it.

If I hear 'I've got to take this' one more time, I'm throwing the next phone out the window. I just wish she'd told me she needed money, but it was so like her to think of everyone but herself.

"It's the caterer," Barbara called from the hallway. "I've got to get ready for the evening. You take it easy for a few hours."

"Let me help you, please."

"No, I'll have help from the others in the village."

"Barbara, I mean I have to help you. Otherwise I will sit in the room and work myself into a snit. By the time of the party I'll be ready to strangle Derrick."

Barbara laughed, wiping her eyes and trying to catch her breath. "You can help, but no murder tonight."

I agreed and walked to the elevator with her.

The party began at six with an open bar and a catered buffet. Dress was to be casual, but my clothes were not designer casual, a fact I discovered when one of the women came up to me. She was about thirty, with flowing hair the color of wheat and eyes a green you get only from contact lenses. She asked me to get her a glass of pinot noir and pronounced the words carefully lest I misunderstand. I pointed in the direction of the bar and left her standing in her Louboutin sandals and her Chanel retro dress.

I managed to find Barbara talking with some of the local merchants. She welcomed me into the conversation.

"Who are all these people?" I asked after she introduced me to Sally Berthold, George Randle, and Michelle Devon.

"Don't mind them." Michelle twisted the stem of her wine

glass, staring briefly into the contents before glancing at me. "Hixon brought most of them. It's a fundraiser, and he wants them to see how the 'little' people live, those of us with 'small businesses' as opposed to the real businesses."

Barbara snorted. "Like Hixon Industries. If it hadn't been for his father, Derrick wouldn't have a dime."

Sally shook her head. "Nope. He doesn't run Hixon Industries. He has managers who do that. Derrick isn't competent to run a toilet."

"George owns Mountain Brooke Boutique," Sally explained. "I own Special Treasures, a vintage items and clothing shop. But George does all the really upscale clothing."

His outfit was impeccable. I was beginning to wonder what all this emphasis on clothing was all about.

Barbara said, "Michelle owns the Plump Muffin, a really excellent bakery. She made many of the sweets for this party."

"I'm going to have to visit your shops before I leave later this month," I said sipping some excellent wine.

"Barbara said you would be here almost a month." George lifted a wrapped shrimp from a tray passed by a server. "You're on vacation?"

"I'm retired and I'm a visiting professor at Laurel Mountain University. I'm also an author, and my writing group has been kicked out of their archive room in the Falls Bend library because of some renovations. So I thought I'd take this month of August and visit an old friend."

Barbara and I grinned at one another, but we were interrupted by a shadow falling over the group.

"Well, I'll be! It is you, Jessie Laconia Griffin." Derrick sidled up to me.

I felt my aura bristle in protection. Barbara and the others suddenly found something else to do and I was left alone with Mr. Slimeball. George hesitated a moment; I wondered if he was worried about me. Sally stepped back and tugged George's sleeve. He followed her.

I turned to face Derrick. His hair was styled to emphasize his face, and the stylist had left just a touch of gray to give the illusion of maturity. His face held no lines and his smile might have reached his eyes if everything between hadn't been botoxed to within an inch of skin.

"Hello, Derrick." I forced a smile.

"I didn't expect to see you, but I should have, knowing that you and Barbara are friends."

"I didn't realize she was letting her property be used as a fundraiser for your run for the state senate."

He nodded at someone passing by and returned his gaze to me. "I've been helpful to the merchants in this small town. It's necessary to keep small businesses running, as they are the heart of American economics."

"I vote in the Walnut Springs district, not Centre County."

Derrick sipped his drink, a fizzy, odd-colored concoction, as he studied me. "I heard about your aunt's death. She ran some sort of business?"

"Yes, she left me a house and a strip mall, Laurel Mall to be exact."

He nodded as if shaking loose some memory. "You're retired; can't be making much of a pension. If I remember, you were at some small university in New Mexico."

This guy had a problem with small. "I manage." No way was I telling him about Aggie's investments and the money she left me in addition to the house and mall.

"You always just managed. You know, I would never have dumped you if you had been able to rise above your upbringing."

I gagged at the outrage sweeping through me. "I dumped you, if you remember."

He chuckled. "Nonsense, I dumped you. You always dressed for comfort. Every party we went to you wore slacks, sometimes even jeans."

"I was doing fieldwork, if you remember." Why were we getting into this?

"Yeah, I visited your work site once. It looked more like a blue-collar hangout than an actual university sponsored excavation."

I fought to control my tremble of fury. Some of those people at that site were now dead as a result of being in the way of art thieves in Mexico. They were good people trying to tell the story of the world's past.

"What you couldn't handle was the rain-drenched ground, and me sitting with two feet in an open grave while I ate a center-cut bologna sandwich. We had to hurry because the bulldozers from Hixon Industries were gunning up to smash any record of the ten-thousand-year-old burials."

Derrick leaned forward and some of his drink sloshed from his glass. "Hixon Industries gave money for that salvage excavation."

"And we couldn't get it done in time, so Hixon Industries covered the site and built its headquarters over it." I could still feel the faint echo of outrage from the bodies we hadn't recovered.

"Derrick, darling, she doesn't work here." The woman who'd asked me for the wine came up to him and shoved her arm possessively around his.

"My wife, Andrea." He recovered quickly, the mark of a good politician.

"You and Derrick went to college together." Andrea studied me again and found my clothing subpar.

"We were in graduate school at Penn State." These two should do well in Harrisburg, if someone didn't kill them before they got to the state capitol.

Andrea smiled and tugged on Derrick's arm. "We have important donors to meet," she suggested. The two went off to annoy someone else.

The party dragged as Derrick and Andrea circled the room discussing whatever topic of the moment came up while preening as the perfect couple for a senate nomination, maybe later governor. I stepped outside and found a path leading around several garden beds filled with flowering plants.

"He demanded the money by the end of this week." The man's voice was just above a whisper.

"She hasn't got the money," a woman's voice replied. I recognized it as Michele Devon.

"Honey, he wants this place, her house, shop, and land. He doesn't care about her. Barbara is the tip of the iceberg. Once he gets her place, he'll drive us out of business and build that stupid development he's been talking about."

"You're right, Evan. He's after all of us and we don't have the money to stop him."

The remainder of the conversation drifted away from me as the couple walked farther into the darkness. I thought of following but decided not to since I wasn't familiar with the grounds.

As I left the garden area, I caught sight of George Randle hurrying around the side of the house. There were a few people on the porch when I returned, and I got caught up in a conversation about development and urban sprawl. I really didn't want to contribute anything, but the five members of the group were tenacious, and I wound up spending nearly an hour discussing archaeology and salvage sites.

It was eleven-thirty when I finally got away from them, but I couldn't find Barbara or Michele. Sally and George were in the kitchen arguing about something, and I stayed away from that. I was about to sneak upstairs when Andrea Hixon came running in from the porch.

"I can't find Derrick," she shouted at me. "Have you seen him? Where is he?"

"How the hell do I know?" I replied several decibels lower. "I haven't seen him or you since we first spoke."

Andrea twisted her skirt and shivered. "I can't find him, and no one's seen him."

"Have you tried the gardens?" I suggested.

Andrea shook her head and held out her hands in front of her. "He can't stay out there long. He's got allergies."

"This is a strange place to hold a fundraiser for a man with allergies." I didn't remember Derrick having allergies, but he could have developed them as he aged.

"I don't care what you think, you're wrong." Sally rushed from the kitchen and almost collided with Andrea.

George followed quickly but stopped a few feet away from Andrea. Sally turned right and stomped into the main yarn room Barbara used for her business. It was dark to discourage anyone from entering during the party. There was a thud and Sally shouted an obscenity as she fell. This was followed by several unintelligible words and a scream.

I raced to the room and felt alongside the wall for the switch, flooding the room with light. Sally had rolled away from a man's body sprawled on the floor with two knitting needles sticking out of him. One was in his abdomen and the other in his throat.

Seeing what she lay next to, Sally screamed louder and

scuttled away until stopped by a basket of alpaca yarn. The body was Derrick's. My first thought was that there was very little blood for someone who had been stabbed in the throat and abdomen.

Andrea moved next to me and screamed a long piercing sound, causing me to cover one of my ears. I pushed her gently out of the room and told George to call the police and ambulance. It took him a few seconds, but he pulled out his cell. His hands shook as he dialed and his face was white and clammy.

"Keep everyone out of here," I ordered. "And get Andrea away from this place."

George pulled Andrea away as her wailing subsided into sobs. I coaxed Sally out of the alpaca yarn and out of the room. Then I blocked the entrance with a side table and two chairs while we waited for the police.

State Police Detective Richard O'Mara arrived with the ambulance and two police cars. God only knew what George told them. O'Mara removed the table and went into the room to check Derrick, but I knew the man was dead. So did O'Mara.

The whole process of questions and interviews took several hours. I was on the wicker couch on the porch when O'Mara touched my shoulder, awakening me. I hadn't been interviewed yet. We discussed how I knew Derrick and when I'd last seen him. Since many people had confirmed my whereabouts, I had a built-in alibi.

"The others told me that you never checked the body," O'Mara said. "Why?"

"I knew he was dead. There was so little blood. And I didn't want to disturb the scene."

"I checked with the Falls Bend Police Department. Detective Manelli said you were a forensic archaeologist and historian, among other things."

"I'm retired and I analyze artifacts and excavate sites. I've seen my share of dead bodies, and Derrick was dead. But those needles, it makes no sense. It looks like he didn't put up a fight. Why didn't he scream? There were people around."

"I'll talk to you tomorrow," O'Mara said. He walked to his

car, leaving me to wonder exactly what Manelli had told him.

Two days later the crime scene was released and Barbara was free to open her store again. I helped her clean the room. There really wasn't much to do except for the drink that Derrick had spilled. Enough remained that the police had taken it as evidence. Barbara and I did a small ceremony and smudged the room using sage and lavender to get rid of any lingering negativity.

Barbara was busy opening the store when two officers arrived and asked her to accompany them for questioning. I protested but Barbara shrugged it off and asked me to take care of the store until she returned. I told her to get a lawyer and not answer any more questions without one.

"I'm innocent," she said on her way out of the shop.

Please. I've heard that before. How many people get into trouble with the words I'm innocent? Don't they know their rights? Don't they watch television? I called Sam Barton, my friend and the lawyer handling my inheritance, and asked that he find a lawyer for Barbara. He promised to call later after he made the arrangements.

"I'll pay for the retainer."

"I know," he said and broke the connection.

I spent the afternoon dusting and arranging the store. There were no customers and there was little more to do. I found a pair of mittens that had dropped behind arrangements of finished hats and scarves set in various baskets. When I lifted them I noticed something that looked like a small Tic-Tac except for the blue color. I used a tissue to pick it up and examine it, noting that there was a number impressed on it inside a tiny white circle. It was a pill. I dropped the mittens on the top of the scarf and hat pile and hunted for one of the small envelopes Barbara used to store tiny buttons. I found one, dumped the pill into it, and pocketed the envelope.

At five I closed the store and went to my bedroom. I stood there wondering if I should look at Barbara's medicine cabinet and finally decided I needed to do so.

But my search of the cabinet was fruitless. She had some prescription medication, but nothing looked like this pill.

So I called my good friend Jan Whitmore, chair of the biochemistry and forensic departments at Laurel Mountain

University. "Jan, I need your help."

"It's about your friend, isn't it? It's all over the news about Hixon's death and now your friend's arrest."

"No one told me she'd been arrested. Damn, I haven't been paying attention to the news. But I may have something that will help Barbara. I found a pill in the room where Derrick was killed. I'm surprised the police missed it. Probably because it was hidden behind some mittens."

"Your friend's pill?" Jan suggested.

"No, I checked and she takes nothing like it. I've never seen anything like it. I'm sending photos to you with a description." I took some photos of the pill with something to indicate its size and emailed them. "Jan, please see if you can discover what this pill is."

"Will do. You're right. It isn't anything I've come across. Did you use that spooky shamanic sense to try and feel what the pill was?"

"Yeah, and it felt like a chemistry lab. Call me when you find out anything." Just because I can sometimes sense information about objects doesn't mean it's a spooky shamanic sense. I've seen other people do this who were not shamans.

After my call to Jan, Barbara finally called to tell me that she'd been arrested for Derrick's murder. I couldn't breathe for a moment. I was very glad I'd alerted Sam.

"Don't say anything to the police, Barbara. I'm getting you a lawyer."

"But I have to explain about Derrick," she protested.

"Anything you say can be held against you and twisted by the prosecution to make you look like a knitting-needle killer. Just say nothing until you get back here. Talk to your lawyer and talk to me. No one else. Promise me."

"Very well. But I'll look silly."

"Well, better silly than in jail." With that I broke the connection.

Sam Barton returned my call that evening to say he'd found a defense lawyer and she would have Barbara back by tomorrow. I scrounged in the refrigerator for the leftover food from the party. I was looking for something to drink when I saw a container of liquid that looked like what Derrick had been drinking, complete with fizz. I opened it and found it was fermented apple cider. The label said "Evan's Best." Apparently Evan made it from local apples. I tasted it and it was definitely fermented. I wondered about Evan selling something slightly alcoholic, but I knew nothing about his business.

I ate and took a call from the lawyer, Leslie Getz, who told me the police could not hold Barbara even though her fingerprints were on the needles. They were her needles, and her prints were smeared. The autopsy report would be available in the morning and she'd bring a copy when she brought Barbara home. I told Leslie that I would pay her retainer. She said Barton had already confirmed this and wished me a nice night. With that thought I went to bed.

I jerked upright in bed. Yes, I'd heard something. It was a shuffling noise, faint since I was on the third floor, but my window was open and it sounded like someone was moving around in the room with all the yarn. I sleep in more clothes than most people wear outdoors, so I simply slipped into my flats, grabbed my cell, and headed downstairs.

I reached the first floor and suddenly thought that this was not a good idea, as I had no gun. I would've had a gun had I been in my own home. There were sensor nightlights on the stairs and ground floor, giving me enough light to see into the kitchen. I grabbed a rolling pin from Barbara's open utensils area, thinking how prosaic, a rolling pin.

I slunk toward the yarn room and turned on the lights. As light filled the room, the prowler turned and stared at me in surprise.

"Derrick?" He was white and somewhat transparent and the needles were still in place. "What the hell are you doing here?"

"I'm dead, and I can't move on until my murderer is discovered. Something is holding me here." He kept staring at me. "Hey, you can see me."

"No shit. And you woke me. What do you mean, you're trapped here?" I shivered at the thought of giving him a ceremony to cross over. That would tax even my late aunt's abilities.

"I don't know." He seemed so pathetic that I almost took pity on him.

"Can't you get rid of those knitting needles? You look ridiculous with them sticking out of you."

He shook his head. "I can't."

"Who killed you, Derrick?"

"I don't really know."

Now, I've seen ghosts before, and every ghost who was a murder victim can't remember who killed them. It's as if they suffer some post-traumatic stress afterlife disorder. It would make my life so much easier if they could remember.

"Can you remember what happened?" I finally lowered the rolling pin to my side.

He shook his head. "I didn't even know I was dead until someone stuck the knitting needles in me. Jessie, you've got to help me so I can get unstuck from this place. There's so much yarn and stuff. I need to go elsewhere." And he was gone.

God, I hate ghosts. Getting him out of here would be my first priority, just to give Barbara some peace. The guy was a pain while he was alive; she didn't need him as a creepy ghost hanging around. I put the rolling pin on the counter, turned out the light, and went back upstairs. Guess the smudging did no good, since he was still here in disembodied form. Maybe something else — silver, holy water — but no, he wasn't a vampire, just a very nasty piece of work.

I crawled into bed and settled back. Then I again sat upright. What did he mean he didn't know he was dead until someone stuck knitting needles in him? That meant he was dead before the needles were inserted. That was why there was so little blood. And if that was the case, the autopsy would confirm it.

At home I might have called Manelli about what I'd learned, but O'Mara probably wasn't ready to accept the word of a shaman visited by the ghost of her former boyfriend. I'd wait until I met with the lawyer and got the autopsy report.

The next morning, after breakfast, Leslie Getz arrived with Barbara, who hurried into the house and made for the elevator. "I need to take a shower and get that jail-house feeling off me."

I glanced at Leslie, who shrugged. "She was just in the

county jail, separate cell, even had her own clothes."

"Probably just feels creeped out, as anyone would," I replied, knowing that Barbara, as a sensitive, would feel more than just creeped out. "Do you have a copy of the autopsy?"

Leslie shrugged again. "I have a preliminary report, but some of this is being kept confidential for now. All I really can tell you is that he wasn't killed by the knitting needles, and toxicology is not back."

There is an old Spanish saying: The horns of a dilemma are often on the same bull. It was so true in this case. That little pill I'd found now loomed large as one of the horns. But if I gave it to the police, Barbara could be arrested. Hence the second horn.

"Leslie, I need you to please wait here until I speak with Barbara. It's crucial."

Leslie had good instincts and I suspected she knew something was wrong. So she dropped a copy of the preliminary autopsy report on a nearby table and walked into the yarn room, intent on investigating the former crime scene while I ran up the stairs to Barbara's room.

Barbara was wrapped in a robe, ready for a shower, with fresh clothes laid out on the bed. "Jessie, what's wrong?"

"In the first place, I shouldn't have run up two flights of stairs, and in the second, look at this. Do you know what it is?" I dumped the pill onto the glass top of her dressing table. "No, don't touch it."

She jerked back her hand and studied it. "I've never seen anything like it. What is it?"

"It's a pill." I explained how I discovered it. Barbara had no idea how it ended in the corner beneath a pair of mittens. "It's not yours?"

She shook her head, but I already knew that. I shoved the tiny pill back into the envelope again, using a tissue, and hurried back to Leslie. She was waiting when I got to the bottom of the stairs.

"What's the problem?" she asked.

I showed her the pill and explained where I had found it and that Barbara didn't recognize it. I told her I had checked the medicine cabinet first, thinking it was one of Barbara's.

"I could say it may or may not be relevant, but we both

know that it is and that it was found at the crime scene. But this was after a search by the police that wasn't a good one. You'll have to let them know. It's best to be upfront about this," she said.

"I agree."

I shook hands with Leslie. She left and I placed a call to the state police detective. O'Mara was in and listened to my story. He said he'd be out in half an hour and not to touch anything else in the yarn room, where the body had been.

My cell vibrated. Jan was on the other end, nearly breathless. "Oh my God, Jessie, do you know what that pill is?"

"Now why would I've called you if I'd known?"

"Do you know what a MAOI is?"

My brain hurried through some biochemistry and came up with monoamine oxidase inhibitor. "Yes. Is that what the blue pill is? I thought those were older anti-depressants."

"Well, yes and no." Jan sighed. "That little thing is related to Selegiline, or more commonly Eldepryl. But not the stuff that's on the market. No, that little baby is Seledil and it's a new, more powerful drug."

"What!" I looked at my phone for a moment before returning it to my ear. "It's still an antidepressant?"

"Oh, yes. Where did Barbara get it?" Jan asked.

"She didn't, as far as I can tell. She came home this morning and said she never saw it before. Is it for real or a placebo?"

"Drug protocols are strict, but from what I have read about this, the pill is no placebo. The formal testing was done. There is just a series of additional small group tests, and one of these is in State College. And guess who is running the tests?"

No, it couldn't be. The only thing that company ever did was electronics. "Hixon Industries? When did they get into pharmaceuticals?"

"About five years ago," Jan replied. "I checked their website, and this is the first foray into this specialized drug. It's a serotonin uptake inhibitor."

"Could Derrick have gotten hold of this drug?" He owned the place. Why not?

"I don't know. Maybe, but why? If you take this drug you can't drink any wine, anything fermented, or take allergy medications. You can't even take St. John's wort capsules. It will cause a massive heart attack. The dietary restrictions on this drug are tighter than for the other MAOIs."

I moved to the table where Leslie had left the preliminary autopsy report. Cause of death? Yep: Derrick had a massive heart attack. But the report was listed as preliminary until the toxicology data was completed.

"Jessie, are you still on the phone?"

"Yes, I'm reading the prelim report. Derrick died of cardiac failure big time. Shit! Listen, Jan, I have to go. I think the police just arrived. I'll call later." That bull just grew another horn, a big one.

I saw Detective O'Mara through the screen door and waved at him to enter. He came into the room and I suggested that we go into the kitchen and have some coffee. He agreed. Once we were seated at the table, I explained what I'd found and where and handed him the envelope.

"Did you touch this?" He indicated the pill inside the envelope.

"Only using a tissue," I said.

"I'll have to get at least one investigator to go over that room again," he said while pocketing the envelope.

"It's not Barbara's," I said. "In fact, it has to belong to someone from Hixon Industries."

O'Mara's face took on a wary expression. "Why? Do you know what it is?"

I explained my call to Jan and her response. At Jan's name, he relaxed a bit and I realized he knew who she was. She was well-known among law enforcement for her trained technicians and her experimental work in forensics. "I have no idea who got this drug, but you have to be in the test group to get it. Most drug protocols are very strict."

"And easily circumvented by clever people." O'Mara took a sip of coffee. "Though from what you say, this drug is very dangerous."

"It's a real killer." Whoops, bad pun. I added aloud, "And that's probably what killed Derrick." I quickly took another sip to stop from saying anything else.

"Manelli warned me about you, but you're most likely right. The coroner said the massive heart attack was induced.

He suspected some sort of drug. Toxicology just hasn't come back yet."

I placed my mug on the table. "Even if they know it's an MAOI, they might not know that it's part of this special study."

Barbara entered the kitchen and stopped when she saw O'Mara sitting at the table. He rose. "I was just leaving," he said. "Your friend will explain it to you."

After he left, Barbara and I sat and talked. I needed to know more about the people around Derrick and the people at the party. And I was curious about Evan's fermented apple juice. For if that was what Derrick had been drinking and he had Seledil in him, it probably helped to kill him.

Barbara promised to do a luncheon and invite Sally, Evan, Michelle, George, and Andrea if she'd come. Barbara was writing out a shopping list as I went to get the mail and newspaper. I stood at the mailbox to open the paper and nearly dropped the mail.

"Oh, crap!" I read the headlines of the Center Daily Times. Hixon Industries was being investigated by the IRS for money laundering and embezzlement. The chief suspect? Derrick Hixon. It seemed that his death caused the investigation to be made public.

A quick scan of the story revealed that Derrick had embezzled at least a hundred million dollars and patents for pharmaceuticals. Not only was the IRS after him, but so were several drug companies. Which explained how he could get his hands on the Seledil. I doubted that he was depressed. In the land of depression, Derrick was a carrier.

I made coffee and Barbara and I drove to the grocery store to shop for the luncheon. Everyone had RSVPed, even Andrea. I wondered what she'd be wearing.

By one-thirty the following afternoon, everyone was seated in the screened-in gazebo that had been built in the middle of the flowerbeds on Barbara's property. It was raised a few feet and gave a view of the gardens and the vegetable plantings beyond them.

Barbara outdid herself by serving her special seafood platter with shrimp, crab wrapped in bacon, mushrooms stuffed with crab, and shrimp and lobster rolls. There were additional platters of fresh fruit and vegetables. She served wine. The intro cocktail was a tequila sunrise.

The fresh veggies were courtesy of Evan, and Michelle brought pastries and crusty French bread. George arrived dressed to advertise that his store also sold men's upscale clothing and Andrea arrived wearing some couture fashion cut too low at the neck and too high along the thigh. Worse still, it was a sparkling cobalt blue. The rest of us wore everyday casual. What was this thing about clothing with George and Andrea?

Everyone tucked in except Andrea, who picked at her meal with the excuse, "I have to watch my figure."

"You need a bit more food," Barbara said. "I know that Derrick's murder was a shock, but you can't stop eating altogether."

"Your clothes will hang on you worse than they already do," George added while stuffing a baconwrapped crab morsel into his mouth.

"Shut up, George." Andrea smacked her fork on the table. "From now on I can pick out my own clothes. Derrick had awful taste, and you encouraged him to buy all the time." She knocked back her cocktail, followed by a wine chaser. Then she refilled her glass to near over-flowing before George snatched the bottle away.

George coughed and took a sip of wine. "You've no taste. Besides, there's no money since the IRS froze everything at Hixon and his estate. You'd better eat here unless they left you money to buy food."

"That's enough," Barbara insisted. "This is to be a luncheon, not a fight."

"Evan, did you serve Derrick any of that fermented apple cider at the party?" I asked as I munched on a shrimp.

Evan nodded. "It was the strangest thing. He wanted some of it, but not wine. He just wanted it to look like he was drinking. He said he couldn't get drunk."

That solved one problem. "Andrea, you said Derrick had allergies. Did he take any medication for them?"

Andrea sniffed her shrimp before taking a tiny bite. She shook her head. "He had an aversion to medications. Rarely took an aspirin. He just put up with the sniffling."

Barbara and I looked at each other across the table. If

Derrick hadn't taken the Seledil, who was it meant for? How did it end up in his system? He was accused of stealing patents. But if he had the patent, why would he have needed the actual drug?

Sally asked, "Is your store finally open for business again?"

Barbara nodded. "Yes, though I don't want those needles back, ever. And the crime scene people took a pair of mittens when they came back yesterday."

Andrea glanced at Barbara. "Why?" She was breaking her bread into tiny pieces.

"Seems they think the person who stabbed Derrick used the mittens to hide their fingerprints. Mine were smeared on the needles, but they're my needles. I don't want the mittens back either."

George hiccupped after sipping more wine. "He was stabbed to death with knitting needles. I may never look at a knitted item again."

"You ass," Andrea shouted as she stood. "You can't easily stab a person with a knitting needle. You have to make a small cut first to open a wound."

Birds chirped, insects hummed, even the ice in the bowl supporting the wine cracked, sounding like a gunshot. I hadn't read the entire preliminary autopsy report that Leslie left, but I just bet it said there were nicks at the throat and stomach not due to the needles.

"Did you use the mittens to cover your hands —" but I never got to finish. Andrea tore out of the gazebo and headed for her car. She gunned the engine and sped from the driveway, sending a rooster tail of gravel in her wake.

"Excuse me a moment," I said and ran into the house. Barbara had filed the autopsy report with other stuff Leslie left for her. I pulled out the report and finally skimmed the entire thing. The toxicology had not yet been completed, but the pathologist noted the nicks on the neck and stomach where someone had made openings with a knife.

"I wonder what knife she used?" The utensils used that night were from the catering service. I wondered if O'Mara had checked with the caterer to see if any knives were missing.

"Well, the party's over." Barbara came into the kitchen with a tray of leftovers. Evan and Michelle followed with the rest.

I came into the kitchen from Barbara's office, which was tucked away in the yarn room. "My question is did she kill him?"

George came into the kitchen with the empty wine bottle. "Bitch stabbed him."

"No," Barbara said as she placed the tray on the counter. "Jessie discovered that he was poisoned. If she stabbed him, he was dead before that."

George placed a hand over his mouth. He slowly let it fall to his side. "Those damned pills. Derrick said Andrea was depressed and he had something that would make her feel better."

"Did you see the pills?" I asked.

George shook his head. "No, but — but he gave me something to hold for him. He said it was an insurance policy. He was leaving Andrea. Oh, my God." George dropped the wine bottle in the recycling bin and hurried from the house.

"Why would Derrick give George anything?" I asked. "Why do you think?" Sally said.

"Derrick and George?" Barbara gasped. "Oh, yuck! I thought George had better taste in men."

"I tried to tell George to dump Derrick that night at the party, but he said he loved him," Sally explained as she placed a tray of fruit on the counter.

Forget the horns of the dilemma. This bull just grew a rack of antlers.

"The service for Derrick is tomorrow," Evan said. "Maybe you should call that police detective."

"He'll be there. Question is, did Andrea kill Derrick or merely use the knitting needles to implicate Barbara?" I said.

The local funeral home held an open-casket viewing of Derrick. After the viewing, those attending the cremation would drive to the small chapel adjacent to the crematorium. Andrea left first but Barbara and I hung back waiting for George. I watched as he leaned over the body, placed something in Derrick's coat pocket, and hurried away.

My mouth hung open. Derrick had been planning to leave Andrea for George? What had George put in Derrick's pocket?

"Ready?" Barbara asked.

George met us at the door and the three of us left as the funeral director closed and locked the casket. I drove Barbara's car.

"Oh, you've got to be kidding, George!" Barbara removed a tissue and I realized that she wasn't crying but laughing. "Derrick was gay? Holy Queen of the Angels, he'd never get a senate seat in Pennsylvania. But it's so funny because he was such a hypocrite."

"Yeah, well, I know Andrea killed him. I just can't prove it."

The drive was short and everyone filed into the small chapel next to the crematorium and found a seat. Barbara and I sat next to George, Sally, Michelle, and Evan, directly behind Andrea and members of her family and Derrick's brother and mother. I looked around but O'Mara was nowhere in sight.

The casket was brought in and placed on a conveyer device that would take it into the furnace room after the service. The minister began the service just as Barbara whispered to me, "I have an idea for proof." She turned to George and raised her voice. "What did you put in Derrick's jacket pocket before the casket was closed?"

George turned a startled face to Barbara. "What — what are you talking about?"

"Jessie and I saw you. And by the way, George, I'd hope you'd find someone better than Derrick."

The minister droned on as Andrea turned and faced George. "What does she mean? What did you put in Derrick's pocket?"

"It was an insurance policy, you bitch!" he snorted. "You freak!"

"You weirdo!" he countered.

By now no one was paying attention to the minister. Something far more interesting was taking place in the two front rows.

"It was bad enough he was leaving me, but leaving me for you? No, no! That was unacceptable," Andrea shouted.

Derrick's mother fainted. Andrea's brother tried to shush her, but she had no part of shushing. The minister stopped and gave a signal to the funeral director and the conveyer began to move, the casket slowly advancing to a curtained-off area.

"What the hell did you put in his pocket?" Andrea shouted.

"I told you, an insurance policy. I didn't want his money, Andrea. I wanted him."

Andrea opened her Juicy Couture bag and pulled out a forty-five. Everybody within three pews hit the floor. From the floor Michelle was busy dialing 911. Evan was holding onto her.

"What was it?" Andrea demanded, waving a gun that was far too big for her.

"A flash drive with the Cayman Islands bank account numbers," he stammered.

Barbara looked at Michelle. "Be sure that you tell the police that."

Before anyone could stop her, Andrea leaped from the pew and jumped onto the conveyer just as the casket entered the curtained area.

"No, Andrea!" her brother shouted as the casket rolled on, followed by Andrea.

I ran from the pew to the curtained-off area, thinking to grab Andrea, but she was already through to the furnace room. I raced from the chapel around to the side but stopped long enough to set Record on my cell phone. I yanked open the door to the furnace room. Andrea was banging on the casket. She let off two rounds into the furnace. One employee made for the open door, leaving air in his wake. I stepped inside.

The casket was stopped. Andrea demanded that it be opened. The other two employees were cowering beneath the conveyer belt.

"Open it," she demanded. "I want my money! No one is burning it."

"N-No one burns a casket," one of the employees whispered. "We take out the body and remove all metal and other stuff. We return it to the family with the ashes. We need a clean burn."

"Open the damned casket!"

"You murdered Derrick because he was running away with George," I accused.

"Well, it wasn't you he was running away with," she

grunted. "Besides, he was a prick, always telling me I needed to be dressed to the hilt and George had such good taste in clothing. Shit!" She started toward me. "All that money he embezzled he hid in a special account. No wonder I couldn't find the account numbers."

Andrea waved the forty-five and I ducked to the side of the door as George shoved his way into the room. "Jessie said you poisoned him."

"Those pills he got were for me. He was going to kill me. But I knew what they were and took them from his pocket at the fundraiser. I slipped one into his drink. And wham, bastard dies in Barbara's yarn room."

"I found one behind the mittens you used to put in the needles," I said, hoping to keep her talking until the police arrived. Apparently Detective O'Mara had skipped the cremation.

"Damned lid fell off and I had to pick them up in the dark. I thought I got them all, and I tossed the mittens behind that pile of knitted stuff. I used the needles to make Barbara guilty. Bitch still owes the estate $20,000."

"One pill rolled into the molding and hid there," I said. "Put down the gun, Andrea. I'll give you the money."

"Open the damned casket and get the flash drive," she ordered.

One of the workers unlocked and opened the casket. George took the drive from Derrick's pocket. He scuttled behind me and held out the drive.

"Give me the drive," she said, advancing on us in her five-inch stiletto heels.

"Come and get it," George sneered.

I took a step to the side and reached for the wall. I inadvertently shoved some long round tubes to the floor and they rolled into Andrea's path.

"Stop, Andrea," I shouted as she reached the tubes.

"When I finish George, you're next, Jessie." She took one step in her stilettos and staggered as they caught between the tubes. Andrea fell forward inches from me and I stepped aside, grabbing the forty-five as she flailed out, trying to break her fall.

"Gee, Andrea," George said as she hit the floor. "No red bottom on your shoes. Must be Louboutin knock-offs. You should buy originals; maybe then you could keep your footing in a crematorium."

Barbara, O'Mara, and I sat in the gazebo drinking Evan's fresh apple cider and nibbling on a tray of munchies that Barbara had fixed. The day was warm, insects buzzed, the cider was delicious, and Andrea was in jail.

"Your recording won't hold up in court," O'Mara informed me. "But we got a partial print from the pill, and Andrea has been confessing to anyone who will listen."

"Doesn't she have a lawyer?" Barbara asked.

O'Mara chewed slowly and smiled. "She does. Leslie Getz."

I chuckled. "Well, she can pay that bill on her own. Leslie doesn't come cheap." I should know, as I just paid the bill for the work she did for Barbara. "The $20,000 I gave Andrea to repay Barbara's loan won't go far."

"No matter." O'Mara snatched another shrimp from the tray. "She's claiming insanity and spousal abuse."

"He was going to kill her," I said.

"So she says. Who knows? A jury may believe her."

"What about George?" Barbara asked, munching on a pecan cookie.

O'Mara sighed. "No charges. He gave up the flash drive, and I think he realized later that Hixon would have gotten rid of him. Derrick had only one ticket to Brazil, one way."

"I feel for George," I muttered. "I have lousy taste in men too. I dated Derrick, but at least I dumped him."

Barbara smiled. "George will do fine. His shop is booming. Murder is titilating, and people will visit the place and the village shops."

"If Andrea had buried Derrick, the flash drive might never have come to light, especially if Barbara hadn't started that altercation. The body would never have been removed and any metal taken from it," O'Mara observed. "He'd have taken it with him, in a manner of speaking." I reached for a pecan cookie and watched Barbara bag the rest and offer them to O'Mara.

He accepted and rose to leave. "Are you staying for the rest of August, Jessie?"

I nodded. "Only two weeks left, and I can get some work

done here."

He left without another word. I wondered whether he hoped there would be no more excitement.

"You will come back next May when Evan and Michelle get married?" Barbara asked.

"Of course I will. Evan told me the wedding will be held in the gardens here."

Barbara nodded. "They will be in bloom and lovely in late May."

"And it's a wedding. What could go wrong at a wedding?"

Character Bios from Marge Burke

Gwyneth Sue Gates is quiet and over fifty. She would rather listen than talk and would never stand out in a crowd. Her passion is history, and she volunteers as a tour guide for the local historical society. Gwyneth likes to think she's in control, but Tazz will tell you otherwise.

Tazz Gates is a black and white lab/springer mix with a long, full tail. He has very expressive ears. He is full of energy, always ready for adventure, and extremely loyal. Mostly he thinks he's a person. Tazz's inspirational detective is Santa's most resourceful reindeer, Prancer.

Tazz & I hope you like these. love, Marge 2016

WOOF!

What Happens in Vegas

Marge Burke

I was trying very hard not to shame myself. It wouldn't do to lose my cookies over Utah. My Gwyneth would be so embarrassed.

How I even found myself on a Learjet, nose pressed against the window at heaven-knows-how-many feet in the air, is a pure amazement to me. One minute Gwyneth was talking on the phone to her boss about a convention, and the next minute we were on this plane zooming across the United States. Of course, time is relative to me, so I'm sure it wasn't just a minute. But you get the picture.

One thing is very clear to me, however. Had it not been for the corporate jet, I would not have been panting at 30,000 feet. At least not with my tongue dripping slobber onto the window. I would have been crated and stuck in the belly of some Boeing 727, jostled around like a leaf in a windstorm in complete darkness. Thank heaven Mr. Boss likes dogs. Loves dogs, actually. And he took a liking to me right off.

I felt a little queasy when the wheels hit the tarmac and pressed my shoulder against Gwyneth. She put her arm around me and kissed my forehead. She has a way of calming me down; but then, I can wrap her around my paw, as well. I guess you could say we are the perfect team. First things first, though, and we both made a pit stop. Me first. Then we went downstairs.

Gwyneth grabbed the luggage spewing from a black hole onto a rotating floor that left my already-spinning head spinning, and I staggered out to the curb. Several people were stowing our gear into the back of a … Holy Bigness. A limo. I had never seen a limo like this, with fur walls, leather seats, black lights, and even a bar. Someone opened a bottle of water, poured some into a cup, and held it out to me. I lapped away, hoping that the obvious wouldn't happen until I could find a fire hydrant or at least a palm tree.

"I'm glad you could bring Tazz on the trip, Gwyneth. He's a great addition to our party." Water Boy scratched my ear.

"I can't thank you enough for including him, Jeffrey,"

Gwyneth said, taking a drink of Diet Pepsi. "I have a hard time leaving him behind these days."

"The hotels have no problems with pets, as long as they're leashed," Mr. Boss added, smiling. I noticed he had a beer; Gwyneth and I don't drink, but I already knew that this crowd would fit right into the party life of Vegas. We planned to go our own way during free time, so we could explore the city. I couldn't wait — I'd especially heard a lot about M&M World, and I wanted to see this four-story wonder for myself.

The Bellagio Hotel welcomed us. I should say it overwhelmed us.

"I wish you could see colors, buddy," Gwyneth said, looking up. "That is beautiful!" She pointed to what must have been colorful glass flower petals reflected from the ceiling, and a ginormous glittering horse stood in a frozen prance in the center of the lobby. There was an entire room filled with igloos, penguins, frozen tundra, and ice sculptures. I was pretty sure I didn't want to go in that room. It would be very cold on my little paws — it was real snow and ice, right?

But in no time we had our key and were settled into our suite. The windows were low enough for me to get a glimpse of the city; Caesar's Palace and the Rio were right outside our window, and they glowed with multi-colored lights. I'm not sure why Gwyneth thinks I don't see colors. I'd like to set her straight about that. Because I do. Maybe just not all of them.

The entire city glowed with lights. The reports were right-on: This city never slept.

We were curled up on the bed, watching the history channel, when Gwyneth looked at her watch. Then she squealed and jumped up, grabbing her jacket, the hotel key, and my leash. We took off at a run. I had no idea where we were going: down the elevator, out the side door, running along the rounded sidewalk toward the street.

Suddenly the water beside us erupted with lights and sound, dancing and spurting to the music. We stood, fascinated, watching the fountains burst with some unseen force. People around me were ooohing and ahhhhing about the colors, but I guess I didn't see all that. I could, however, feel it from the inside out, along with the light spray of the water on my fur. That was probably the most amazing thing I had ever seen in my short life, and I was too captivated to even move.

I realized that Gwyneth still clutched the leash in her hand and had not even fastened it to my collar. I nudged her, and when she reached down to rub my neck, she realized it as well. Ah, there. We were safe now, all hooked together.

We had just turned around when I saw a little commotion near the sidewalk. Several people were watching a tree. Now I like trees — they serve a definitepurpose for me – but this one appeared to be very small and ordinary. As I watched, the tree moved. Hmmmm … maybe not so ordinary. I let out a quiet bark, and Gwyneth turned around. The tree was indeed moving. A small step to the left, then the right. A branch would move up, then down. For the life of me, I couldn't tell the difference between that tree and the one beside it.

"Would you look at that," Gwyneth said, grabbing her camera. But it was too dark, and she couldn't get a clear image of the human tree. It was more like a real tree than the ones around it. I could well imagine chasing a cat up that tree. I was sorely tempted to lift my leg, but as always, Gwyneth sensed my next move and nixed it. That would have been something to write home about, though.

Slowly we walked back to our room, neither of us speaking. Well, I generally didn't speak in the same way she did, but I could communicate when necessary. I think we both felt that we just needed to reflect. That was cool.

It must have been about 4:00 a.m. when the alarm on the phone rang. I leaped off the bed and barked once as Gwyneth grabbed the phone.

"Crap!" she fussed, trying to shut it off. "I forgot to change the alarm." I stood panting until she had things under control. "We have another two hours to sleep, puppy. Let's get to it."

She rolled over and I hopped back on the bed, easing my way toward the headboard. I always waited until she was asleep to actually cuddle, but in the morning, my head would be on the other pillow, and when she opened her eyes, she would be staring into my deep brown ones. Ah, bliss.

This time when the alarm went off, I knew it meant up and at 'em. I did my usual morning stretch while Gwyneth threw on her gym shorts and tank top. We trotted down the hall until we came to the elevator. Well, I trotted; she walked. This was crazy, in my opinion. We got shoved into this little room with no windows and a bunch of buttons. Gwyneth pushed a button and the bottom dropped out of my stomach. She seemed unconcerned, but I was seriously convinced that we might be plummeting to our death. When the door opened, we were in the lobby.

Quickly we found the designated pet relief area – such a quaint name! – and got back in the elevator. This time we were in it for only a few seconds when the door opened and we stepped into a room full of sweaty people on machines. Yikes. I kept my tail to myself, thank you. I didn't want to be someone's ground meat.

I was relieved to recognize that crazy belt treadmill thing that Gwyneth had at home, and soon she was running without going anywhere. Seemed pretty silly to me, but it made Gwyneth happy, and her happy is my happy. So I curled up on the spare towel and people-watched while she puffed, but I was glad to finally be heading back to our room.

She was about to step back into that plummeting room again when I heard her gasp. I stood my ground and growled.

"Shhhh! Tazz! It's okay, really!" She turned to the person stepping out of the elevator. "Dr. Lang! What are you doing here?"

"Gwyneth!" He reached out and gave her a huge hug. "It's the annual dental convention and training seminar. It's always held in Vegas."

"Oh, right. I remember hearing that before. You have a photo in your exam room, right?"

He laughed, and I liked the way he laughed, even though he hadn't petted me yet. I really like the behind-the-left-ear thing.

"Who's with you? Your wife? Office staff?"

"Just me this year. Alexis stayed home with the kids; too many sports events, and they'd miss too much school." He looked at me sort of sideways, as if to determine what he actually thought about me. "I left the office in capable hands."

"I'm sure the girls will handle things." She paused. "Dr. Lang, this is Tazz. He's my best bud, and we go everywhere together." She smiled at me, and I knew that everything was okay. I barked once, my "wanna be friends" bark.

"Hey, Tazz. I've heard about you. I'm honored to finally meet you." He not only scratched behind my left ear but rubbed my chest and patted my snout. Great guy, this.

By now a woman had stepped out of the elevator and was standing quietly behind Dr. Lang. She looked a little peaked and was doing a little nervous-type thing with her hands. Her eyes were kind of wide and tense looking.

"Gwyneth, Tazz, this is Maryann, my former intern. She now has her doctorate in specialized dentistry and is teaching one of the classes over at the MGM later today. I didn't even know she was going to be here." The doctor introduced everyone all around.

Maryann and Doc exchanged glances, and I know that Gwyneth saw them. She furrowed her brow and looked at me, but just for a second. It doesn't take much for us to communicate.

"We'd best be going," he said. "Want to do a little spa workout before the sessions start." One more pat on my head and a wave to Gwyneth, and they disappeared through the swinging doors to the right.

"That was strange. We'll have to keep my eyes open to see what that was about, won't we?" Gwyneth said as we entered the elevator. We soon had our day well under way.

We had a grueling day of convention sessions and rabbit food (yuck) for lunch. By evening Gwyneth and I decided we needed to stretch our legs. Everyone else was going to the Hard Rock Vegas for drinks, but again, Gwyneth and I don't drink — except for diet soda.

"Let's walk through Caesar's Palace, pup," Gwyneth suggested. It was connected to our hotel, so we wove our way through the casino, around the gaming tables, and past the bars.

I was a little concerned about Gwyneth. Did she think we were in Rome? I really thought Caesar had died a few days ago. But then time is not relevant to me, as I mentioned earlier.

We turned a corner and I stopped dead in my tracks. However did we get outside? I thought it was getting dark outside. But the sky here was bright blue, with white puffy clouds. We seemed to have stumbled into a village, almost like a Brigadoon, with cobblestone streets and ancient storefronts. It did feel like we were walking the streets of ancient Rome. I didn't know much about money or prices, but I could tell just by the way those stiff lady mannequins were posed in the windows that whatever was in there was way past our means.

I looked up to see Gwyneth's mouth hanging open and her eyes wide like Frisbees. She took several tentative steps and I slunk alongside, trying to take it all in. We both seemed to hear the sound of splashing water at the same time and moved toward a center courtyard.

Holy Coliseum. We had transcended not only time but space as well. How had we gotten to Rome without leaving the building? Directly in front of us was a fountain, with Zeus or some unholy god seated in the center, while several life-size statues — or were they real people pretending to be statues? Or statues pretending to be real people? — stood ankle deep in the water paying homage. The whole thing was supported by marble columns, ancient ruins with centurions holding spears. They were poised at the very top, illuminated against the blue sky spattered with those puffy clouds. It was almost too much to take in.

Gwyneth sighed in ecstasy as she snapped photos with her digital camera; I took the opportunity to slurp a few laps of water. Goddesses held urns that spilled water into the pool. Ahhh, so cool and refreshing. I may have overdone it, though; where exactly were those pet-relief areas?

We twisted our way back down the cobbled streets, but after about fifteen minutes it became obvious we had no idea where we were. We stumbled around through the bars and past the casinos, trying to find our way. There were several gambling kiosks, and a cage with young girls dressed in nothing but feather boas hanging from the bars. Shameless. Those boas looked almost alive, the way they undulated. I'd sort of like to try it, though. I think my tail could do that.

We finally managed to get back to where we started. I felt immense relief and was strolling happily to the lobby when Gwyneth stopped short. I looked up quizzically and saw her staring at that Maryann girl we had met yesterday with Dr. Lang.

Gwyneth and I moved closer and watched with the crowd that had gathered. It was obvious that something huge was going down. The guy next to me muttered something about winning big money. We pushed in farther and saw some huge dude with his hand on her shoulder. He was applying pressure, and she winced as he tightened his grip. Gwyneth tightened her grip on my collar and I pushed against her leg.

"Sorry, pup," she whispered.

As I stood there, a buzzing began to tingle in my ears, and I shook my head fiercely. It almost sounded like a Japanese beetle had climbed down my ear canal, something that had happened before and let me tell you. It wasn't just a buzz, actually; it was more like scrambled voices. I couldn't make out what they were saying, but I knew this wasn't good. We canines get feelings about these things.

Someone else at the slot machines started shouting accusations, something about cheating, and the big dude pulled Maryann back and nodded. She picked up her chips and moved toward the little office in the back. The dude had a tight grip on her elbow. I looked up and saw that Gwyneth had watched the whole thing transpire.

We wandered around some more. I think Gwyneth could have spent days exploring the casinos. At some point we turned around and ran smack into Dr. Lang.

"Gracious!" Gwyneth gasped, righting herself. "I'm so sorry. I wasn't watching where we were going."

"No problem." He reached down to scratch my ear, but his heart wasn't in his hand. "Have you seen Maryann? She was to meet me for dinner to go over her notes." He indicated a folder with pages poking out in all directions. His face turned a tomato shade of red and his smile was lopsided. "I'm not real organized."

"Apparently not." Gwyneth smiled. "As to Maryann, I saw her earlier; she may have gone to the ladies'. Why don't you just wait over there by the lounge area? I'm sure she'll be along."

"I'll do that. You two have a nice night." He strolled off, his eyes sweeping the crowd.

"I don't like that, Tazz. Maryann looked very frightened, and Dr. Lang was definitely concerned at her absence. Something's up."

I agreed.

Mr. Boss sprang for all of us to go see Love – Cirque du Soleil – at the Mirage. I could not believe the way those performers were flung through the air, dropping from the ceiling and springboarding from one stage level to the other. They were decked out in costumes of every type, from feathers to flowers and then some.

As I watched several octopuses dangle above me, I let my gaze wander through the dim light. That was when I saw them. Doc and his ex-intern were in the corner seats below us, but Gwyneth didn't appear to notice them. Maryann was clinging to him in what appeared to be desperation, while he was focused on the performers.

I glanced up again to watch the octopus under the sea over my head and became totally mesmerized. When I looked down again, Dr. L and Maryann were gone.

Strange of them to leave in the middle of the show. Especially when it was so amazingly terrific. I trotted with Mr. Boss's group back to the hotel, listening to them chatter about Love. But my mind was stuck on Dr. Lang and his ex-intern.

The next morning we skipped the convention and decided to explore. After watching another rumbling water show in front of the Bellagio — Gwyneth never seemed to tire of that — we made our way over to the Venetian. We went down a set of twisted steps, got in line, and next thing I knew we were in a gondola, floating along a little canal with some guy in a striped shirt and a flat hat guiding us along with a pole.

Before I even realized what was happening, we were inside a building that was outside. How in the world do they do that? The outside-inside of this building was ancient ruins, three stories high with torches illuminating the arched windows. We went through a tunnel and were suddenly in a marketplace, with people milling around shopping and eating. I could eat. I can always eat.

As we passed the little bistro, Gwyneth nudged me. "Look, puppy."

I looked. It was Dr. Lang with Maryann, going over those sloppy notes. Her eyes looked glassy, like she had been awake all night or had been crying. Dr. Lang just kept talking (guys don't notice these things — except for me, and I'm an exceptional kind of guy) until Maryann stood, took the folder, half-heartedly hugged Dr. Lang, and left. We floated past without either of them noticing us, and soon were back on dry land.

We explored until after dusk, having munched and

snacked our way up one side of the street and down the other, weaving in and out of hotels. We watched the pirates and the mermaids and the ships at Treasure Island, and I was seriously afraid we were going to get blown into the next state if those cannons misfired.

Darkness had just settled in when in front of us there was a huge flare-up and a volcano erupted, spewing lava and fire everywhere. That was pretty amazing, since it was in the middle of a small pool. The ground shook and the air echoed with thunderous explosions. This must be what they refer to as firewater. Hmm … What a wild, crazy city.

We walked through the Flamingo and immediately spotted Maryann. She was playing some table game and the big dude was behind her again. Gwyneth stopped, and Dr. Lang came up behind us.

"I wonder what she's doing. She doesn't gamble." He seemed to take it all in, from the crowd around her to the dude with the grip. Doc leaned around a few people. "Are you okay?" he asked Maryann.

I could see the fear in her eyes, although she smiled and nodded. The BD (Big Dude, for those who don't understand dogisms) shoved him back.

"Stay out of this." His fierce glare said he meant business.

"I was talking to the lady," Doc said, trying to push closer to her.

BD said something to Maryann, and she picked up her chips. They walked back toward the casino window that had a sign about collections, but Doc intercepted them.

"Look, buddy, leave her alone. She's —"

"I don't think you heard me. I said, stay out of this. She owes me, and until she pays, it is none of your affair." He stepped between Doc and Maryann and they disappeared into the crowd.

"Well, what do you make of that?" Doc asked no one in particular. I barked, reminding him we were there. "I hope she knows what she's doing. Her track record at the Rivers Casino back home is horrible. She makes a point to avoid it these days."

"She didn't look too happy," Gwyneth agreed. "But I'm not sure what we can do. I will, however, keep my eyes and ears open."

"That's a good idea. I'll pay closer attention myself." Doc turned to look at Gwyneth, then seemed to realize where he was. "How about we all have dinner tonight? I'll ask Maryann, too. Maybe we can get to the bottom of this. I'm not one to let sleeping dogs lie."

He grinned at me and scratched my right ear. Wrong ear, but that was okay. It still felt good.

"I've got a voucher for New York, New York," he continued. "We could have dinner, then maybe ride that rooftop roller coaster."

"I don't do roller coasters, but we'll meet you both for dinner. 8:30?"

"Yes. That's fine." He looked over his shoulder, and I could see he was still puzzled over the Maryann thing. "I'll catch up with Maryann, and we'll see you then. You too, pup." And he was gone.

We were at New York well before the time. I stood there on the street looking at the hotel, which actually looked like a street in New York City. There were dozens of building fronts, all shapes and sizes and colors, with that crazy looping roller coaster flinging itself around on top of the whole affair. Made my stomach loop just looking at it. Not for me, thanks.

We walked around the building a few times, down the block, and across the street, but by 9:00 I think we both had the sinking feeling that we had been stood up. Just to be on the safe side, Gwyneth and I went inside and asked if Dr. Lang or Maryann had been there, or if there were reservations, or if possibly they were waiting at a table. Doc's name was indeed on the list for 8:30 pm, but he had not shown up or canceled. Thanking the hostess, Gwyneth went outside, playing with my leash like she does when she's in deep thought.

Back at the Bellagio, we asked at the desk if Dr. Lang was in his room. They called but got no answer.

"Did he leave word that he was going out?" Gwyneth asked the clerk.

"No, nothing here in the notes," the clerk said, glancing at the counter. An older woman who was working in the same booth leaned across toward us.

"Your Dr. Lang did say he was going out. To meet a couple of ladies, I think he said. He was going to stop at M&M

World and grab some purple M&M's for a friend, he said, and a little bag of doggie treats, too. They have everything over there. I love that place! Four floors of nothing but M&Ms-- candy, books, games, clothes, pet toys. You name it. I always buy presents for my grand-kids there before going home to Kansas to see them. He may have just got carried away in there, looking at everything —"

"Thank you!" Gwyneth patted Grandma's hand and smiled, and we took off. M&M World was down the street a few blocks, on the other side by MGM Grand. She ran, I trotted. Delicious. Great stretch of the legs.

We arrived breathless and went through every inch of that place, but no Doc. And no Maryann. It's amazing to me that Gwyneth didn't even pause to check out anything. Maybe she picked up on my sense of unrest. There was definitely something going on here, with Maryann and now with Doc. I just hoped we'd have time to come back here. Those were some awesome M&M puppy treats there on the third floor.

We were back at the Bellagio in time to see the fountains, this time to the tune of "Proud to Be an American." It was mostly lost on Gwyneth. She was just leaning against the fence, staring over top of the splashing, rainbow-colored water show. I knew how she felt. I was worried, too.

Instead of going inside, she moved across the sidewalk and sat on a park bench. I sat beside her, leaning against her leg with my head on her knee.

"What should we do, pup? I can't imagine Dr. Lang being so casual about an appointment. I've been a patient of his for over 23 years, and you can learn quite a lot about someone in that amount of time. Plus he's one of our customers at the dealership."

"I can't call his wife. I don't know their number." She sat tapping her foot, making my head bounce up and down. I was getting a headache.

"I can, however," she said, pulling out her cell phone, "check in with his answering service. He's on my speed dial."

If anyone in the world needs a dentist on speed dial, it's Gwyneth. She has the worst luck with breaking teeth and popping crowns of anyone I know. Once she broke off a back tooth eating ice cream — go figure — and a crown popped off one morning when she was eating her oatmeal. Luckily the lumpy crown made itself known in the bowl of smooth oatmeal, or it would have been one crappy way to lose $1,200. Oh. Sorry for the pun.

"Uh, yes. Hello. My name is Gwyneth Gates, and I'm trying to locate Dr. Lang. We're both here in Las Vegas and I was wondering if he's checked in for messages this evening at all."

She nodded and murmured a few responses. "Thank you very much. Yes, yes I will. You, too." She shut the phone.

"Well, he usually checks in about 8:00 p.m., but they wouldn't tell me if they heard from him. Confidentiality and all that. She asked me a lot of questions, and I think they were fishing for information, too. Something is going on, pup. Something not good."

We walked back toward our room, but Gwyneth was extremely distracted. I kept walking past the elevators toward the shops. She just kept on walking beside me, looking around but clearly not seeing anything.

I pulled her toward Ye Olde Christmas Shoppe, knowing she wouldn't protest. Gwyneth is a true holiday fanatic, and although she doesn't usually make purchases, she loves to look. I led her around the store until we came to a display of Santa, his sleigh, and all nine of the reindeer. I saw Prancer right away, and very cautiously I sidled up as close as I could get. I nudged Prancer with the tip of my cold nose – I am very healthy – and then for extra measure I jangled the little bell on the sleigh's reins.

"Tazz! Don't touch the displays!" Gwyneth pulled at my leash, but I did this twist thing that I can do with my neck and slipped my collar. Before anyone could even protest, I escaped through the door and took off toward the garden room. It was the best place for an undercover dog to meet an undercover reindeer.

Gwyneth had looked up the Bellagio online before we left home. We saw the different ways the gardens were designed throughout the year. Last winter it was bright and colorful in honor of Chinese New Year. Right now, it was an arctic tundra. There were giant snowmen, huge snow-covered trees, dogsleds with fake dogs hitched to them. One husky had pretty eyes. Ooh la la! The most amazing things, though, were the igloos. Some even had smoke coming out of their chimneys. I made my way down the path, over the little bridge past a humongous elk, and peered inside the biggest igloo.

Sitting inside on a folding canvas chair was Prancer. He was wrapped in buffalo robes, holding a fishing pole and staring into a hole in the ice. A sea otter lounged at his feet, and a string of fish hung from a hook on the ceiling. He looked at me and motioned me inside. I stepped gingerly on the ice floor. Wait. It wasn't really ice. Was it?

"Well, Tazz. What brings you to the Frozen Arctic?" Prancer bounced his pole a bit, making the string jiggle in the "water."

"What are you doing?" I asked, ignoring his question.

"Ice fishing is a great way to unwind after a hard day. We do a lot of that at the North Pole, you know. Lots of ice and snow up there. This is nothing. But again, what brings you to my humble igloo?"

I filled Prancer in on the mystery: how Maryann was acting strangely, how Dr. Lang had disappeared, and that Gwyneth was worried. "I think she suspects foul play. Dr. Lang is nothing if not punctual and reliable, and he would not just disappear like that."

"Hmmm." Prancer reached down into a bucket beside him and pulled out a tiny fish. The otter opened his mouth. Prancer tossed the fish and the otter caught it, swallowed, and lay back down.

"I really think it's too cold for a swim, don't you, Tazz? I believe there are inside pools that are heated and can be used all year long, but generally speaking, going swimming fully clothed in the middle of the morning is not a good plan. You never can tell when that opportunity will present itself, though, so be on the lookout." Prancer snuggled deeper inside the robe and smiled. "You'll know when you see it."

I really wasn't sure about that. Sounded rather vague and off the subject to me. But I'd just have to be alert and pay attention. Prancer hadn't been wrong yet.

"Gwyneth will be frantic. I'd best get moving." I backed out the door of the igloo and right into an abominable snowman. "Oh, sorry, sir," I said. Then I realized he wasn't real. At least I didn't think he was real. I wasn't taking any chances. I was outta there.

Turning, I leaped over the bridge and landed on the path,

right at Gwyneth's feet. She had the leash in her hand and looked hot enough to melt the entire garden area if it were real snow. It wasn't real snow, right? Anyway, she was fuming.

"Tazz, you come with me right this minute. You gave me the fright of a lifetime. Who knows what could have happened to you? There are walking trees out there, and dancing fountains, and erupting volcanoes, and roller coasters on top of hotel roofs, and who knows what else. You, my four-legged friend, will stay right with me from now on, do you understand?"

I knew she meant business, so I submitted to the reattachment of the collar and followed her meekly to our room, where I settled in for a long winter's nap.

Over breakfast the next morning — after another session on that moving belt thing — Gwyneth discussed the case with me.

"Here's what we have. We have Maryann gambling, which Dr. Lang said she never does and was lousy at when she played for fun at the Rivers Casino. We have the big dude who seems to be strong-arming her everywhere she goes. Then we have the dude and Dr. Lang getting into a verbal altercation in the Flamingo.

"Now Dr. Lang has disappeared and no one has heard from him, including his answering service. I checked with them again this morning, and they said his wife hasn't heard from him since last night about 6:00 p.m."

Gwyneth finished her fruit and half of her bagel, then gave me the other half. Garlic doesn't always agree with me, but beggars can't be choosy, so I wolfed it down. I'd be spouting garlic breath big time, but then so would Gwyneth, so that was cool.

"Let's take a walk, pup. We have to figure this out."

Gwyneth and I walked through the lobby, out past the glass horse by the front desk, and into the street. There were several souvenir shops on the other side of the street, so we decided to check them out. It was really funky here, because to cross the street you had to go up a set of stairs, across a bridge with glass railings, and down some steps on the other side.

Much safer, but the bridge was lined with people begging for money, or painting pictures, or playing music, or just sitting with their dogs against the glass wall. There were street prophets standing on soapboxes shouting about the Lord, right next to shady-looking men slapping cards in the air, inviting gentlemen of the city to be entertained by ladies of the night. I wanted to bark at them, "Get a real job!" But since I couldn't speak human, I just walked beside Gwyneth like the respectably employed dog that I was and kept going.

We bought a few T-shirts, a hoodie, a deck of playing cards (it was Vegas, after all), several refrigerator magnets, and a travel mug. Then we crossed another bridge by a group of palm trees near the Luxor and headed back to the hotel.

We were trotting down the street when we saw this quaint little wedding chapel. It was the bottom floor of the Cosmopolitan, and the whole side wall was glass panels. There was a little altar with a trellis behind it, decked with white flowers and ivy.

But the amazing things were the chairs. Each wooden chair was painted to look like the back was a person sitting there, audience for the ceremony. I guess a lot of people come to Vegas to get married and don't have anyone else to attend. Perfect solution, I guess. Not for me, though. I'm a confirmed bachelor. I may look, but I never touch.

Gwyneth laughed and commented out loud that were of like mind.

There was even a couple standing near the back. She was dressed in a long white gown with a veil; he was in jeans, Nikes, and a Pink Floyd T-shirt. Whatever.

As we moved forward, I saw a sign. I can't always read — I have only basic letter recognition — but this I understood. It said something about ballroom dancing and synchronized swimming. Both on the fourth floor. Now that intrigued me! I dragged Gwyneth over to the hotel door and jumped in as it revolved past. She had no option but to jump in, too, or I would have been separated from her.

The elevator door was open, so I dashed for it. We reached it as the door was closing, and I yanked her inside. The door closed and we were on our way.

"What are you up to, Tazz?" she asked, irritation obvious in her voice. She adjusted her packages and pulled her hair from under her purse strap on her shoulder. The door opened on 3, but I wouldn't budge. She looked at me, perturbed, but the door shut and we were off again.

At 4, I slunk quietly out the door and sat down. She eyed

me strangely, as though she had finally figured out that I had something up my sleeve — er, fur.

We sneaked down the hall and around the next corner. I stopped on all fours and pushed against Gwyneth. She looked up and saw Maryann with the BD. He had her pushed against the wall and was poking his finger right in her face. This couldn't be good. She was crying and trembling and very upset.

Gwyneth grabbed my collar and pulled me behind a huge potted palm. I knew she was trying to hear what was being said, but with his back to us, we couldn't make it out. The Big Dude dragged Maryann through a set of double swinging doors to their left. Gwyneth strained to hear, but everything was muffled now.

Then suddenly I had that buzzing in my ears again, and it was voices. Only this time I recognized the voices. One of them was Doc, and the other was Maryann. They weren't talking to each other; it was just that I heard both of them at the same time. I shook all over, trying to clear my thoughts, and my collar clinked. Gwyneth grabbed it, and I tried to stop shaking my head.

The noises were in my head, but they were also coming from the room behind us. I pulled on Gwyneth and pushed against a second set of doors a few feet down. She signaled me to be quiet. I nodded. Then we slid into the room.

It was a kitchen of sorts, with stainless-steel counters and appliances and utensils spread out all over the center island. The noises were coming from a huge commercial-size radio on the counter.

"It's a shortwave radio, Tazz. It's picking up a signal from somewhere close." She got it. She tiptoed over and fiddled with the knobs until one band had a clear signal. I heard Doc.

"I'm telling you, I don't know anything. But I'll find out, you can be sure, and this will not go unpunished."

"Oh, so the big-shot doc thinks he can scare us! Hey, boss. Did you ever think that someone you trained in your safe, high-class little office would stoop to installing electronic devices in teeth?" BD laughed.

"It's supposed to pick up the radio signals from the electronic boards programmed into the games, so we know what to play to beat the system." He sneered. "But something went wrong. The signals are scrambled."

The word diabolical came to my mind, but I didn't know

what it meant. I was guessing it meant nasty. Just plain nasty.

"I think she messed this up on purpose, didn't you, little lady?" There was no mistaking the threat in BD's tone of voice.

"The casinos scramble the signals for that very reason. They all do it." Doc sounded like he was talking through clenched teeth. Like he was trying to stay in control or something. "If you'd done your homework, you'd know that."

Gwyneth moved carefully over to the swinging doors with the small window near the top; she peeked through. I could see through the crack between the two doors.

BD had tied Maryann's hands behind her back. Doc was sitting in a wing chair, his ankles and hands duct-taped together. A curtain tassel strapped him to the arms of the chair. BD was pointing a gun at him. I gulped. I don't, in any circumstance, mess with dudes with guns.

They were still talking.

"He forced me! I owed him a lot of money. We'd lose our house, and we have Joe's medical bills, and I couldn't let Joe know. He'd never get better. I had to do what he said—"

"Can it, chick. We don't want any sob stories." DB shoved her against the wall.

"Leave her alone!"

BD sneered. "Who's gonna make me? You?"

Dr. Lang's legs were taped together at the ankles. He tried to pull his wrists away from the chair arms, but he was stuck. So it's true what they say about duct tape.

Then I saw it. On the wall behind the Big Dude was a panel of buttons. There were words but there were also symbols. One was a disco ball — I looked up and saw several overhead. Must be for the ballroom, which was set up for dancing. Chairs were pushed back against the walls, with small cocktail tables between them for casual conversation, cocktails, and ladies' purses.

There were several buttons for different lights and the P/A system with the microphones. That was pretty clear. The last button was big and round and had one of those red circles with a line through it, and a swimmer in the center. Under the button in bold letters read POOL.

In a flash, I slipped my collar, slammed through the door, and raced to the far wall. One jump and I hit that button, and the motor began to churn. I leapt across the widening gap in the floor and watched in horror as BD and Maryann slipped into the water. The gun went flying and BD choked, arms flailing.

"Help! I can't swim!" he screamed, splashing and thrashing in the water as the floor kept moving toward the walls. I saw Maryann turn over onto her back and float, her head above the water, her feet paddling to keep her above the surface. Just as Gwyneth grabbed a knife from the counter and headed to Doc, his chair toppled into the pool.

She was in the water before I could move. The chair was heavy and pulled him down, and I saw panic on her face. She wasn't a hold-your-breath kind of lady. She grabbed the back of the chair and hung onto the side of the pool, but she couldn't move. I saw her glance toward Maryann, who was bobbing in and out of the water.

I swam over to Maryann and shoved her to the side. When I pushed her against the side of the pool, she could keep her head up. Gwyneth's eyes widened. She took a deep breath and let go, and she and Doc both went under. She sliced the tape on his right wrist, then came up for a breath. She dived back under and grabbed the chair, kicking furiously until Doc's free hand could grasp the pool edge. He hung on and she headed for Maryann.

As Gwyneth set about cutting them both loose, BD was still screaming.

"Let him sink," Maryann whispered. "Just let him sink."

"We can't do that. You know we can't."

When Maryann climbed out, I swam over to the side and she pulled me up. "Good dog. You are an amazing animal, you know that?" She hugged me despite my soaking wet fur.

Doc was finally free and climbed out as the chair sank to the bottom. He helped Gwyneth up. They were trying to find some way to subdue BD and drag him out of the water when Security showed up. Apparently an alarm went off all over the hotel when the pool floor opened.

It didn't take much effort to pull BD out and have him in tight custody before the police arrived. First time I ever saw a card shark that couldn't swim!

Everyone was talking at once, and there was a strange echo as their words bounced back from the short-wave radio in the kitchen. Gwyneth and Maryann were wrapped tablecloths, and I shook myself nearly dry.

I heard Prancer's words echoing in my head. "Swimming with their clothes on," he had said. And "in the middle of the morning," and "unexpected opportunity."

"Be on the lookout." I knew what that meant. I had seen an episode of some sixties' TV show where the kids were dancing at a high school prom when someone hit the button and wham! They all took a dive, like it or not. I had just recreated the scene. Quite well, I might add.

Someone slipped me a huge bone, and I just curled up on the rug in the corner and let them all sort everything out. Much-deserved treat. I'd done my part.

"That was some detective work, Tazz," Doc said, pushing back from the table and wiping his mouth on his napkin. He looked at Gwyneth.

"Who would have guessed that Maryann could install the transmitter in that dude's tooth and then he could force her to be the other half of the team? Would have worked like a charm, if the casino didn't scramble short-wave transmissions. Oh, and if Tazz hadn't broken up the act. Does he do this type of thing often?"

I looked at Gwyneth expectantly. I didn't like to toot my own horn, but I had been pretty successful solving some crazy crimes recently.

"Actually, yes he does. Mostly it doesn't make the papers because the authorities are embarrassed to be bested by a dog."

Doc laughed. "Well, that I understand." He reached over and scratched my left ear. Ah, heaven. "I'd be inclined to deny it if he took up dentistry and wrote the textbooks."

"I'll bring him to my next appointment. You can teach him everything you know."

"Thanks, but no thanks. We'll let him stick to playing detective."

"Fortunately for all of us," Gwyneth said, winking, "he wasn't playing."

Touché.

EPILOGUE

It was finally September and Manelli pushed on the red door into the archives room to find almost everyone in place in their old comfy chairs. In fact, except for a new coat of paint and a polished floor, he would never have known the room had been emptied, though a few of the writers sported tans. As one they stared at the old oak table, which held an impressive array of snacks.

"Glad to see everyone back here bright-eyed and bushy-tailed, whatever that means." He came to a screeching halt when he saw the new jet-black coffee contraption along with a twirly tree of cups boasting various flavors. "What is that?"

Jessie spoke up. "The chief of police gave us that for being so patient about our room."

"You mean it's a present?" Colleen asked.

Merris said, "This will never work. We'd have to wait in line for coffee."

"Has anybody tried it?" Nick asked.

Cassie dashed in and almost dropped her bowl of cookies. "What the —" She picked up the gift bag that must have contained the coffee system. "How did this get here?"

"The chief gave it to us," Jessie said. "Guess we have to use it. They must have pitched the old one."

Night Train tilted his head to one side. "Maybe we should try it. It's all we've got now."

"Why don't you take it, Cassie," Mary Alice offered. "We didn't get you anything for your honeymoon — and we're all afraid of it."

Cassie stared at the contraption. "I gave this to the library. I recognize the gift bag."

Manelli stared at her as though she gone run mad. "Why would you do that?"

"Because someone gave it to me for a wedding present and I didn't know what to do with it."

They all chuckled at the same time.

"Never fear. I took the old pot home to wash," Cassie said. She pulled it out of a bag. "I bought fresh coffee too."

A sigh of relief enveloped the group as Merris and

Gwyneth set to work making real coffee. Cassie put the coffee system back in the gift bag and dropped it into the large trash can, then went to her seat.

Merris stared into the trash can and pulled out the gift bag. "Waste not, want not. I can sell this at my shop."

Manelli glanced around at the group. "I've had enough phone calls to convince me none of you have been idle. Let's hear about your cases. Who goes first?"

Greensburg Writers' Group and Ligonier Valley Writers

The is the third anthology created by the Greensburg Writers' Group, an offshoot of Ligonier Valley Writers. GWG members are as strange as the members of the Sleuths and Serpents featured in the book. Many of them also belong to Ligonier Valley Writers: thus their generosity of time and talent in creating this collection.

In 2016, LVW celebrates thirty years of enriching experiences for readers and writers alike, an amazing accomplishment for an all-volunteer organization. Among the programs sponsored by LVW are an annual student poetry contest for grades 4-12, an annual horror story flash fiction contest, and The Loyalhanna Review, an annual full-color literary magazine. The two contests include cash prizes as well as publication for the winners.

The Loyalhanna Review publishes high-quality writing and art, most of it by western Pennsylvanians.

LVW presents guest speakers and programs for the community and workshops for writers. It also helps beginning and experienced authors with spinoff critique groups. There they can share their work and get solid advice from other writers on how to improve their stories, novels, essays, plays, and poetry.

All of these things cost money, something most writers sorely lack. So members of the Greensburg Writers' Group have created this book to raise funds for Ligonier Valley Writers. Check out www.LVWonline.org and take part in the fun.

About the Authors

Thomas Beck, a father, grandfather, and retired nursing supervisor, has lived in Southwest Pennsylvania his entire life, except for a stint as a naval corpsman. Writing from his home in the mountains near Acme, Pennsylvania, he draws on past experiences and creative imaginings to weave together baskets of tales for the reader's enjoyment. He has written three books of short stories. Reams of Haiku, other stories, and poetry fill his work areas. He recently won first place in a local competition, describing the places, people and history of southwestern Pennsylvania.

Marge Burke's crazy life includes working at three auto dealerships, juggling two grown children, five grandkids, teaching Sunday school kindergarteners, falling asleep reading, doing historic research, and playing in the dirt (flower gardens). Oh, and writing. She has been published in newspapers, magazines, and anthologies, and has two published historical novels, Letters to Mary and Fields of Blue. Check her out at www.margeburke.com and on Facebook. Tazz has been an amazing inspiration and companion.

Judith Gallagher lives on a mountaintop in western Pennsylvania, where she writes and edits textbooks on subjects ranging from math to mythology, from finance to physics. She is also writing a five-book fantasy series called Tales from Tirnanog. You can write her at jgallagher@LVWonline.org.

Barb Holliday lives with her husband and daughter and three spoiled dogs. She is passionate about poetry, and dabbles in mystery writing.

Michele Jones is a diehard Penguin, Steeler, and Pirate fan — really, a diehard anything-Pittsburgh fan. Family, writing, cooking, and sports are passions for her. Michele is a published memoir writer, short story author, and poet, but she loves writing paranormal, horror, and thriller fiction. She moderates a local writing group in her hometown and critiques and beta

reads for several published authors. Follow her online at
www.michele-jones.com, Twitter @Chelepie,
www.facebook.com/michelejoneswriter,
Google+ http://google.com/+michelejoneswriter

Barbara Miller has been teaching in the Writing Popular Fiction
MFA program at Seton Hill University since its inception in
1999. Her nationally – published historical romances have been
sold worldwide and translated into at least 14 languages. She
has published mysteries, children's novellas, and a picture book.
She and her husband, Don, live in western PA on their farm,
Weavers Old Stand, with a pack of unruly dogs and a passel of
inspiring cats. You may email her at scribe@fallsbend.net or
visit www.fallsbend.net.

M. A. Mogus's formal education is in physics and biophysics,
subjects she taught at a university until retiring. But she's
always been interested in archaeology, history, and forensics.
She did work in archaeology and also served as a museum
director for a short time. History and physics appear in her
writings and include "what if" ideas. Her interactive murder
mystery plays have been performed by nonprofit organizations
as fundraisers. She writes both fiction and nonfiction, designs
and creates jewelry and fiber arts, and loves plants. She has six
published books. The latest is Cloud Walker with Wings ePress.

Ronald J. Shafer, a graduate of Seton Hill University's Writing
Popular Fiction program, writes for children as well as adults.
His stories have appeared in several local and regional
magazines. He enjoys hunting, fishing, listening to classical
music, and reading.